LIKE WINGS, YOUR HANDS

LIKE WINGS,
YOUR HANDS

a novel

ℬ

Elizabeth Earley

Red Hen Press | *Pasadena, CA*

Book Design by Mark E. Cull

Library of Congress Cataloging-in-Publication Data

Names: Earley, Elizabeth, 1977– author.
Title: Like wings, your hands : a novel / Elizabeth Earley.
Description: First edition. | Pasadena, CA : Red Hen Press, [2019]
Identifiers: LCCN 2019018068 (print) | LCCN 2019020074 (ebook) | ISBN 9781597098069 | ISBN 9781597098236 (print)
Subjects: | GSAFD: Bildungsromans.
Classification: LCC PS3605.A7586 (ebook) | LCC PS3605.A7586 L55 2019 (print) | DDC 813/.6—dc23
LC record available at https://lccn.loc.gov/2019018068

The National Endowment for the Arts, the Los Angeles County Arts Commission, the Ahmanson Foundation, the Dwight Stuart Youth Fund, the Max Factor Family Foundation, the Pasadena Tournament of Roses Foundation, the Pasadena Arts & Culture Commission and the City of Pasadena Cultural Affairs Division, the City of Los Angeles Department of Cultural Affairs, the Audrey & Sydney Irmas Charitable Foundation, the Kinder Morgan Foundation, the Meta & George Rosenberg Foundation, the Allergan Foundation, the Riordan Foundation, Amazon Literary Partnership, and the Mara W. Breech Foundation partially support Red Hen Press.

First Edition
Published by Red Hen Press
www.redhen.org

ACKNOWLEDGMENTS

This book and its characters have spent so many years (seven now) in my head and the manuscript has taken many forms. So many people along the way have helped shape it. Thank you to my family—Biliana, Nico, Michael, Jerel, Cora, and Jude—for your daily doses of inspiration. Thank you to early readers of this manuscript: Carol Davies, Susan Evans, Michael Sullivan, Corinne Gartner, Carly Leahy, Mary Earley (aka, Mom), Heather Outlaw (aka, bestie), Iudita Harlan, and Caroline Zimmerman. And thank you to that psychic in Sedona who told me that I should re-read *Bid Time Return* and that it would be an important influence on the final revision. Thank you to my ex-spouse and current friend, Lucy, who had my back during the years I spent conceiving and writing this story. And thank you for your maturity and forgiveness that allows us to harmoniously co-parent. Thanks, too, to my generous blurbers: Gina Frangello, Peter Nichols, Lily Hoang, and Gayle Brandeis.

Thank you ultimately and eternally to Aimee Bender, who judged this book the winner of the Red Hen Press Women's Prose Prize. I am humbled and deeply honored.

Thank you to Kate Gale, Tobi Harper, Monica Fernandez, Natasha McClellan, and the rest of the team at Red Hen Press for your hard work and dedication.

Thank you to Rosalie Morales Kearns for being a kick-ass publicist and all-around coach for the business side of writing.

Many unending thanks to Seth Fischer for being a brilliant editor. Thank you for being my secret sauce/ secret guru/ secret weapon who tears my shit up and helps me take it to the next level and then the next—to the level of just killing it.

And never least, thank you to the love of my life—my soul mate, my seal mate, my best friend—Biliana Angelova, for everything (every single thing).

for Biliana

LIKE WINGS, YOUR HANDS

1. May 13, 2015: 20,000 feet

On the plane to Bulgaria, Marko's mom had to catheterize him in his seat. She placed a blanket over his lap for privacy. Marko was watching baseball on his iPad but only the games he had saved on the device because he didn't have Wi-Fi. Sitting beside his mom, he was careful to avoid opening the secret folder where he had his private links and files. Marko noticed how tense and nervous his mom was when she catheterized him. She moved quickly, like a bird. Marko didn't like to watch her thread the tube into the tip of his penis. He was always disturbed by how far she seemed to push it inside his body—was there really that much space in there?

Watching made math happen in his head, unwilled. Sometimes he could see sounds, smell colors, taste shapes. And sometimes, when he saw the unfeeling parts of his own body interact with anything—his own hands, his mom's, objects, the outside world—the math happened. It wasn't just math; it was a vivid, visceral, sometimes painful experience of numbers. The numbers moved in his mind. Sometimes they'd fly fast—that's when they hurt. But sometimes they were slow. They could be dark, almost black, or they could be blindingly bright, or somewhere in between. Each number was a three-dimensional shape with a color and a texture. The number seventeen, for example, was mostly blue, a little yellow, round but not perfectly round—more like an ellipsoid—and it had a smooth texture like marble. Nine thousand and fourteen was rough and dry but also soft like wool, diamond shaped, and beige. Every number between zero and ten thousand had color and shape and texture. And because every feeling Marko experienced, physical or emotional, also had shape and color, each corresponded to a number or a set of numbers. So sometimes, when Marko didn't know what he was feeling in words, he would know in numbers. He would think: *I'm feeling 4,372, which is a yellowish-brown, sharp-edged asymmetrical triangle.*

The math happened when his unfeeling parts came in contact with anything that had to do with spatial navigation in the half of his body whose boundaries he couldn't sense. The numbers came together to give him the perception of the precise location of each point in space where his body ended and another thing began.

Marko pressed his face into his mom's hair: long, straight and black threaded with gray. He inhaled her smell—which he associated with home—leaned back, and looked at her. He could see his reflection in her eyes: two tiny hims staring back. His face was long and narrow, his wire-rimmed glasses perpetually slipping down the bridge of his nose. His voice was deeper now that he was fourteen and his pubic hair was thicker. He had a single brown mole sprouting two coarse hairs on one pale cheek, matching similar moles on his mom's neck and body. His hair was dark blonde and fine, unlike his mom's thick, black mane. He changed his focus from his reflection to her eyes, their colors like autumn in New England: brown and burnt orange and yellowish green.

Being 20,000 feet in the sky, trapped inside a metal tube, hurtling forward at hundreds of miles per hour gave Marko an uneasy feeling in his stomach. It wasn't quite sick but almost. Any time there was turbulence, Marko imagined a gust of strong wind flipping the plane and sending it spiraling down to crash into the ocean below. At this speed the surface tension of water would be the same as that of pavement—he knew because he had looked it up—and he imagined the plane as it smashed apart, all the scraps and all of the people and limbs and Marko's wheelchair would sink to the bottom of the ocean floor, catching in the dense foliage of kelp plants to gather algae thick as moss.

"He has spina bifida. Paralyzed from the belly button down," Marko's mom said to the woman seated next to them in the three-seat row. The expression on the woman's face in response was as familiar to Marko as the sound of his own name.

"I'm sorry," she said, which was the soundtrack to the familiar facial expression. If it had meaning, it would have been mildly offensive to Marko because it would mean she was sorry about who he was—sorry about his heaviness in her mental notebook, the burden his existence was to the imaginations of able-bodied people—but thankfully, it was as hollow as the look of pity it accompanied. Unfortunately, the words didn't seem to have lost their meaning to his mom, because she looked even more nervous.

To calm himself and distract himself from his mom's nervousness, from the tube threaded into his penis, from the potential crashing of the plane, and to counter the swirling math, Marko decided to concentrate on something else. He looked for all of the printed numbers he could see around him and added them all up, dividing the total by three. If it were a clean divide, one that resulted in a whole number, then he was safe and the plane wouldn't crash. If there were a fraction left over, he would simply add those numbers to the whole number and divide by three again. He would repeat this until he got a whole number as a result.

In the midst of this mental arithmetic, Marko's mom pulled his arm down a little roughly. He wasn't even aware that he'd had his hands up in front of his face again until she yanked on him. He tried to keep them down but they sprung back up involuntarily. He put them down again and kept them at his side, but when he did, he wasn't able to do the adding and dividing in his head. His thinking was stuck. He started to panic. His hands went back up.

"I'm sorry, sweetie, can you hold still for just a moment until I'm done here?" His mom's voice was soothing. He dropped his hands again and tried to relax. But then turbulence happened and he still hadn't gotten to a whole number!

He quickly decided on another way to keep the plane safe. He listened for anything he could overhear from people on the plane, any words he could make out from their conversations. If he whispered those same words aloud to himself three times and then did it again with the next words he heard, the plane would stay safe. Marko listened. It was hard to hear voices over the roar of jet engines. He thought he heard "that was funny" after someone nearby finished laughing. Marko lowered his head and whispered, "that was funny" as quietly as possible three times.

"You okay?" His mom asked. He looked up at her. She smiled. He nodded, listening for the next words. But now she was done catheterizing him and she got up to go throw out the waste. Marko looked at the woman in their row. She was 92 percent uneasy being left alone with him. To make her feel better, he tried to make conversation.

"I'm going to meet my grandfather for the first time in Bulgaria," he said. She gave him a nod and a tight, fake smile. Her uneasiness wasn't reduced. In fact, it went up a few percentage points. He decided to take it up a notch and over-share.

"It all started six months ago when I found this book and my mom's journal. And this box that I could lay down in and sort of time travel and have weird dreams." He pulled out the book and held it up to her. The same strained smile stared back and her uneasiness had now topped out at 100 percent. She got up and walked off down the aisle. He was free to use his hands again, so he went back to the more comfortable task of addition and division.

2. May 13, 2015: 20,000 feet

On the plane to Bulgaria, Kali saw the high view of the past nineteen years of her life since she'd left there to come to America. The years contained so much—falling in love, having another abortion, having a baby, falling out of love, getting divorced, watching him leave their child, accepting her mother, Lydia, as the surrogate other parent to her son when she hadn't even filled that role for Kalina as a child. Only Lydia called her Kalina anymore. In Bulgaria, before 1999, she had always been Kalina. In the States, after 1999, she was Kali.

When Kali left Sofia, she went to the South Shore of Boston to be a nanny for wealthy children there. Lydia followed her six months later. Kali's host family let her mother stay there with Kali for a few months until Lydia herself found work as a nanny. Lydia's wealthy children belonged to a family with a townhouse in Cambridge and a mansion in Lincoln, Massachusetts.

Kali recalled all of this while she catheterized Marko. She was embarrassed to have to do it right there in his seat, but there was no other option. His wheelchair was gate checked and she couldn't carry him to the tiny airplane lavatory. She put a blanket over his lap for privacy, even though he seemed oblivious. He was busy with his screen time. He was watching reruns of Red Sox games. Kali knew he'd rather be watching porn, or "kissing videos" as he called them. He had a cache of videos of people kissing, both people and cartoon characters, actually—a vanilla collection that he allowed his mom to know about. But Kali was aware of the harder core stuff he had hidden behind a password-protected folder. She'd thought about making him get rid of it, but decided to let him be. There was the inevitability of it on the one hand, him being a teenage boy much like any teenage boy, but then, on the other, was the heartbreaking part. The part Kali couldn't bear to think about. What kind of romantic life would he be able to have with no sensation in his pelvis—no sensation anywhere below his waist?

Kali knew that sex is 95 percent mental—that the pituitary gland is the hub that produces all the chemicals that make the body feel so on fire about it. And Marko's pituitary gland was alive and functioning, so why couldn't he have a full and active sexual life, even without the use of his penis? Even without a partner? Thus, the videos. Kali couldn't deprive him that.

The woman in the seat next to her in their row was staring unabashedly at Kali prepping the catheter. She looked away when Kali inserted it into Marko's penis, and then looked back when she re-covered his lap. Kali made eye contact with her and she looked away.

"He has spina bifida. Paralyzed from the belly button down," Kali said. The woman gave her that look she knew so well. It was a look of admiration and pity that Kali couldn't stand. It made her nervous to have it this close to her. She fought the urge to slap the woman, to knock the look right off her face.

"I'm sorry," the woman said. Kali didn't respond. She went about taking the cath back out, as the bag was nearly full. Marko was moving his hands rapidly and rhythmically, so Kali couldn't get a steady hand on the tube. She grabbed his arms and pinned them down, which startled Marko. Immediately, she regretted having been so rough with him.

"I'm sorry, sweetie, can you hold still for just a moment until I'm done here?" she said, apologetic in tone. It worried Kali slightly that Marko held so still and was so quiet while she removed the tube and cleaned him up.

"You okay?" she asked. He nodded and she smiled. With the used catheter and bag gathered up, she needed to get up and dispose of everything and wash her hands. She gave a look to the woman next to her and started to rise, aware even as she did that it was a simple luxury—this bearing of weight on her legs—that her son would never experience. As the woman stood up and moved aside to let Kali out, that thought made her aware, more intensely than usual, of how completely this basic guilt was woven throughout her life and everything she'd done since Marko had been born fourteen years prior. This brought her thoughts, again, to Lydia and when she first came to the States.

Kali moved carefully down the plane's aisle, absorbed in the memory. Lydia had come initially, or so she said, to merely visit Kalina. But after a month and a half lapsed and her mother was still there with no plans of leaving and dwindling money, Kali began helping her look for work. Kali understood that Lydia didn't want to return to Bulgaria and be alone with her father, Todor, who was chronically depressed and who routinely threatened suicide, to the extent that it no longer had any shock value left. Kali herself had just stopped talking to him shortly after moving away, not wanting to bear the emotional burden of his pain.

The kind of work that could sponsor a visa and keep Lydia in the United States for longer than six months was abundantly available in New England, given all the rich, white people having kids. After Lydia found a family to nanny for, Kalina didn't stay at her job long. She left and became a student, going to graduate school for psychology. That's where she met Marko's father, Zach, and started that whole journey. Looking back now, Kali could see the inevitability of it all—like a black line running across the clear sky, its unwavering trajectory carved solidly against a dramatic canvas of deep blue.

Kali, Zach and Marko spent whole days with Lydia at the mansion in Lincoln, swimming in the pool, lounging in lawn chairs in the family's acres-big backyard. After the parents divorced, the man promptly remarried a much younger Russian woman who didn't like Lydia. With the kids grown and off to college, Lydia soon found herself out of the mansion and back on her own in a country that still didn't feel like home.

Marko was six at the time and Lydia came to live with them. Kali, having become integrated into the yoga community, connected Lydia with people she knew at the ashram—a spiritual yoga retreat in the suburbs. Lydia was able to get a small apartment there and a job cooking as well as another part-time job at the local Montessóri school. This way, Kali was able to visit her at the Ashram and sometimes leave Marko there with her for a few days so she could get away. To Kali's mind, it was the perfect solution; Lydia could also come to the city to visit Kali and Marko, but they didn't have to be on top of each other. She loved her mother, but too much time together often led them down a path of buried resentments from older, deeper wounds.

And now Kali was headed back to Bulgaria for the first time in fifteen years. She opened the door to the little airplane lavatory, disposed of the catheter bag, and washed her hands. She thought of her son. Marko would see Sofia for the first time and meet his grandfather, Todor, who Kali thought might actually, finally, be dying for real. When Lydia had told Kali she was going back to stay with him because he was sick, she had known it must have been serious. Faced with the reality of his death after having been estranged from her father for nearly two decades, she decided, somewhat spontaneously, to return and see him one last time and let him meet his grandson.

When Kali walked up the aisle to return to her seat, she squeezed past the woman who had been sitting next to her headed in the opposite direction, looking uncomfortable. Marko must have over-shared something with her, Kali thought, then laughed to herself. She returned to her seat to find her son, face upturned and illuminated by the sunlight streaming in through the window, hands carving elegant arches and angles in the space before his face.

3. December 13, 2014: Cambridge, MA

Marko sat in his room and stared at the wall to think. It had been a year since his dad moved out and went to California. Marko didn't mind that his dad was gone. In fact, he preferred it to when they had all lived together. His mom and dad had fought a lot. And Marko didn't get as much one-on-one attention from his mom when they all lived together. Sometimes he acted like he did mind because that would get him more attention, but he only did that a very few times when he was feeling extra lonely (number eleven) or extra uncomfortable (number fourteen). In fact, he didn't even want as much one-on-one attention from his mom anymore. What he wanted was to *know* her—to know her 100 percent, or at least 80 percent. He knew her only 17 percent. His mom never talked to him about what she felt for anyone but him. She never talked about what made her afraid or lonely or what she wanted out of life. Marko knew that wasn't malicious. She was doing it to protect him. She wanted him to feel safe, and if he knew she was fallible (which he knew she was), she worried he would not trust her.

Because he wanted to know her more, he started asking her questions. He would ask about her friends and if she was dating anyone, but she would answer with short, meaningless phrases like "so and so is a good person" or "I'm not interested in dating." When his questioning didn't lead anywhere, he decided he would have to be a detective and find out for himself.

One practice his mom had started since he turned fourteen was leaving him home alone sometimes. He could create this alone time if he asked her to go and get him something.

"Mom, can you please get me a smoothie from that health food store? I really have been craving one," he said that second Saturday afternoon in January when it all started.

"When was the last time you had one, honey?"

"It's been weeks," he said. He felt a little bad because he knew that they were expensive and that his mom never had a lot of money. She never told him she couldn't afford something, but he knew.

"I'll pay you back," he said, knowing he could not. Still, he liked to think that eventually he would find a way to earn money and be able to not only pay his parents back for taking such good care of him, but also help to take care of them.

"It's not about the money, babe," she said, "I just don't know about going out in this weather."

"You go without me. I'll wait here," Marko said and smiled. His mom smiled, too. She knew he was proud to be trusted on his own for a little while.

"Okay, I'll go get you a Green Goddess, how about that?"

"Yes! Yay!" Marko pumped the air with his fist, which she loved and which always made her laugh and hug him.

As soon as she closed and locked the door, Marko wheeled himself into her bedroom. He looked inside her drawers and opened the various small containers on her dresser, but all he found were earrings and hair barrettes and clothes and underwear. He went to the small bookcase just behind the wall inside her room and scanned the spines. He was familiar with the books his mom kept next to her bed. He'd read most of the English ones, but not the ones in Russian, Bulgarian, and French. His mother's fluency in four languages was something he admired and envied, but he'd never had the patience to learn other languages. There was too much to learn and to think about in English.

He recognized a new book on the shelf and he picked it up. It was a hardback book with a gray cover and the words:

THE
UNBEARABLE
LIGHTNESS
OF BEING
A NOVEL BY
MILAN KUNDERA

He opened it and flipped through it. There was some writing that was highlighted on a page: *What does this mad math signify?*

This was how Marko first read the line, and he was so excited to find his own latent, burning question in print in a book under his eyes that he nearly threw the book to the floor. Was this author writing about the mad math in his head? Did he have the mad math, too? Marko had never considered this phrase before exactly, but he thought it was an excellent name for the numbers and shapes that operated in his mind: the mad math.

But when he reread the line, he saw that he'd misread it.

"To think that everything recurs as we once experienced it, and that this recurrence itself recurs ad infinitum! What does this mad myth signify?"

Myth. A much different word than math.

Still, she had highlighted it, so it must mean something to her. Or had someone else highlighted it?

He turned back to the front of the book and saw an inscription on the title page. It read: "To Kalina, my firstborn: this will help you perfect your English and heighten your thinking. Let it make you smarter, and more interesting! All my love, Papa."

Marko's heartbeat quickened. His mom never talked about her father and Marko had never met him. All he knew was that he lived alone in Bulgaria and was a sad man. Marko's mom had a brother who died, also named Marko, and she talked all about him, but never their father. The inscription in the book was dated January of 1985. A quick calculation. His mom would have been eleven years old. If she could read it when she was eleven, then Marko, being fourteen, could certainly read it.

Marko replaced the book on the shelf and picked up another book, a journal. Its cover was blank yellow fabric, worn and a little dirty. Was this her diary? Even handling it made him feel guilty. He knew that diaries were for secrets, and not for anyone else to read. Still, he needed to know her better. It was important, more so than he could explain. It was like there was a deep well inside of him and he was stuck at the bottom. Knowledge about his mother was a rope that he could hold onto, one that could possibly lift him out.

He opened the journal. Inside, every page was filled with his mom's tiny print handwriting. At first, he avoided reading it, feeling ashamed. In the back was a stack of papers. He unfolded one and saw that it was a letter to his mom from his grandfather. He knew that she rarely spoke to his grandfather—they'd been estranged for most of Marko's life. He couldn't resist. He read the letter and then replaced it. He then read several pages of the journal, careful not to lose track of time and read for too long.

Satisfied, feeling that he did know his mom just a bit better, he closed the journal and returned it to the shelf. He wheeled out of the room just in time to hear the key unlocking the door. His heart pounded and he felt lightheaded. He glanced back toward her room to check for evidence that he'd been there. He saw none. The door opened and his mom stepped inside. She had a brown paper bag and two plastic cups filled with green sludge.

"I got us scones, too," she said, smiling. But then her smile fell off. Her mouth was a straight line and her forehead crinkled.

"What's wrong?" she asked.

"Nothing, why?"

"You look guilty. Did you do something?"

"Uh, no. I just have to poop, I think."

"Oh, ok, let me get you on the toilet," she said, and put down the cups and the bag. She crossed the room, lifted him out of his chair, and carried him to the bathroom. She grunted when she put him down.

"You're getting too big for me to carry," she said. Marko knew she was trying to make him feel better. Even with the growth hormones he'd been taking, he hadn't gained much weight. While the hormones had caused him finally to start puberty, and while his legs and arms seemed somewhat longer, he was still only 65 pounds.

On the toilet, he helped her pull his pants down and remove his diaper and he was embarrassed to see an erection there, between his legs. Where had that come from? He felt his face heat up and he started stuttering.

"It's okay, it's fine," she said. "It happens, no big deal."

But it was too late. Marko was crying and covering his penis. The feeling it produced in him was unbearable and insatiable.

"Honey, why are you sad?"

But Marko wasn't sad. Whatever he was, he didn't understand, and it was overwhelming enough to make him have to cry. His mother said nothing more. She looked at the wall over his head and bounced him on the toilet seat, waiting for poop to come out.

4. December 13, 2014: Cambridge, MA

K alina sat in the office of the shrink. She couldn't believe she had actually shown up this time. The shrink, clad in gray tights and a form-fitting skirt, came out through the plain white door and welcomed her in. The room was furnished from Ikea. Kali knew this because she loved IKEA. It was her favorite thing about America, even though it was from Sweden.

The shrink was not ugly and not pretty. Perfect for a shrink, Kali thought. She sat on a simple green loveseat couch unadorned with pillows, across from the shrink. The shrink asked Kali about when she came to America, so Kali told her about how she didn't have money back home in Bulgaria, and how she got a job at the American Embassy taking care of military children. She learned about rice crisps and milk in a carton. One family adopted her as a nanny. When the mother's sister had newborn twins, they sent her to the U.S. to help take care of them. January, 1999.

She landed in New York City. The age she had on her ID was 23. She felt nine.

The dumpy hotel she stayed in had a view of a brick wall. She marveled at the city surrounding that brick wall, vibrating with life and stinking of piss.

She lived in Swampscott and took care of the twin babies.

She stayed for eighteen months until she went to school. She received a scholarship for being foreign and smart and got a degree in psychoanalysis.

She got a job and made two hundred dollars per week.

In school, she met her ex-husband. They had similar values. Children, society, family, money. They were married when she was 26. He was 24. She got her papers.

She had an abortion after the first pregnancy and that destroyed the marriage. The second pregnancy was an attempt to save it. She didn't show up for her 20-week ultrasound because she thought she was on top of the world. She gave birth on December 12th.

She remembered the midwife looking between her legs with a look on her face like she had just watched a car wreck. The midwife wouldn't look at Kali. It was early in the morning. The baby was taken away from her. It felt like hours they were gone. She was left alone in the room. She delivered the placenta and lay there. Finally, she got up, even though she wasn't supposed to. She had to find her baby and hold him. She made it to the hall and saw five people in white coats coming toward her. As soon as they approached, her legs collapsed. She fell against the wall and slid down to the floor. She stayed on the floor while they told her everything that was wrong. It wasn't just one thing. It was five or six things.

Major spinal, brain, and heart surgery. Because of all the surgery and recovery, the baby had to be on morphine for six straight weeks and developed an addiction. He was then on methadone for morphine withdrawal symptoms. The shrink listened patiently. Kali stopped talking. The shrink blinked her eyes. Her brown hair, cropped short to chin length, moved slightly. Otherwise, the shrink was very still.

5. December 13, 2014: Cambridge, MA

*J*ournal entry dated September 27, 2005
  My favorite place in the city is a cemetery. I visit every Sunday but my favorite season to visit is autumn. The tops of the trees are burnt orange and flame red, the leaves are curling and coloring and letting go to blanket the graves to crunch underfoot. Nowhere else in nature is dying so beautiful.

  There is a still, green pool in the valley formed by the connecting of several hills. A sloping path surrounds it and winds through grassy plateaus, perfect for sitting and not being seen. When I sit at the banks of the pool at dusk, I watch the dragonflies being born. There are two important observations:

  First, the buzzing of this new, exotic life stands in stark contrast to the stillness offered by the surrounding dead people. In the cemetery an essential fact emerges in sharp relief: life is perpetuated by death.

  Second, the new dragonflies emerge from within the pond on the stems of foliage. Another important fact: life supports life. Also, things rise to the surface and the world decides to let them in or not.

  They climb up and out of the water as nymphs, their larval stage of development. They have hatched from eggs lain in the water. In the right temperature of water, larvae will hatch from eggs in less than a month. The larva or nymph will grow quickly, feeding on small bacteria in the water. Some nymphs are passive growers, sitting and waiting for prey bacteria to come within reach. Others hunt.

Tetralogy of Fallot causes low oxygen levels in the blood. This leads to blue baby syndrome. The classic form includes four defects of the heart and its major blood vessels: Ventricular septal defect (hole between the right and left ventricles); narrowing of the pulmonary outflow tract (the valve and artery that connect the heart with the lungs); shifted verriding aorta (the artery that carries oxygen-rich blood to the body) over the right ventricle instead of coming out only from the left ventricle; thickened wall of the right ventricle (right ventricular hypertrophy).

Nymphs swim by forcing the leftover hydrogen from the chamber housing the gills, which acts like a jet to propel the nymph forward.

Spina bifida, or SB, is a neural tube defect caused by the failure of the fetus's spine to close properly during the first month of pregnancy. Infants born with SB sometimes have an open lesion on their spine where significant damage to the nerves and spinal cord has occurred. Although the spinal opening can be surgically repaired shortly after birth, the nerve damage is permanent, resulting in varying degrees of paralysis of the lower limbs.

A nymph has a flexible lip that rapidly extends up to a third of the length of its body to help it capture prey. As the nymphs grow, they will switch to hunting larger insects, including mosquito larvae. Large nymphs can capture small tadpoles and fish. Nymphs will molt or shed their skin ten to fifteen times before they are mature.

Hydrocephalus is a buildup of fluid inside the skull that leads to brain swelling. This fluid is called the cerebrospinal fluid, or CSF. It surrounds the brain and spinal cord and helps cushion the brain. Too much CSF puts pressure on the brain. This pushes the brain up against the skull and damages brain tissue. Hydrocephalus may begin while the baby is growing in the womb. It is common in babies who have a myelomeningocele, a birth defect in which the spinal column does not close properly.

Dragonfly nymphs take up to five years to mature; years spent below the surface of the water, growing stronger.

It is the only species I know of that remains so vulnerable for such a length of time—almost as long as the human animal.

As the nymphs mature, the wing pads form and elongate. Colors gradually become visible through the translucent skin. When ready, they will move to the surface of the pond and start to breathe air. In the evening, nymphs climb up the stems of vegetation. Their first swallows of air cause their skin to split down the back. Gradually, the adult emerges. The wings slowly unfold as blood is pumped into them. Recently emerged adults are soft and exposed. They often don't survive their first few hours as adults because they make such excellent prey. It will take most of the night for the wings to harden before the adult dragonfly is ready for flight.

I watch them until I can't hold my eyes open anymore, or until I get too cold. They're so still, creeping out of the nymph skin almost imperceptibly.

Sometimes I go in the morning, before sunrise. I like to see the first light of dawn reveal their shed skins, like abandoned outfits of clothes cast off from new lovers.

The babies under glass in the NICU require more patience. No adult emerges overnight from an infant. These are the nymphs just hatched from eggs. They are not the hunters. They take the longest to mature, the most care. They are the most delicate.

That evening, Marko watched a cartoon where a monster was depicted dragging itself around by its hands with short, lifeless legs and no feet. Perhaps it was a ghost and not a monster because it seemed to float more than drag. It reminded Marko of the dark body—a part monster, part ghost—that floated inside him; occupying the space inside his despair with incredible gravity and mass. When the dark body pulled Marko in, it made him hit himself. Although it was Marko's own fist punching his own face and head and chest, it was the dark body that was hurting him and leaving bruises. But the ghost-monster in the cartoon didn't look at all like the dark body. It looked happy and harmless and light in its weightlessness.

Marko believed that the black box warnings on all of the medications he had to take had a weight that pushed down on him and bent him forward. In real life, he had scoliosis, but as his mom said, there's a metaphysical reason for all physical conditions. He took two medications for his heart condition; one medication for his hydrocephalus; and a couple of medications for complications of his SB. He spent a lot of time looking up information about the medications he took on the Internet. That's where he saw the black box warnings, which gave him so much of feeling number one, fear, that he nearly lost himself to the dark body. Just a few of the weighty warnings he discovered inside of the heavy black boxes:

- Cerebrovascular insufficiency
- Cardiovascular disease
- Hypertension
- Diabetes mellitus
- Thyroid disease
- Prostatic hypertrophy
- Addiction, abuse, and misuse
- Life-threatening respiratory depression

Of course, Marko spent time looking up each of these potential conditions as well. It all got heavier. There was too much weight tethered to Marko to ever be able to float. Marko envied the black-box-warning-free ghost-monster and its ability to float. Getting from one spot to another without his chair took up a lot of energy. One time, he caught his mom trying it out—to move across a room without using her legs. He woke up earlier than usual and dragged himself out of bed. He was trying to be extra quiet in case his mom was meditating or sleeping. He glimpsed her as soon as he hit the floor and nearly gasped. There she was, coming out of the living room into the small hallway and to her bedroom. She let her legs drag behind her and stood upright on her arms. Each step forward with her arms was like a new, one-armed push-up combined with the effort and weight of dragging her legs. She grunted but she managed it. She was strong and built small, so it was easier for her than it would be for someone else.

Marko had felt a strange mixture of sadness and pleasure to see his mom drag herself along the ground. On one hand, he didn't like being imitated or mocked. On the other hand, he was pleased that his mom cared enough to want to know what it might be like—to share in his hardship. Marko had sat on the floor and held these conflicting truths in his hands, the way his mom had taught him. "We have to learn to sit with opposites, as though we were holding one in each hand, and just let them both be true," she had told him.

He'd been meditating the same way almost every day since that day. Sometimes, they practiced sitting meditation together, finding opposites to sit with like happy and sad or good and bad. Sometimes, Marko sat with two sets of feelings so tangled he didn't even have numbers for them, like the feeling he experienced when surrounded by a group of adults having a conversation he couldn't completely follow and then hearing them all laugh and not knowing what was funny. Or the feeling he felt when his mom touched his body in a place he had no sensation except an idea of numeric value or color in a way that seemed both built in and totally unrelated to his body. Over time, Marko got so good at the sitting meditation, and could do it for such long stretches, that it became like a waking sleep for him where he sometimes had vivid dreams.

Marko was more like the ghost-monster when he was little. He remembered the platform with wheels he scooted around on and how much easier that made it to get anywhere, how it sometimes felt like floating. But ghosts and monsters weren't real. He wondered if he was real. Real, he decided, meant being alive in the world. Reading his mom's journal entry about his conditions and the gestation of dragonflies made him remember when she first talked to him about what was wrong with him. He had been told that his condition was rare. In fact, he had three distinct conditions, each of them rare. So he was very, very, very rare.

Could he be both rare and real? He had required so much medical and surgical intervention to be kept alive and in the world. He, alone, had not been capable of staying alive and in the world. So did that count as real? He sat and thought about this for a long time. Then he held being real in one hand, and being rare and not real (and a ghost and a monster) in the other hand. He held them there together and felt their unequal weights.

After sitting that way for a while, Marko saw a group of yellow bodies hovering above him in the room, giving off light. They had heads and torsos with tiny arms and no legs. One of the bodies spoke to him, but not out loud with words. It spoke to him in his mind with thoughts. It told him that he was connected to another place, a *real* place, through a rope of light in his chest. Marko looked down and saw the light coming out of his chest like a luminescent rope. Under the light was something dark, something black. Marko was alarmed.

"What is it? What do you mean, a real place?"

"When people are born," the yellow body said, "it's as though they're dropped from a plane. They accelerate at first, both horizontally and vertically, and the change in direction and speed are difficult to adjust to. They spend most of the time during the fall adjusting to the physics of falling. Once adjusted, they spend time fearing impact. But impact never comes: the body keeps falling for a long time. So where you are now, what you are, is a body moving in space in relation to other bodies moving in space. You're on a rotating planet hurtling in an ellipsoid pattern around a sun, which is also rotating. And the whole system, all the planets and the earth and the sun, is orbiting something else. The compounded directions and velocities are unfathomable to you, but you're so used to it that it seems as though you're sitting still right now. If it weren't for your perpetual motion, your body would break apart into a million pieces."

Marko squinted at the yellow body and the other bodies around it. His thoughts were tripping over themselves, trying to keep up. Thinking about the perspective from outer space this way, being alive in any kind of body was all unreal and absurd. He was zooming around in a huge matrix of motion with everything else: falling through space for the entirety of a life. Not just growing used to it, but actually held together by it. Marko thought about the math in his head, the numbers and equations. They compensated for his lack of sensation but also gave him anxiety and made him feel tired sometimes.

"What is the place that's real?"

"It's where bodies aren't needed because there is no falling. There are no forces of gravity. There are no kinematic equations. No cause and effect. What is just is, and it is free. Pure consciousness, pure thought."

"Time for bed," Marko's mom said. He opened his eyes and saw her standing there, her black hair aglow with yellow light already receding from the room.

"Did you have a nice meditation? You were there for a long time," she said.

"How long?"

"Over an hour. It's late. Get yourself to bed."

Marko held his arms up to her. He felt too tired to pull himself up into his chair. She leaned down and gripped him under his arms and legs and then lifted him from the floor. He closed his eyes and watched the math; numbers swarming to build a matrix in three dimensions of his legs hanging over his mother's muscled arm.

6. December 15, 2014: Cambridge, MA

The next morning, Marko woke and listened for the sounds of his mom leaving the house. Many days, she snuck away to do sadhana, an early morning yoga practice that was supposed to take place during sunrise. (Although, as Marko had argued several times, the sun doesn't actually rise at all; it's just an illusion caused by the rotation of Earth.) The morning after Marko discovered the journal, he listened hopefully, wishing hard that she would go to sadhana that day. He'd barely slept just thinking about the journal and wanting to get back to it as soon as he could.

Marko closed his eyes and listened hard. He imagined his ears growing large and bending toward the hallway. He heard silence so loud it hummed. Finally, after what felt like an hour of big-eared listening, she woke up and got dressed for sadhana. Knowing she would check on him before she left, Marko did his best pretend sleep when he heard her approach his room. And then she was gone.

With the diary back in his hands just minutes later, Marko felt bright yellow anticipation. He opened it to a random page in the middle. Staring up at him from its pages was a sketch of the wooden contraption she kept under her bed. "I lay inside of it and it helps me feel calm," she'd told him when he first saw it. That didn't make much sense to Marko, but he'd accepted her explanation without much further thought. Now, with a diagram of it in her journal labeled, "dream bed," Marko's interest level went up 250 percent. He turned in his chair and strained his neck to see the dream bed under her bed. Blanketed in shadow, its blonde wood façade seemed to glow as though subtly lit from within. He replaced the journal and climbed out of his wheelchair. More quickly than he thought possible, he was on the floor beside the dream bed.

At first, he thought he would have to pull it out from under the bed to get inside of it, but then he realized that the side of it opened from hinges at the top. He lifted it and peered inside. It looked like an empty box, coffin-like in shape. Inexplicably, he was drawn to be inside of it in the dark. He lay back and began sliding sideways into it, which was more challenging than he had expected. To move his lower half inside, he had to grab his pant legs and slide each limb over. First, he had to get as much of his legs and hips into the box as possible, which held the side up and open enough for him to lay back and slide his top half in.

Once inside, Marko let the side flap close and he was in complete blackness. Then something happened that had never happened before: the math and the colors disappeared. He could no longer see in his mind what he was feeling and where his body was in space. There was nothing but blackness, inside and out. In fact, he realized he couldn't even feel his own weight on the floor. It was as if he were afloat, but not even that—he wasn't there anymore.

Sound came first: he began to hear a voice speaking rapidly, but he couldn't make out the words. They were muffled, like he was hearing them from another room. Then, light and shape began to form. And then he was there, fully there.

He was seated in a chair. He felt different in his body. At first, he couldn't think of why but then it occurred to him suddenly and he looked down at his lap. He could feel everything: his feet, his legs, his groin! But what he was looking at were not his legs. They were strong and very tall. It was a strange, vivid dream, he thought. There was pain in his feet. They were sore, maybe from too much use, and it was exquisite. He looked up at his surroundings. There were bookshelves lined with books. There were boxes with more books along the floor.

The voice he heard resumed speaking and he turned to see a man seated behind a desk.

"Do you agree?" the man said. He had an accent similar to Marko's mom's. He was dressed in a dark gray uniform. Marko realized that perhaps this was not a dream and that he was somehow in possession of someone else's body in some other place, perhaps some other time. But it was real. He was real. It came as a relief to put the correct language to the state—the phrase itself like a cold lake in which to dive, a bracing immersion. The man was staring at Marko, expecting him to say something.

"I have to use the bathroom," Marko said. The man scowled and nodded. Marko stood. Feeling the strength and sturdiness in his legs, he gasped and smiled. The man instinctively smiled back, just briefly, then returned to scowling. Marko walked from the room. The act of walking was automatic—Marko had access to this body's muscle memory. What he did not have access to any longer, however, were the colors and the math. He felt confused and disoriented without them.

In the restroom, Marko went first for a stall but they were small, open partitions without doors and latches. He'd hoped for more privacy. Because here he was, in a man's body, in an able body, and there was one thing he had to do before anything else. He stood over the small ivory oval and, hands shaking, undid his pants. Taking the penis in his hands, the sensation was overwhelming. It immediately grew larger and ached in his open palm. He nearly passed out from the crushing commotion in his body set off by an erection he could feel. Again with access to muscle memory not his own, he deftly worked his hand to relieve the ache until he ejaculated. The orgasm nearly moved him to tears. What remained was sweet exhaustion coupled with a kind of satisfaction he had never known. He cleaned up with toilet paper and went to the sink to wash his hands.

Marko stood in front of the mirror and stared. He traced his fingertips across this strange and beautiful face, the foreignness of which heightened the sensation of touch to electric proportions. A dark, clean-shaven, lean face and thick, black hair. Eyes so dark they were almost black. His hands trembled. He felt it all—the floor beneath his feet, the water on his hands, the ledge of the sink pressed against his thighs, the air against his skin. He smelled the odor of the soap he used to wash his hands. He tasted the bitter flavor of his mouth. He leaned forward, closer to the mirror, searching for any sign of himself in those eyes.

That's when he felt it, the dark body, starting to take over. It was a black cloud moving over the open sky of his mind, tuning into any pain in this body and intensifying it, blurring his vision.

The soreness in the borrowed feet had turned into throbbing pain. Marko sat on the bathroom floor and removed his shoes to stretch and move the feet. This provided no relief, but rather made it worse. The burning pain rose quickly through his legs into his spine, radiating across his hips and lower back. Marko cried out. He fell to his back and stared at the ceiling, watching it disappear. He heard the door open and was aware of someone entering the bathroom. Before he could stop it, he was gone, back in the dream bed in his mother's bedroom.

For a brief moment between, Marko experienced delicious nothingness—a moment in which he was all essence, with no physical conveyance attached—and he loved it. Only in experiencing it did he realize it was something he'd always wanted: to be free of his body.

The moment passed. Marko awoke in the dream bed, suffocated and hot. He pushed open the hinged side flap and slid his head and torso out, gasping for air. The room was bright and cold, the math resumed, and Marko saw his disappointment at leaving the borrowed body as a brown, flat oval in his chest. But it wasn't being in an able body that he regretted the loss of so much as the in-between place of existing as pure essence. He looked at the dream bed tucked away under his mother's bed and marveled. She'd done it. His mother had figured out a trick for slipping essence from form.

Marko heard the door open and his mom call his name. He quickly pulled himself out and dragged his body back toward his chair. Marko's mom walked in as he was trying to climb back into it but finding he lacked the strength. Also, his back hurt more than usual. There was a particularly sharp pain directly in the center of his back on his spine, right around where he went from feeling to not feeling. What's more, he felt the echo of the pain in his feet from the other body. Kali helped him, lifting him from under his arms up onto the seat.

"What are you doing in here?" she asked.

"I came in to look for you then just wanted to sit on the floor and meditate," he said. He didn't want to admit he had gone inside her dream bed and risk her not allowing him to do it again. He saw her journal replaced to its correct spot on her shelf and was grateful he'd thought to put it back before going into the dream bed. But his mom wasn't buying it. Her forehead was creased into a skeptical expression.

"Something strange happened while I was meditating," Marko said. He would give her a scent of the truth, just enough so that she would feel satisfied he was telling her everything. Her skeptical expression melted into curiosity. She said nothing. Her face was a question.

"I felt like I had no body and was just me without any weight or form."

Kalina glanced toward her dream bed and Marko got nervous (two). Maybe he had just given it away.

"How did that feel?" she asked.

"Amazing."

She smiled a sad smile and then rolled his wheelchair out of her room. Marko watched the carpet in front of him disappear beneath him and ached for that feeling to return.

7. December 21, 2015: Cambridge MA

She knew this shrink was a bad idea. Walking home from her second session, Kali felt the tides of guilt. Guilt now pervaded everything. The concrete she walked on, her ribcage, the glass-and-chrome tumbler she used for her decaf coffee takeaway, the coffee itself, hazy memories of Thailand and Bulgaria, the vein-like cracks in the pavement, the weather, the orbits of planets, the air, the rust-orange patches of skin on her mother's elbows, the kisses. Especially the kisses. Zach became needy after Marko came home from the hospital, she remembered.

"Your mother's always here taking care of my son," he'd said, moping, hulking in the doorway to the bedroom.

"I'm grateful that she helps me with our son," Kali had snapped. He slunk in and sat on the bed. Lowered his head into his hands.

"I need help, Kali."

She didn't say anything. She kept busying herself, folding all the clean laundry from the dryer then putting it away. After she was finished, she took up a cloth and dusted every surface in the bedroom.

"I need help," he repeated.

"I can't help you."

He stood abruptly and crossed the room to her, grabbed her hips and turned her toward him. He kissed her so hard it was painful. His grip tightened and he forced his tongue into her mouth. She turned her face away and his tongue slipped wetly across her cheek. She twisted away. He glared at her.

"I can't help you. I can't have sex with you. I won't do anything for you. I have nothing to give. Everything I have goes to this baby and there's nothing left for you. Go somewhere else if you have to have attention." Kali stated it calmly, as a matter of such solid fact that there was no room for appeal. His face registered its truth. He looked defeated. Tears filled his red, worn eyes. He turned and walked out before one of them could fall free. She wiped the wetness off her face and went back to dusting. Marko had been a baby then. He was sleeping in the next room; his oxygen machine whirred. His heart monitor beeped rhythmically, reporting a normal heart rate.

It went on that way for years.

"You're my wife," he'd said. "We have to have intimacy."

"You want sex?"

"Yes."

"Okay, let's try it." Kali realized that she didn't have to desire sex to have it. She could simply do it. The idea was a revelation. And yet. Kissing him felt like guilt. Pressing naked against him felt like guilt. The act itself was guilt being stabbed deeper and deeper into her. It wasn't right. She had to say no the next time. And the time after that. Again, she invited him to go somewhere else with his needs.

Then came the day when Kali walked into the bedroom to see Zach jump in his chair and close the browser window he had open. The implication was obvious: he wanted to get caught. She sat at the edge of the bed and stared at him. He looked tormented. He was too thin; his cheeks had hollowed and his eyes seemed sunken deep into his face with coffee-colored pockets beneath them. His handsomeness had been trampled under the weight of this baby. She knew then that he felt it, too—the sense that they were being punished. He only knew about the one abortion Kali had had with him. He didn't know about the three others before that. He didn't know how early on Kali became voluntarily sexual. Her genitals had been touched and licked and pen-

etrated by many people. It started when she was only twelve or thirteen. Even before that, there had been the masturbating.

Now, for the first time in her life, sex was the furthest thing from
her mind. She felt no desire for it and the memory of the desire for
it bordered on disgusting. She'd kept her history a secret from Zach.
She'd kept it a secret from everybody. The only person who knew was
her mother, because Lydia paid attention. Lydia watched knowingly
when Kali slunk into the house in the thin light of morning. She took
Kali to get the first abortion. She was angry and wanted Kali to feel
punished.

Later, when Kali looked at Lydia over Marko's head as she held him
or bathed him or moved him in and out of his chair, Kali could see that
Lydia saw that Kali finally felt punished.

Thinking these thoughts, after her visit to the shrink, Kali walked
into her apartment and went to Marko's room and saw his hand lifted
up in front of his face. She walked in and looked down at him. He
trained his gray-blue eyes on her and smiled. Kali's punishment was
her reward.

8. December 15, 1984: Thailand

Todor was in love with his wife, Lydia, when he married her but he knew that she was not in love with him. She married him because he was wealthy, but he didn't understand this, because she herself was a doctor. She would make enough money to live well with any man. Still, Todor didn't question her. He was just satisfied that she accepted his proposal, regardless of her reasons. They bought a house in Sofia, Bulgaria. They had children right away, first a girl and then a boy. Kalina and Marko.

Lydia denied Todor sex most of the time after the children came. And even when she did give him sex, she was cold and dispassionate about it. It came to be that the only way he could bear it at all was to turn her face away from him and enter her from behind. At first, it was because her vacant eyes and stone face would kill the mood for him whenever he accidentally looked at her. But then, after doing it that way several times, it was because her body was strong and small like a boy's, and Todor could pretend that she was a boy. It excited him very much, this fantasy. So when she started to deny him consistently, he grew lonely and hungry for touch. But not the touch of another woman.

At 28, Todor looked older than his 35-year-old wife, which was part of his attraction to her. Her maturity far surpassed his own, but it didn't show on her face in the soft way of aging. It showed as toughness—a chiseled quality to her features and resoluteness in her eyes. While Todor discovered his sexual attraction to his own gender to be specific to younger, more feminine-looking men, his attraction to the opposite gender was specific to older, harder-looking women.

In 1984, Todor was stationed with his family in a suburb of Bangkok in a gated diplomatic community called Grafton. It housed diplomats from around the world, including young diplomats in training. Todor was a trade ambassador. He established mine building contracts and mining-related trades with the Thai government. On their second day there, a young man knocked on Todor's door. It was six o'clock in the morning. When Todor opened the door, the boy gave a salute. Todor, forgetting he had a cup of coffee in his right hand, made to return the solute and splashed hot coffee against his chest, the crisp, white uniform shirt instantly soggy brown. His chest burned, but Todor barely noticed the pain, so taken he was by the boy's beauty. He was tall and thin with black hair and eyes so deeply brown they looked almost black. Todor realized this was because they contrasted so sharply with his very pale, unblemished skin.

"Sir, may I help you with your shirt?" he asked. Todor snapped out of his reverie and looked down at himself. Coffee had also spilled down the front of his trousers.

"Well, this uniform is a mess now, isn't it?"

"Sir, you should take it off and I will have it cleaned for you." Todor gazed at the young man. There was a feminine tilt to his hips and the way he held himself. When Todor next spoke, the boy's gaze fell to focus on Todor's mouth.

"I'm clumsy. You should not feel obliged to clean up my mess. Come in, please," he said. He knew right away that the young soldier was gay. The knowledge made him feel vulnerable and superior at the same time. When the boy walked in, one broad shoulder brushed past Todor's shoulder and Todor smelled cloves. The scent overpowered the bitter scent of spilled coffee. As the boy crossed the room, Todor noticed that he limped. His feet were turned in, toes pointing toward one another.

"Sir, may I sit?" he asked.

"Yes, please, sit," said Todor, "act at ease."

"Thank you, sir."

"Call me Todor. What's your name?"

"Emil, sir. I mean, my name is Emil. Pleased to meet you, Todor," he said. His cheeks reddened, making him look adolescent.

"Emil, what can I do for you?"

"Sir, I mean, Todor, I have come to ask for your help. I want to stay at Grafton but they want to send me home. My feet, they're bad, but I can walk normally with braces. That's how I got through the interview process without anyone knowing there was anything different about me. But coming here, my braces were taken from me, and I can't walk normally without them."

"What do you mean your feet are bad? How are they bad?"

"They have a problem in the structure of the bones and joints. They're twisted so that my feet point in. It causes nerve pain, which I have learned to overcome. I had braces specially designed to fit my feet and turn them back out, which allows me to walk normally."

"Walk normally with pain?"

"I'm used to the pain, sir. I don't even feel it."

"Can you run?"

"Yes, sir, with the braces, I can do anything any other man can do."

Todor sat across from him, noticing during their conversation that his eyes kept falling to Todor's mouth. This made Todor want to look at the boy's mouth, which was exquisitely shaped.

"What became of the braces?"

"I don't know, sir."

"And who wants to send you home?"

"The Thai government, sir."

"Emil, I told you, call me Todor."

Emil blushed again and glanced at the floor before meeting Todor's gaze with surprising confidence and saying, "Yes, Todor."

Todor felt a fleeting jolt in his stomach as though he were in free fall for a single second.

"I will work on recovering your braces. Meanwhile, I will find work for you to do here, for me," Todor said. Emil looked at Todor, wide-eyed and slack-mouthed.

"Thank you, Todor," he said, causing the same explosion of sensation in Todor's stomach. Just to hear Emil say his name caused a stab of pure pleasure in his gut.

At first, Todor gave Emil odd jobs to do: get his uniforms cleaned, shine his shoes, bring him coffee, deliver messages. Each of these tasks kept Emil away from Todor most of the time. Todor found himself searching for a task he could assign to Emil that would keep the boy in his office. He realized that most of the built-in shelving space in his office was empty. So one day, he and Emil went to a used bookstore in Bangkok and bought several boxes of books, all in English. He then asked Emil to organize his bookshelves.

"Never have I seen so many books in English," Emil said, unpacking the boxes.

"The clerk at the store told me they were donated to the local library by an American when he left town. The clerk then made a donation to the library and they offered him the books. I like reading books in English, so I decided to buy them all."

Emil pulled out each book and inspected it. Several in succession about anatomy and physiology. Another several medical texts about the prognosis of various rare diseases. A smattering of ancient Greek philosophy. And several books on physics. When all the boxes were empty and the books stacked on the floor in groupings by subject, Todor and Emil regarded the collection as a whole.

"No fiction," they both said, nearly simultaneously. They laughed.

"Except, look," Emil said. He pulled a gray book from a box and held it up.

THE
UNBEARABLE
LIGHTNESS
OF BEING
A NOVEL BY
MILAN KUNDERA

9. December 16, 2015, Cambridge, MA

The dark body living inside the despair could pull Marko in at any moment. When it did, it was like a blackout. Marko didn't remember what had happened when he came to. Often, a stressful situation could trigger it. Sometimes at school, when things got to be particularly stressful or scary, Marko would slip off with the dark body and come back later. Often, this would happen in the middle of a class when a teacher was saying something Marko wasn't following or when another student was staring at Marko the way the other kids who aren't in wheelchairs sometimes do. Marko never made a decision to slip off, it just happened.

When he came back, the feeling was like waking up from a dream. He could remember scraps of what had happened but not all of it, and it would fade fast. Sometimes, he would have hit himself and screamed in the blackouts. But that stopped happening for a while and instead, when he woke up from these states, usually nothing would have happened and everyone would be just as they were before. He had just lost a bit of time. Until the day after his first trip in the dream bed, when something went very wrong.

A girl who sat next to Marko in class pushed his books off his desk and then laughed. Another kid behind Marko laughed, too. That was the last thing Marko remembered before he slipped off. In his dream,

Marko watched the dark body float around the ceiling of the class-room while everyone in the class was frozen still, like a movie on pause. Darkness from the dark body started to drip like melted wax over everyone and everything in the classroom until it was all covered and encased. Marko himself held his breath until his lungs burned, and when he inhaled finally, the dark body came rushing thickly into his lungs and made him cough. When Marko came back from his dream, the girl was crying and someone was pulling his chair backward, out of the classroom. When he got to the principal's office, the teacher parked his chair and sat in front of him.

The teacher said, "Hitting yourself is bad enough, Marko; I can't always stop you from doing that. But I won't let you hit the other children." Marko was terribly confused. Had he hit someone? He wanted to ask but he couldn't get his mouth to open or his voice to work.

"Marko," the principal said, "why did you hit Amy?"

Marko was stunned. He looked at his hands, then back up at the principal, and then at his teacher. The two men were waiting for him to answer. When Marko tried to speak, he laughed. He didn't mean to laugh, and nothing was funny, but he laughed anyway. Marko could see it was the wrong thing to do—the teacher didn't look pleased at all—but he couldn't stop laughing once he'd started.

"Call his parents," the principal said and slammed his pen down on his desk. Marko laughed harder. He tried to stop but couldn't. He covered his face with his hands to stifle the sound. He felt himself being wheeled out again and he looked through his fingers. The teacher parked him at the front of the office and walked away to talk to the man at the desk, the school secretary. Marko had been in the office before, the time he'd written with permanent marker on the teacher's desk. He'd done it because one of the other boys in class, Ryan, dared him to. He'd had no choice. The teacher had asked Marko why he did it. Marko looked at Ryan, who was giving him a warning look. Marko had started laughing that time, too, and he went to the office where they called his parents. They were calling his parents again.

10. December 17, 2015: Cambridge, MA

Marko woke the next morning feeling majorly hungry. It was feeling number four and it was flat, square, and nearly black. His belly felt inside out. He even lifted up his shirt and looked at it to see if it looked different, but it didn't. It gurgled and ached. He placed his hand wide across it and lay back. Why was he so hungry? Then he remembered: he had refused dinner the night before. His mom had been on the phone talking from about five minutes after they got in the door all the way through dinnertime. She didn't even talk to Marko at all. She just talked *about* him to other people. Marko was so used to hearing her talk to doctors on the phone about his medical issues that he'd learned to tune it out. He played a game of checkers by himself, but he couldn't really play because checkers needs two players. He moved the chips around the board and then stacked them, red on black on red on black, into a tall tower that, in the end, he tumbled with a touch of a finger.

At school one time, he and another boy had set up an elaborate trail of dominos. The trail went in loops, around objects on the table, up over a book and back down again, ending at the edge of the table. When they pushed over the first domino together, it seemed like the dominos were falling one after another for the longest time. He watched each and every domino fall, the cause and effect of one domino bumping into another, knocking it over to bump into the next. When the last domino fell from the table and clattered onto the floor, he looked over the remains. Overlapping dominos lay in the same pattern, roughly, as the boys had arranged them.

While looking at the fallen dominos, he'd felt something he couldn't quite name. He couldn't decide if it was happy or sad (seven and three), triumphant or defeated (twenty-four and thirty-two). It was the same feeling he felt now tumbling the tower of perfectly stacked checkers. There was a satisfaction to it (sixty-seven), but also a little regret (seventeen). Altogether, he decided it was a pleasant feeling that he would like to reproduce at key moments—moments like this one where he felt lonely (eleven) and sad (three). The satisfaction-regret feeling somehow soothed the powerful and large loneliness that held the dark body.

While she talked on the phone, his mom cooked. It was all boring food: mung beans, brown rice, vegetables, salad. He'd rather eat some cheese puffs and pizza, which he got sometimes at his grandma's apartment. His grandma always told him not to tell his mom that she let him eat that stuff, so he never did. Until that evening, at least; now he decided that he would tell her, because he was mad. When she finally hung up the phone and called to him, she had the table set already.

"Come and eat, sweetie," she said. He didn't move.

"Marko come on, it's time for dinner," she said, her voice a little louder and harder-edged.

"I hate that food. Grandma lets me eat cheese puffs and pizza." Silence followed. He stretched up from his position on the floor to see her in the kitchen or dining room. There was a large, square, glassless window in the wall between the living room and kitchen and also between the kitchen and dining room, so that he could see all the way across the apartment. He couldn't see her. It seemed like a long silence. Just about when Marko was going to apologize and drag himself into the dining room, she sighed loudly.

"Fine, you're not eating then," she said. Marko was shocked. He didn't know what to say. He felt a large lump of sad and mad and frustrated accumulate right in the middle of his chest. It got so big that it made his eyes water. He saw her cross into the kitchen with the food. He heard a loud bang and thump. The faucet turned on. The refrigerator opened, then closed. Something went in the trash. Then the faucet went off and Marko's mom walked past him to her room, where she closed the door behind her.

Marko burst into sobs. He had to, the lump was that big and pressed so hard on the place inside him where sadness lived. It pressed out the crying that was always there, not too far below the surface. When the lump came, he didn't have the strength to hold down the crying. Even when the lump wasn't there, he sometimes tired of holding it down and had to have a good, long cry just to let it out.

A few minutes passed and his mom came back. She picked him up without saying anything. He swatted at her and screamed, still crying. She held her head back away from him and carried him into the bathroom. She pulled his clothes off and set him on the toilet. She filled the tub. She put him in the warm water up to his chest, settled him in his bath chair. She scooped water with her hands up over his back and shoulders. She wet his hair. She shampooed him, gently massaging his head.

Marko's crying slowed and then subsided. Even though she didn't say anything to him, her touch was gentle and loving. When his mom handled him, held him, washed him, touched him in any way, he could feel a powerful love and a deep kindness in her hands. It was more real than her words. Marko didn't look at her through the whole process. She didn't speak to him. At one point, she started humming and mumbling one of her chants.

After the bath, she catheterized him.

"Hold this, please," she said, handing him the bag that filled with his pee. He took it and held it and looked away while she threaded the tube into the hole at the tip of his penis. He didn't like to watch. When he watched, the numbers moved too fast.

Looking at the floor of the hallway outside the bathroom door, the numbers in Marko's head moved more slowly. He knew when she was done, even before he felt the increasing weight of the bag in his hand.

After his bladder was empty, Marko's mom put a new diaper on him and helped him into his pajamas and then lay him in bed. She placed the book he'd been reading (the Kundera book) on his bed before she walked out. Marko tried to read but couldn't concentrate. He read just the parts his mom had underlined or starred. Eventually, he fell asleep.

He lay there the next morning hungry as could be. He checked the time and saw that it was way too early to wake his mom: 4:30 a.m. He would get something to eat himself. Marko slid himself to the floor and crossed the room to his chair. After a few attempts to pull himself up, he realized it would be easier to get into his chair from his bed: he could slide from his bed to the seat. He unlocked the wheels of his chair and pushed it up against the bed. Then he tried to get back up into bed. He pulled at the comforter, but it only slid off the bed. He couldn't lift his arms high enough to get the necessary leverage.

Marko gathered the comforter underneath him in hopes that it would lift him closer to his bed or the chair. He was able to get his arms onto the bed, but there was nothing secure to hold for pulling, only the sheet, which would slide off too. Conceding that it wouldn't work, Marko abandoned his chair and dragged himself to the kitchen. It was a slower and more tiring way to move.

None of the lower cabinets had food, only pots and pans and cleaning supplies. He looked up at the counter and saw the edge of a bag of something. He lifted his arm, tried turning his body to lift it higher, but he couldn't reach the bag on the counter. He slid along the floor to the refrigerator, which he could reach and open. He looked up and saw the container with his dinner that his mom had put away last night. He imagined it filled with beans and rice and a savory sauce. His stomach grumbled. Opening a lower drawer inside, he found an apple and some cheese. He closed the door, leaned against the wall, and ate the apple. It was a green apple, and the sour-sweet taste made him pucker. But it was delicious, the tastiest apple he'd ever eaten. He ate all of it, even almost all of the core. Then he unwrapped a Kraft single cheese slice and ate it. He did that with nine more individually wrapped slices.

Marko sat on the floor surrounded by his apple core and cheese wrappers. He wasn't able to reach high enough to throw his trash into the garbage can, so he made a small pile of the refuse against the base of the can.

Marko didn't feel full, but he didn't feel so hungry anymore either. From where he sat on the kitchen floor, he couldn't see anything over the high walls. The house was dark and quiet. He listened for noises. He heard the sound of a plane in the distance, then a car passing by on the street outside, then another car. Under all of that was something else, a little hum he couldn't place. No birds were singing yet, not a hint of sun. Marko had never been afraid of the dark, but there was something spooky about dark and quiet put together. It was like the quiet made the darkness even darker. He closed his eyes and continued to pay attention to the sounds—sounds that confirmed he was not alone in the world. There were other people all around, all the time.

Just then, Marko heard his mom stirring in her room. She must be getting up for her very early morning yoga and meditation. Suddenly, he was scared. He didn't want her to find him like this in the kitchen. Hearing her approach, he wished he could disappear into the floor. He put his hand over his face and closed his eyes. Light pushed through.

"Marko?"

He opened his eyes and blinked against the brightened room.

"Honey, are you okay?" She walked to him and crouched down. She pulled his hand from his face. He opened his eyes. He couldn't think of anything to say. She looked at the pile of trash. He watched her face. A line formed between her eyes, and the corners of her mouth turned down. Then her eyes brightened and she smiled.

"I see you had some breakfast," she said, and tousled his hair. She threw the trash away and picked him up.

Marko didn't go back to school that day or the next day. Then he didn't go back to school at all, because he would be starting a new school. During the days, his mom had to go to work. She would come home for lunch to feed him and take him to the bathroom, but then she would leave again. The rest of the time, he was alone in the apartment.

11. January 5, 2015: Cambridge, MA

Over the American commercial holidays, which Kali decided not to celebrate so formally now that Zach was gone, she actually missed going to her shrink. She was starting to understand why people paid so much money to have someone listen for an hour each week to their secrets and stories about their troubled lives. It was nice to have an objective stranger there to witness it, one with whom no reciprocation was required. On her first visit back, after exchanging pleasantries about the American commercial holidays, the shrink asked Kali about the time of Marko's birth.

"Tell me about what happened after Marko was born."

After Marko was born, Kali lived in the neonatal intensive care unit. The NICU. She was the only mother who wouldn't leave. They gave her a nametag to wear around her neck: *Kali, Marko's mother.* All the parents wore nametags like this, as if they were at a party. And like any good party, there was also alcohol. Kali became used to smelling alcohol on the breath of the other parents. She knew it as the smell of other people's grief.

Kali became synesthetic some nights, intoxicated by sleeplessness. She could have sworn that she heard the pink lungs praying. The pulpy interiors, shiny under plastic wrap, hummed little lullabies. The sounds of the ventilators and respirators and various monitors were slimy against her skin—a very specific patch of skin on her middle back. She began to scratch it regularly to relieve the sensation of slime.

"You have a chronic itch there, on your back. You scratch at it all the time." It was one of the NICU nurses.

Kali hadn't heard her coming. She told her it wasn't really an itch. She was a night shift nurse; Kali had seen her before and never spoken to her. Her eyes were kind. Somehow, she understood what Kali meant. She said, "Oh, I know. It's an irritation almost, down beneath the skin. Right? Like on your spine?"

Kali remembered saying something pathetic like, "I don't have a backbone. I feel so weak all the time, so crumpled." The nurse spent some time reassuring her, which Kali hated and loved at the same time. She tended to do that, fish for reassurance or compliments, and then feel like she was going to throw up when she got them because of how contrived they were. How ingenuine. So the nurse told Kali how strong she was for being able to be there with Marko and blah blah blah. But then, Kali recalled, she said something interesting. The nurse wondered why people associate strength with the backbone in the first place. And, she had gone on, why is love associated with the heart? She said hearts are the strongest, most active organs in the body. Backbones hold everything up with flexibility and buoyancy, like love. So it should be the other way around!

Backbone = Love

Heart = Strength

The nurse talked to Kali about her chronic itch. She told Kali about a woman who had a chronic itch on her head and how, in her sleep, she would scratch and scratch it. The woman could control her scratching during the day while she was awake. But at night when she slept, she scratched the side of her head in her sleep. Every morning, she woke up with blood on her pillow and a fresh wound on her head. She went in for tests. Everything was normal; only there was this circle on her scalp where skin was replaced by scab.

So the lady tried everything from bandaging her head to wearing hats to bed, but she always found a way to get at it in her sleep. One morning, she woke up and found a greenish fluid on her pillow. She pressed some gauze to her head and went to the doctor. The doctor called an ambulance—it turned out she'd scratched clear through her skull into her brain and the greenish stuff was brain fluid.

Kali didn't believe it. Nobody could scratch a hole through bone. But then the nurse told her how it happened. The woman had been scratching the spot so long, re-opening the wound so often that bacteria had surely gotten in there. This could have led to an infection that softened the skull, allowing her to gradually scratch through.

Kali thought about this: Brains and bodies work together, inseparably. The brain is not an autonomous organ. The body is actually as much a part of the brain as the fingers are the hand.

Likewise, the itch is inseparable from the scratch. The itch-scratch reflex activates higher levels of your brain than the spinal-cord-level reflex that makes you pull your hand away from a flame. And no doctor or scientist has been able to figure it out. There's no specific nerve fiber responsible. The nurse thought it was because the brain and the body are one organism. A distress signal from the brain produces a deep itch in the body.

Which means the body produces thoughts. Different parts think different thoughts.

Kali had looked at Marko: his chest tube, his urinary catheter, his pulse oximeter, his nasal cannula. Every part of his body was cut into—a tiny bundle of violated skin. The thoughts his body made would be too much for a baby. Too much for his mother. As though reading Kali's mind, the nurse said: "He's on enough morphine to not feel any of that. Enough not to think."

12. January 5, 2015: Cambridge, MA

There were three things that Marko's mom told him never to do:
1. Don't presume to know what the future holds
2. Don't mind the not knowing; never fear it
3. Never deny any experience that comes to you; embrace everything to be total

Marko took these directives 100 percent seriously. He understood intuitively rather than intellectually that what it equated to was neutrality. For as much as culture and society idealized hope, Marko recognized, it's a limiting prospect. Investment in any specific outcome precluded openness to anything, to all things. It's a tether that can easily become a prison. Marko had read something in his mom's journal that he thought a lot about:

Freedom is in the mind and spirit of the person who embraces the expanse of possibilities, including the great possibility of getting something other than what you think you want. Many times, people get what they think they don't want and it turns out to be more of what they wanted than they even knew.

The raw materials of the universe create thick webs: threads crisscrossing and connecting everything in complicated, indecipherable, shifting ways. A tug in one spot in one corner of a galaxy causes a shift a billion miles away—in a corner you'd never guess was related. Wide swaths of any life, the great majority, lie well beyond the influence of personal preferences. Yet there is an intricate design at work—there must be.

Marko more than intuited this as fact; he knew it when he started seeing the math. Even though the math happened automatically and was triggered by physical, spatial interaction with the unsensing parts of his body, after a while just the anticipation of such interactions could trigger the calculations, effectively making Marko psychic. In other words, he sometimes knew what was going to happen before it happened. It had to do with the way his mind interpreted time spatially.

From where Marko sat in the month of January in 2015, he could look back and to the left at the past decade. Each year of his life had been like a step in stairs. But the staircase was spiraled (not in a perfect circle, but rather long and narrow like a tall oval), with each rotation a decade, and now that he was fourteen, he was in the middle of a turn. The last thirteen years stretched out in a loop behind him: down and directly to the left, he saw the moment he was born. It was so close, he could almost touch it. Yet at the same moment he was rounding the corner to the next decade, up and to his right.

This is why Marko hesitated in going back in the dream bed. As much as he wanted to be in an able body again and experience the nothingness of the in-between, he sensed something bad would happen to him there. It somehow made him more vulnerable to the dark body.

Still, this psychic sense gave Marko feeling number one, fear— which was like pink sandpaper—because it seemed to directly contradict the three 'nevers' that his mom made him promise to follow. Marko had always kept his promises and he didn't want to change that. As he wrestled with how to fit this psychic sense into a world governed by these three rules, he had an idea. The third 'never' was to never deny any experience that came to him but to embrace everything. The math and the shapes and the colors—they were an experience coming to him. When they foretold a series of events, this was also an experience coming to him. His embracing and not denying this experience meant that he should pay attention and intervene where he thought necessary.

Besides, words, Marko understood, were open to interpretation and carried varying meanings. He remembered with a little bitterness when he had discovered this to be true. As a small child, Marko trusted language to be sturdy and consistent. His father had asked him: "Would you like to go on an adventure with me?" Marko didn't know what the word "adventure" meant, but he deduced from his dad's tone and the glint in his eye that it was something wonderful. Without much thought, Marko answered that yes, he did want to go on an adventure. So when the word "adventure" was first used to describe an outing he had with his father in his jogging stroller, where his dad had zoomed him off road, through the woods, over gravel and roots and around huge, looming trees, past people and dogs, around ponds with exotic, long-necked creatures that Marko had never seen before and that he learned that day were called ducks and swans, he associated that event with the word absolutely. The next time he heard the word, it was his grandmother speaking it. She wanted to know if Marko would like to go with her to the ashram. She said that it would be an adventure. Marko answered with a confident yes, knowing what was in store but skeptical that his grandmother was capable of delivering it the same way his father had done.

The indignation he felt when it turned out to be a series of chores—sweeping floors and cleaning windows and lugging trash—something that was patently not the exciting, fast, and freeing encounter with nature he'd had with his dad but in fact exactly opposite, was his first experience of the hot flush of betrayal. It wasn't his grandmother who'd betrayed him, but the word and its ability to blithely shed one meaning and slip into another at will. It was the beginning of his mistrust of language and its ability to never be precise in conveying intended meaning. It was why, as he grew older, he chose to talk less and less, especially about things that mattered.

In no realm was this more applicable than that of Marko's relationship with his mother. She was such a colossal mystery to him that he could never begin to know the myriad expectations she might have not only of him as he was in any given point in time, but of the him he used to be and the him he would become. Throughout his childhood, he had the sense that he was not doing something right by her, but there was no evidence to support this feeling. In fact, all the evidence pointed toward her bold and unconditional acceptance and love for him. Still, this evidence was built mostly of words, which Marko had come to understand were unreliable as evidence because they were so open to subjective interpretation. And because they were easy to utter. Observable actions were more reliable as evidence, and Marko had observed and memorized and catalogued a great variety of actions of his mother's, which, taken as a whole, was rife with internal conflict, contradiction, and unfathomably infinite nuance. In fact, taken as a whole, this body of evidence made up of all her observable actions was as unreliable as language.

This is why reading her diary was so important. After finding it for the first time, he knew he couldn't risk taking it off her shelf again because she wrote in it almost every day. So instead, he took a picture of every page and of every one of the letters folded up in the back with his iPad. He made a password-protected PDF of them and saved it inside one of his homework folders where she would never find it.

13. January 12, 2015: Cambridge, MA

It was time to catheterize him. Every day at 8 a.m., 12 p.m., 4 p.m., and 8 p.m., someone drained his bladder. The task required fine motor skills that he didn't have, so Kali or Lydia or a school nurse continued to do it for him. This morning, Marko woke and got himself out of bed. He dragged himself to his chair and got in it, then went to the bathroom to get his catheterization kit. He brought it to Kali in her room. She pretended to still be sleeping because she liked the way he had of waking her. He would slow down his chair and push the door open ahead of him, then inch in without letting the chair bump the door. The whole process was nearly silent. Kali loved the sweetness of it, because he intended to wake her up anyway; he just wanted to do it with a gentle kiss to her hand and a whispered, "Good morning, Mama."

That time, Kali's hands were in front of her, tucked up against her chest in prayer pose. Kali couldn't move them without betraying that she was awake. He was so quiet there behind her for what felt like a very long time. She wondered what he was doing. She pictured him sitting there looking at her, watching her sleep. He could have just as easily been zoned out, staring at the floor or wall, she knew. But Kali seemed to feel his gaze trained on the side of her face. Kali stirred and turned over. He was bent forward, looking under her bed. Kali shot up and dropped her blanked over the side of her bed. Her dream bed was under there, and she didn't want him asking her about it.

Marko smiled at Kali. He smelled like urine again and, in spite of trying to smile back, Kali frowned. The line instantly appeared between his eyes, and he frowned too.

"What's wrong?"

Kali smiled as big a smile as she could make. "Nothing, my love. Good morning! How are you?" His face relaxed. He looked at her with one eye turned in, something that often happened in the mornings or at night if he was very tired. Kali reached out and tousled his hair. He nuzzled his head against her hand and reached for her. She pulled him from his chair into her lap and held him like a baby. He was still so small. The last time Kali had had him weighed, he was right around fifty pounds.

"Here," Kali said, sitting up and pulling him to the floor, "let's get you cleaned up." Kali pulled off his diaper. It was soaked through. She would have to change his bed sheets again. She cleaned him up and inserted the catheter tube. The tip of his small penis was red and irritated. Kali put Vaseline on it to soothe it, even though he couldn't feel it.

Marko was oblivious. Not just because he couldn't feel anything down there, but also because he wasn't aware of the stigma. As a paraplegic, dealing with urine leaks was as routine and uneventful as visiting the toilet is for non-paraplegics. It simply didn't bother him. It bothered Kali though. At school, his diaper sometimes showed, sticking up over the waist of his jeans. Kali felt embarrassed for him because the other kids could see, and she'd seen them looking.

When his bladder was completely emptied, Kali withdrew the catheter tube and cleaned it.

"Feel better?" she asked, putting a fresh diaper on.

"Yes, thanks," he said, and Kali felt bad. Because he didn't feel better. Of course he didn't—he couldn't feel a thing, not the tube, not the irritation, not the urge to pee. It was Kali who felt better, knowing that his bladder was empty and that he would be okay for at least four hours.

Although many kids with spina bifida could feel when they had to pee, which allowed most of them to actually use the toilet, at least some of the time, Marko could not. Kali used the toilet for Marko only when he had to poop. She would sit him on it and jiggle him around some until a few nuggets come out. Lately he had been so constipated, though, that the pressure built up in his intestines was pressing on his bladder and causing him to leak a lot between catheterizations.

"Mom, do you know why my skin starts to look so wrinkly when we're in the water too long?"

"I don't actually know."

"Because the oil in our skin that makes it waterproof, called sebum, seeee-bum, gets all washed off. Then, the water soaks into the top layer of the skin and makes it soggy."

"How do you know so much?"

"I look stuff up."

14. January 12, 2015: Cambridge, MA

M arko's first day at his new school was something he dreaded (six) and anticipated (ninety) in equal measure. They cancelled each other out, and the result was emotional paralysis. To distract himself from thinking about it and feeling oddly numb, he read *The Unbearable Lightness of Being*.

He read and reread and underlined. He starred a part at the beginning of chapter 16, which read:

> Necessity, weight, and value are three concepts inextricably bound: only necessity is heavy, and only what is heavy has value.

Then, a little farther down, he read something not underlined but that articulated a truth for Marko he'd always known but never been able to put words to:

We believe that the greatness of man stems from the fact that he bears his fate as Atlas bore the heavens on his shoulders.

Marko's mom had told him the tale of Atlas to illustrate for Marko how she and he, but he in particular, were lifters of metaphysical weights that, although burdensome, made them only stronger over time. Marko wondered if this is where she'd gotten it from. He read a couple more pages before he hit PART TWO and decided to stop and save it for later when he would have more time.

With time yet to spare, he looked up things on the Internet. Marko liked stories about outer space and life on other planets. He read articles about Jupiter's moons, Saturn's moon, Venus, and Mars. He understood that scientists looked for life based on finding the chemicals on other planets that sustain life on Earth, but he wondered why there couldn't be totally different chemicals on other planets. Or at least, totally different life, the kind that gets sustained by nitrogen gas and doesn't need oxygen and maybe requires different climates. Like three hundred degrees below zero, or three hundred degrees Fahrenheit.

Marko imagined that beings on other planets would be floating torsos with tails and heads with no necks and one eye. Maybe they would have hair but not on their heads. It would be on the palms of their hands and they would consider those with dark, curly hand hair much more beautiful than those with straight, yellow hand hair. This made Marko laugh out loud by himself at the computer desk.

"What's funny?" Kali was on the floor doing yoga. She was excited to take Marko to his first day at the new school but Marko could tell she was also nervous. Even though she asked the question, she kept doing her set, crunching herself up sideways and counting the number of times under her breath. Marko didn't answer her; he went back to the Internet. He read an article about the heartbeat of the sun, which was magnetic and which was responsible for solar storms and flares. Marko thought about his own heartbeat, and he placed his two fingers on his wrist until he found its steady rhythm. He pictured it with its bovine part sewed in and wondered whether the sun ever had to have an operation. Would they put other magnets inside to fix it? Scientists had also detected that the sun changed its polarity once every forty years. Maybe the sun had an operation every forty years where they switched out its magnets and made it reverse charge. Then he read about "magnetic structures" on the sun's surface. This reminded him of the math in his head, the shapes and how they snapped together and gridded out the perimeter of his body or the shape of the future. He wondered with fascination if he got the math from the sun.

"What are you reading about?" Kali was seated now and breathing heavy. She wiped sweat from her forehead with her sleeve.

"Space."

"What about space?"

"The sun and the planets and stuff." Marko wondered if his mom thought about other life in outer space and if she thought it would be very different from life as they understood it on Earth. Just when he was about to ask her, she announced that she was going to shower and left the room.

By the time they got to school, Marko was thinking about magnets and fireballs one million times larger than Earth. *Whatever operates on the magnetic heart of the sun must be very big and very powerful*, he thought. He looked at the building when they pulled into the parking lot, and it made him nervous (two). His hands started moving and his heart rate picked up. He wondered what made the heart rate of the sun pick up, or if it even did. He thought it probably did, even though it never had to go to a new school.

His mom lifted him out of the car and the math worked in his head. The flaming orange octahedron connected with a blue tetrahedron connected with a yellow dodecahedron made him sure of the sun's influence on his brain. She put him in the seat but he was only remotely aware of this because he couldn't fathom what one million times the size of the whole Earth even looks like. And for it to be that big, how far away must it be? He tried to go inside himself as far as the sun is away from the earth, to sink, sink, sink down so small that the space inside him was as vast as the space outside of him. It was something he could do sometimes, but not this time. He was aware of the building he was about to enter, aware of the bumps in the parking lot and the cold air stinging his face. Then he saw a van with a mechanical lift for kids in wheelchairs. Then they were inside and there were many other kids in wheelchairs. A nice lady came and talked to them and Marko couldn't hear her for the loud nervous static in his head. She showed them around and he took it all in. Everyone was either nice to him or didn't notice him at all, which was a miracle, because at his last school everyone was nice to him (too nice) and noticed him all the time.

Marko saw a sidebar adapter on another kid's wheelchair that had contoured, padded surfaces for resting the arms and elbows more comfortably. Another wheelchair sported an iPad holder and a cup holder. He was fascinated by the accessories; he'd never seen so many wheelchairs in one place before. Before he was completely comfortable being there, his mom was ready to leave. The nice lady offered to let Marko walk out to their car with his mom to say goodbye.

He went with the same sensation that he had when he came—half excited, half terrified. The more prominent feeling was number ninety-one, which was excited. And as they walked back toward the car, he saw something strange in the bare branches of the tree at the edge of the parking lot. Perched on a branch, staring straight down at him, was an owl. Marko was surprised to see it because he had read on the Internet that owls sleep during the day.

"Mom, look at that owl," Marko said and pointed. Kali gasped and stopped.

"It's beautiful!"

"Don't owls usually sleep during the day?"

"He woke up just for you." She squeezed one of Marko's shoulders and added, "It's a good sign."

Marko took a long time to think about that owl and the good sign that it was. He remembered his dad telling him stories about an owl when he was little. In the stories, the owl was just like a person. It lived in a house, had furniture, wore clothes, walked around instead of flying. Marko liked the stories, but something about them always bothered him. He didn't understand it then but he understood it now. He wondered why the owl had to be that way, like a person. Instead, couldn't his dad have made up stories about owls as they really were? Flying around, mating, building nests, interacting within their mysterious hierarchy?

The wordless system of bird culture fascinated Marko. How did they know, for example, which direction was south, and that warmer weather would be there if they flew in that direction long enough? Furthermore, how did they communicate in which formation they would fly and who flew in which position? Any time Marko saw that moving, wavering V in the sky, he stared in wonder. Somehow, it made him feel okay in the world. It was something miraculous that he would never understand, yet there it was. In this way, the birds were proof of something big. Marko didn't know what it was, but he knew that it existed because of the birds, and that was all he needed to know.

As for that owl at the school, Marko thought his mother must be right. That it was a sign of something. Because owls weren't supposed to be awake during the day and they were a rare thing to spot in New England even at night. They kept themselves well hidden. But there it had been, just perched there in a naked winter tree, staring directly at Marko, tracking his progress. Maybe it hadn't been a real owl. Maybe it had been a robot owl that someone very smart had built and put in the tree as a way to spy on people at the school. Marko chuckled to himself at the thought, but then he wondered—what if it was true?

If it was, Marko wished that he were very smart too so that he could build a robot owl to place in a tree outside his mother's window and spy on her while he was away. Then he could know all about what she was doing that she never told him.

Marko emerged from the depths of his thinking to find himself in a classroom.

"My name is Markus and I can't sit up straight." The girl was making fun of Marko and getting his name wrong at the same time. Her name was not Markus, nor was it Marko. Her name was Derekah. She sat directly behind him. Marko thought about making fun of her too with something like, 'what kind of a name is Derekah?' But instead he pushed his shoulders back and sat up as tall as he could in his wheelchair. He looked to his left to see Derekah's reflection in the tinted, floor-to-ceiling window that separated the classroom from the hallway. What he noticed instead was himself and how, no matter how hard he tried, he was still bent forward, however slightly.

"I have congenital scoliosis," he said. It came out almost inaudibly—a desperate, whispered defense.

"My name is Markus and I can't feel my penis," she sang. A few kids in the classroom laughed. Marko instinctively looked down at his crotch. There were his jeaned thighs, flat against the seat of his chair. Atrophied.

"I have spina bifida, and I'm paralyzed from the waist down." But this time it didn't come out at all. The effort to speak became too great, leaden under the weight of humiliation. He felt something pelt the back of his neck and startled. Touching it, he felt its wetness, and another one hit the back of his hand. Then his hair. He looked at Derekah's reflection in the glass. Spitballs. She was pulling another chewed bit of paper from her mouth and loading the small straw again. More laughter from the other kids. Marko felt the dark body then, like a rising tide from the floor. He lifted his chin to the air to keep above it.

"I'm Markus and I do this weird thing with my hands."

Marko's hands were working fast, cutting the chewable air in front of his face. Becoming aware of them, he tried to stop, but it was too late. The dark body swallowed him and he was gone.

Marko surfaced to find himself in the school clinic. He was in his chair with his backpack in his lap. In front of him was a desk with a woman seated behind it. Her face was lit from the computer screen she stared into. Marko noticed her bushy eyebrows with coarse, silver hairs sprouting from them, longer than the black ones.

"Hello?"

She looked up from the screen. Her eyes were deep brown and kind. "Hi there, Marko. You're back. The nurse will be with you in a few moments."

"I don't need to see a nurse. This is just something that happens. I'm fine."

"It's just routine for you to be cleared by the nurse before we send you back to the classroom. It won't be long." She directed her attention back at the screen. Marko pulled his own screen from his backpack and retrieved the PDF file of his mom's diary.

When I was eight, I asked my mother for the first time why people die. She said, "It's because people are born." That made me think to ask why people are born, but the next thought to come after that stopped every-

thing else and no more questions were asked. I had been born. It was my sentence to die. I started to feel sorry for myself, the way I felt sorry for my brother when they left him at my grandmother's house. I started to feel sorry for everybody because they too had been born. Once, a woman who was a stranger caught me looking at her sadly and asked me what was wrong. I told her I was sorry she'd been born and she frowned deeply at me before turning away.

Death seemed like a terrible thing, because the people I had seen die were fighting it with everything and all the people around them were terribly sad when it happened. The first person I saw die was my cousin, who was only 24. A truck had hit him while he was camping with his friends. We went to visit him in the hospital, and when I saw his swollen face I couldn't stop myself from imagining the impact of the truck against his body. I winced imaging the sound it would have made: a wet thump and maybe a cracking sound from breaking bones. He opened his eyes and looked at us before he died. He said five words, "I don't want to die." Tears came out of his bulging eyes, and then he died. Everybody in the room cried. His mother, my aunt, fell on top of him with half her body and yelled, "No!" over and over again while she cried.

The second person I saw die was my great-grandfather, who was very old. He kept trying to sit up and my mother kept pushing him back down, telling him to sleep, sleep, rest, rest. He was very agitated. When my mother told him that he could go, that we would be okay without him, his eyes grew very wide and filled with so much fear that it spilled out and into me and I felt afraid, too. When he died, his eyes stayed wide open and all the fear was trapped there, glossed over with a nothing look. My mom cried very much and pulled his eyelids down over his fearful eyes.

The second time I asked my mom why people die, she told me that it was because they expire like milk. I imagined a bottle of milk sitting too long and being spoiled. But the opposite was true with people, I thought. Our bodies are like the milk and our souls are like the bottle. Except sometimes our bodies die before they expire because of an accident or something, like my cousin with the truck. I wondered then if our souls die too but just a long time later. Maybe they live much longer than our

bodies but still have a birth and a death of their own, like the milk bot-
tle. When I said this to my mom, she smiled and told me I was smart. I
didn't feel smart. I felt very confused.

She is the one who told me that we have souls. She said that what
looks out through our eyes is our soul. At the time, it made me worried
that anything other than me was looking out through my eyes. But then
I pictured my soul as a very quiet, very alert owl hiding in my head. Its
eyes were wide open and it never slept. It felt better to think of it that way.
I was less lonely and not so worried. I do that a lot, even now—when
something worries me, I think of something right away that will help me
feel better about it and not be so worried.

Marko loved the idea of his mom's soul as an owl that never slept. It
reinforced that the owl they saw in the parking lot that morning was
a sign. But so far, his new school wasn't any better than the old one.
Her owl soul reminded Marko of something she'd underlined in the
novel. He pulled it out of his backpack and turned to the dog-eared
page and read:

> The body was a cage, and inside that cage was something which
> looked, listened, feared, thought, and marveled; that something,
> that remainder left over after the body had been accounted for,
> was the soul.

He closed the book and put it away. He wasn't in the mood for reading;
he wanted to think. Marko liked that his mom thought of something
right away to help her not worry. He tried to think of something to
help him not worry about Derekah.

Derekah hadn't struck Marko as a threat when he first met her. Her
small frame, yellow hair, and the child-size wheelchair she rode created an aura of innocence. The only sign of her malevolence were her
thick-lensed glasses that magnified her eyes to appear twice their size—
eyes that reminded Marko of the dark body. The first time he shook her
hand and looked her in the eyes, the hair on his arms stood up. Amaz-
ingly, she noticed. She glanced at his arms then screwed her mouth up

into what Marko guessed was her version of a smile. He couldn't prove it, but he was sure there was a smug satisfaction in it that suggested she knew how intimidating she was.

It had happened only that morning, when the teacher introduced Marko to the other eight kids in the class. He had to shake their hands—a custom Marko never understood and always felt awkward doing. To distract himself from the hand shaking and the scary eyes of Derekah, he calculated the percent of friendship potential each kid had. He'd been aching for a friend, so he paid close attention, ready to do the work his mom taught him to do to make a friend.

"Friends don't just materialize," she'd said, "it takes work." She said it while she was tucking Marko in the night before his first day. As she spoke, Marko could hear the opera music, volume low, playing in his mom's bedroom. She listened to it while she read, though Marko suspected she didn't really listen. She played it as mere background music. She claimed it calmed her mind. But it seemed to do the opposite for Marko. Night after night, listening to it in the dark, when he was more sharply awake and his senses more attuned, he heard thick emotion in the voices. The voices were sometimes high and thin like ghosts; other times hard and threatening like pointed, painted fingernails; and other times lilting and light like angels but in a tinsely way, trembling and distant and cold.

"First, you have to look people in the eye. That shows them you're interested. Then, ask them questions about themselves. People love to talk about themselves. Ask about their parents, their grandparents. Do they have any siblings? Any pets? Where do they live? Any vacations over the summer? What sports do they like?"

His mom's voice boomed over the low current of opera music, and although Marko wanted to pay attention and remember the advice, his awareness clung to the music between her words. He wished that his mom would stop talking just then and that the music could be turned up louder.

"Just keep asking them questions. Don't talk about yourself until later, after you're already friends."

Marko tuned into this last bit. "How do I know who would make a good friend? How do I know who to pick to ask questions?" His mom straightened. Marko sensed his mom was offering something more useful than anything else. Something that would potentially cure Marko's loneliness.

"You'll probably just know," she said. Marko searched his mom's face for signs of humor. There's no way she could have been serious. Just know?

"Sleep tight, bud. See you in the morning." She switched the light off and left. She left the door open. The light in the hall cut into the dark of his room. The opera music serenaded the shadows on the floor. Marko lay awake listening, puzzling out through the voices how he would ever possibly just know.

So in class on that first day, he calculated the friendship potential of each kid based on how certain he felt that he just knew. Blaire had cerebral palsy and drooled when she smiled (61 percent). Christopher rode a wheelchair the same as Marko's but he sat up straight and his legs were muscled (11 percent). Tanya wore braces on her legs and braces on her teeth (33 percent). The twins, Mia and Tia, smiled and laughed all the time and gave everybody hugs (2 percent each). Greg was chubby and screamed abruptly every once in a while (71 percent). Derekah had those scary eyes (2 percent).

Then there was Malik. He had brown skin and black hair and was the only one not in a wheelchair. He was tall for his age and thick. He stood with slumped shoulders, mumbled indecipherable things, and never looked anyone in the eye. But what Marko noticed first about him were his hands. They were bruised, or so Marko first thought, watching them shuffle in his lap or on the surface of his desk as if with a mind all their own. Upon further inspection, Marko saw that Malik's hands weren't bruised but had some sort of a rash. They had darker brown, white, and pink splotches and were somewhat swollen. Malik was the only other person Marko had ever met whose hands seemed to move unwilled. For this alone, Marko gave him a 99 percent. Suddenly, he knew his mom had been right. It was true that he would just know.

But before he had a chance to do the work of making Malik his friend, the incident with Derekah happened and he ended up in the clinic. With all of the students at McKinley having serious medical needs, the school housed a clinic staffed with nurses, psychiatrists, and various other consulting physicians.

"Hi Marko, I'm Nurse Shea."

Marko looked up. She had short, brown hair and a kind, round face. She wheeled him into an office and then sat across from him and shined a light in his eyes.

"Your pupils are back to normal now," she said. Marko blinked. "Your teacher, Ms. Ludwig, called for me when you had an episode in class. Do you remember that?"

"We were waiting for her to come in and start school. Derekah was making fun of me," he said but stopped talking abruptly when he heard the waver in his voice. He didn't want to cry in front of her.

"Where'd you go?" Ms. Shea's face was present and gentle. Marko looked at his lap and noticed his hands weren't there; they were up and going. He made the conscious effort of placing them back down into his lap and keeping them still. Each hand gripped the other, as though holding down two birds straining to take off.

"I don't know," Marko said.

15. January 12, 2015: Stowe, MA

It was Marko's first day at his new school. Kali unloaded his wheelchair from the back of the Subaru and lifted him out of his car seat.
He was attempting to hide the emotion and nervousness he was
feeling, but Kali saw it pass in his expression like weather. Her stomach
was sick with love and pity and admiration mixed with everything
he was feeling—anxiety, insecurity, excitement. She checked him over
while buckling him into his chair, pulled the waistband of his jeans up
and tugged the hem of his tee shirt down to hide the bit of diaper peeking through. She scanned his face for embarrassment but he seemed
not to notice or care. His eyes were frosted glass. His thoughts were
far away—it was a coping mechanism of his when feelings got to be
too much. Sometimes Kali would follow him there and attempt to pull
him back, but this time, she would let him be. He needed to face this
his own way, she told herself. He needed to bear it. Kali knew he was
suffering, that he would suffer, but it was the kind of suffering that ma-
tures into something beautiful. This suffering was going somewhere.

Pushing him through the parking lot toward the entrance, they
watched a white van pull up and block the view of the doors. Kali ma-
neuvered his chair around the van and they turned their heads in uni-
son to see its double doors opened wide and an automated ramp slide
out with a mechanical whir. A boy about Marko's age wheeled onto

the ramp and engaged his wheel locks. The ramp started down. The boy's head was cocked to one side, his ear nearly on his shoulder, and his right hand was bent all the way forward at the wrist. He worked the controls for his wheelchair with his left hand. A small, strange sound came out of Marko as they passed and took this all in. It startled Kali at first, not knowing what produced it, but then she leaned forward and saw the side of Marko's face, his mouth open, and the sound, like the low mew of a cat, coming out of it.

"You okay buddy?"

Her voice instantly halted the sound and Marko closed his mouth and looked forward, establishing again his inner distance. Entering the building, Kali's awareness was especially sharp. Rather than taking it all in, the big picture, she rapidly assimilated a series of small details: the glass panel of a classroom door with a hand-painted rainbow; a potted fern tree, vital and lush, beside a large window; a tall boy walking slowly, unsteadily, away from them wearing a batman tee shirt, a strap around the back of his brunette head holding on his glasses; yellow flags with blue stripes suspended from high ceilings; a balcony on the second story with a motorized wheelchair moving across. After only several steps, Kali stopped and checked her phone for the room number where they were to meet the principal.

"You must be Marko," a voice said. Kali looked up. An older woman with chin-length gray hair and kind eyes emerged from a doorway and approached, smiling at Marko. She reached to shake Marko's hand. He hesitated and then lifted his limp hand. She grasped it and moved it up and down, up and down. She glanced up at Kali.

"I'm Kali, Marko's mom," Kali offered and forced her best smile. Her heart slammed inside her chest so powerfully she worried it would knock her over. The woman fixed Kali in her warm gaze, locked her eyes with Kali's and offered her hand. Kali was instantly put at ease.

"I'm Jane Lewis, the principal. Welcome to the McKinley School. We're so excited to have you." Each phrase was delivered distinctly with a clean pause between, each word articulated precisely.

"We're excited to be here. Aren't we, Marko?" Marko remained silent and still. Kali felt stupid, aware of her accent and the too-high pitch of her fake-friendly voice. Her armpits started to sweat. She lifted her arms to let them air dry, lest half-moons of wetness mar her shirt. Jane pretended not to notice.

Kali and Marko followed Jane across the hall and through the door from which she had emerged only moments before. The room they entered was a large area filled with computer stations. Students, at least half of them in wheelchairs, occupied most stations, hands hovering before touch screen displays. Jane approached a young girl seated in a motorized wheelchair with a touch screen device mounted on a stand extending from her armrest.

"Susan, this is Marko. Today's his first day," Jane said, gesturing toward Marko and Kali. The girl seemed to have difficulty controlling her facial muscles well enough to regard Marko. Her eyes moved toward him and then away while her mouth worked with the effort. She pressed something on her touch screen and a robotic voice sounded: "Welcome. Everyone. Here. Is. Friendly."

The girl grimaced, which Kali read as a smile. She smiled back and said, "Thank you," but her voice cracked. A swell of emotion overcame her and she had to clamp down against it to keep herself composed.

Jane gave them a tour, revealing room after room of happy kids with varying levels of disability appearing fully engaged in their activities, which included painting, making music, reading, and using various pieces of cutting-edge technology. Kali hardly needed to see the rest of the tour; after Susan, she was convinced. Her attention was instead attuned to Marko as they moved through the successive rooms. His reactions were subtle but there. His eyes widened or narrowed, expressing wonder and excitement or skepticism, perhaps fear. His hands were busy, undulating before his face the way they did when he was anxious, the way a teacher at his last school discouraged, claiming it was distracting to other students. Here, at McKinley, they understood it was an unconscious reaction to overstimulation. They called it "stimming." Jane's expression remained utterly neutral when she saw Marko stimming, when she regarded his hands and their undeviating pattern of fluid motion.

16. January 13, 2015: Stowe, MA

Marko sat across from Malik in the cafeteria, watching his discolored and swollen hands unwrap a peanut butter and jelly sandwich on white bread. The crusts had been cut off and parts of the bread were soggy pink from the jelly soaking through. Marko's own sandwich was on multigrain bread and instead of peanut butter, it was almond butter, and instead of strawberry jelly, it was apple preserves with no added sugar.

"Do you like sports?" Marko asked. Malik said yes but did not look up from his sandwich.

"I like baseball," Marko said. A silence followed and Marko realized with horror that he had just broken his mom's instructions. He had said something about himself instead of asking another question about Malik.

"The Red Sox are the best major league baseball team of all time," Malik said.

Marko was excited that they had something in common. He tried to think of something to say next. "I like baseball," he said. Marko realized he'd just said the same thing over again and his heart swelled with embarrassment to the point of rupture. It made him think of a part in *The Unbearable Lightness of Being* that described the woman's face as the deck of a ship and the crew of the ship as her soul. When she looked at her face in the mirror, she searched for the crew of her soul rushing up to deck from below. That's what must be happening to him in response to Malik, he thought. He said, "I feel my soul rushing up to the surface through my blood vessels and pores to show itself to you."

Malik didn't say anything, but a slight smile spread across his mouth.

"That's from a novel I'm reading called *The Unbearable Lightness of Being*. It's my mom's and it's pretty old. I found it and it has lots of dog-eared pages and underlined parts, so it's cool. It's helping me know her better, you know? How she thinks, what she notices?"

Malik still didn't say anything but just stared at Marko with the small smile.

Marko started to say something different when Malik abruptly grabbed his hands and pinned them to the table. Marko, startled, looked at the hands on the table between the two sandwiches and then looked at Malik, who was looking him in the eyes now. Marko's neck and face started feeling hot and he pulled his hands away.

"Why do you do that with your hands?" Malik asked.

"I don't know, it just happens. The doctors call it stimming," Marko said.

"What's that mean?"

"It's short for stimulation. It's something that kids with autistic spectrum disorder sometimes do."

"I have that," Malik said.

"Another thing we have in common," Marko said.

"What's the first thing?"

"We both like baseball."

Malik laughed and took a bite of his sandwich. "Lots of people like baseball," he said.

"Yeah but maybe not lots of people with autism like baseball," Marko said.

"I have 253 spring training games saved on my iPad," Malik said. "You could come over and watch some with me if you want."

Marko smiled. "I like baseball," he said. Malik laughed again. His laughing sounded like hiccups. Marko didn't understand what was so funny.

"Retards!"

Marko turned to see Derekah rolling by behind him. She rolled down to the other end of the cafeteria and sat with Christopher and Tanya and a few other kids that Marko didn't know.

"Why is she so mean?" Malik asked.

"My mom would say it's because she's an unhappy person," Marko said. Malik chewed his sandwich and looked at the ceiling. He seemed to be considering this idea. Marko took a bite of his own sandwich and it turned to clay in his mouth. His mouth turned dry when he was nervous. Marko realized he was afraid that Malik was going to ask him about what had happened to him in class earlier when Derekah was making fun of him. He didn't know how he would answer.

"What happened to your hands?" Marko asked.

"I have eczema on my hands."

"What's that?"

"A kind of rash."

Marko made a mental note to look up eczema later when he got home.

"Why are your legs so flat?"

Marko looked down at his lap. "I'm paralyzed from the waist down because I have spina bifida. I was born with it. So I've never used the muscles in my legs. Muscles grow from being broken. You strain them and they get tiny tears then when the tears are repaired, the muscle builds. So I guess you could say my leg muscles are unbroken."

"Now we have three things in common," Malik said. "I have spina bifida too. I was in a wheelchair for four years but now I wear a brace that helps me walk."

Marko was in awe. Now he was 100 percent sure that Malik would be his friend.

"Maybe I could come over to your house and watch baseball," Marko said.

"I'll ask my parents," Malik said. He was unwrapping his second peanut butter and jelly sandwich, which made Marko nervous. Lunch was about to be over and he still had to finish his one sandwich. And kids were only supposed to have one sandwich for lunch, not two.

"Maybe I could come over to your house and watch baseball," Marko said.

"You just said that," Malik said.

17. February 6, 2015: Stowe, MA

After that day, Marko dreaded seeing Derekah at school but looked forward to seeing Malik. The two feelings, six and ninety-six—being even and round, light and dark—cancelled each other out, leaving a net neutrality that was numberless and that Marko saw as a smooth, cool beige in his chest. After The Incident, their teacher was never late again, making it hard for Derekah to humiliate Marko in the classroom. She still threw tiny balls of paper at the back of h   is head whenever the teacher's back was turned, but this didn't bother Marko too much. He brushed them out of his hair with his hand and went about his day. He met with Malik every day for lunch and they had the same conversation about baseball. Almost every weekend, he went to Malik's house and they watched baseball together. This routine comforted Marko.

It comforted him, until one day when something different happened. It was an unseasonably warm day in the middle of winter, so the kids went outside for lunch. Malik pushed Marko's wheelchair up a grassy hill and behind a row of trees. Without saying anything, Malik lifted Marko from his chair and placed him on the grass, then sat down beside him very close so their shoulders and legs were touching. Malik placed Marko's lunch bag in his lap and reached for his own lunch bag, which he'd dropped to free his hands to lift Marko. Malik opened his first sandwich and began eating.

Marko sat feeling the heat where his shoulder touched Malik's and watching the math calculating where their hips and legs connected. It startled Marko to realize that he was excited. In fact, he wished that Malik would kiss him on the mouth. This wish and the sensations it created were altogether new and the shapes and colors they created were a mesmerizing spectacle.

"Eat your lunch," Malik said, staring at Marko's lunch bag on his lap. Malik paused in his chewing and his hands froze with the sandwich in midair. Marko knew Malik couldn't resume eating unless he ate too. It bothered Malik when routines weren't followed, as it bothered Marko, but this time they had strayed from the routine by coming outside for lunch and sitting in the grass, so Marko couldn't bring himself to eat. It wasn't the place and position in which he normally ate.

"Eat!" Malik said, his mouth half full. Marko withdrew a strawberry from his lunch bag and bit into it. This seemed to satisfy Malik enough to resume chewing. Marko chewed the strawberry slowly. It didn't taste right in this setting. Marko wanted to go back to their regular table in the cafeteria to eat his lunch, but he also wanted to be there in the grass with Malik. The ambivalence paralyzed him, and Malik once again insisted that Marko eat.

"Marko, eat your lunch." Malik sat forward, turned to Marko, and put his hand on Marko's shoulder. Marko couldn't move. Malik pulled another strawberry out of Marko's bag and fed it to Marko.

Marko inspected Malik's swollen, ruddy hand as it held the strawberry aloft in front of his mouth. Malik's fingers held just the green leafy top. Pinched together that way, they looked delicate and strong all at the same time. Marko bit into the strawberry. Its flavor exploded inside his mouth. Some strawberry juice dripped down his chin. As he reached to wipe it away, so did Malik, and their hands collided. Malik grabbed Marko's hand and held it. Marko looked up into Malik's face but his eyes were diverted, looking out past the trees and down the hill toward the school. Marko noticed how long his dark eyelashes were, and how close to his face. How, if he wanted to, he could flutter them against Marko's cheek.

18. February 7, 2015: Cambridge, MA

I n his spare time, which was the majority of the time, Marko enjoyed reading peer reviewed articles in medical journals that addressed, however remotely, any aspect of any of his conditions. While he was reading an article that was published in *Arthritis & Rheumatology* about hyaluronic acid in synovial fluid, he stopped every third word or so to look up words in his medical dictionary. So that he would better remember them for the next time he came across them, he wrote them down in his notebook. He was only in the third paragraph of the article and his list was getting long:

Anaphylaxis: exaggerated allergic reaction to a foreign protein resulting from previous exposure to it.

Angioedema: swelling that occurs just beneath the surface of the skin or mucous membranes.

Concomitant: existing or occurring with something else, often in a lesser way; accompanying; concurrent:

- Articular: of or relating to the joints.
- Arthralgia: pain in a joint.
- Arthropathy: disease of the joints.
- Synovia: a lubricating fluid resembling the white of an egg, secreted by certain membranes, as those of the joints.

- Aseptic: free from the living germs of disease, fermentation, or putrefaction.
- Rheology: the study of the deformation and flow of matter.

Marko was reading this particular article (very slowly) because one of his doctors recommended trying a hyaluronic acid supplement for his arm joints, which hurt a lot. They would inject this stuff into his shoulder, elbow, and wrist joints and it would cushion the joints the way that synovial fluid, the body's natural joint cushioning, did. Marko's own synovial fluid, they said, was breaking down because of the excessive weight-bearing his arms did, which they were not meant to do. It's like the knees of a fifty-year-old overweight person, they said, which is the type of patient they typically used these injectable supplements for.

Another solution for his problem, they said, was to build muscle strength in his arms so that his joints were well supported and not taking the brunt of all the impact. The consequence of this was that his mom and grandma were now feeding him protein shakes and making him lift weights. The shakes tasted bad and the weights were too hard to lift, so he asked for some time to read an article about the supplement and learn about it. His mom was letting him, but he was running out of brain steam and had only been at it for an hour.

"You ready for another round?" It was his mom. She stood in the doorway to his room holding the hand weights that looked deceptively small. Marko's arms ached just looking at them. He looked back at his computer screen. The letters scrambled and blurred together. He closed his eyes and rubbed them. He unlocked his wheels and rolled over to his mom, took the weights from her, and started the curls. She repositioned his arms and corrected his range.

"Remember, you have to lift all the way up until it touches your bicep, here," she said, pressing the weight against his arm. It was those last few inches that were the hardest. He did another rep and squeezed the weight all the way up.

"Perfect!"

She smiled. Her pride was enough to fuel one more full repetition.

"Mom?"

"Yes?"

"I need to talk to you about something."

"Can you keep lifting while you talk?"

He sighed and lifted the weights again. They felt twice as heavy with each ascent.

"There's this girl at school who hates me. She keeps making fun of me and my friend, but mostly just me."

"How does she make fun of you?"

Marko thought of the embarrassing things she said and couldn't bring himself to tell her.

"She calls me names and stuff," he said.

"She's probably having a hard time at home. Maybe her parents are really mean to her."

Marko remembered when he had seen Derekah being dropped off in the morning by someone. It was an older woman with a nice car. She seemed to be doting on Derekah, not mean to her.

"I don't think so," Marko said.

"It's not about you, honey," his mom said. "Can you focus on lifting?"

Marko sighed. "My arms are tired!"

"OK, take a break. I'll get you some water."

She walked away. Marko put the weights in his lap and let his arms fall open. His joints still ached and his muscles burned. He looked at his reflection in the mirror. His arms were skinny. They looked like little, pale twigs. He flexed one arm and inspected its muscles. He imagined them bulging and veiny, the way his dad's arms used to look. His mom came back with a glass of water and he took a sip.

"She called me and my friend Malik gay together," he said. His mom sat on the floor in front of him.

"How do you feel about that?"

It wasn't what Marko expected her to say. He was unprepared for the question and didn't have an answer.

"I don't know."

"How do you feel about Malik?"

"I like him. He's my friend. But we're not gay together." Marko felt the heat in his face. He remembered Malik feeding him strawberries and felt ashamed.

"If you were, that would be okay," she said. This was another unexpected statement. Marko stared at the weights in his lap. His hands were going.

"It's normal for kids to have strong feelings for both boys and girls, or either boys or girls. When I was your age, I had crushes on girls."

"You did?" Marko looked at her. He could see in her eyes that she meant it. She wasn't just saying it to make him feel better.

"I had crushes on boys, too. All my life, I've been attracted to both genders at different times."

Marko was simultaneously thrilled and repulsed. He had the sense she was confessing something to him that nobody else knew. He didn't know where it came from, but the feeling that it was wrong to be attracted to both genders was strong inside him and he was embarrassed (number fourteen) for her.

"Did you tell your parents?"

"No."

"Why not?"

"They wouldn't understand. They're from another time and another country."

"Well, I'm not gay with Malik."

"That's okay too," she said.

Marko put his water down and grabbed the hand weights again. He lifted them once and struggled to pinch his arms all the way closed at the top.

"Here, let's try another way," his mom said and positioned his hands over his shoulders.

"Just press them straight up," she said. Marko lifted the weights up over his head and lowered them back down. They felt much lighter this way. He did it again and got that smile of approval from his mom. He kept going and wondered whether he had told his mom the truth. Maybe he *was* gay with Malik. His mom had friends who were gay and they were nice people. Maybe it wasn't a bad thing to be. Marko wasn't even sure where the idea that it was wrong came from in the first place. Then he remembered. It was his grandmother.

He had been at a yoga class with her and there were two men in the class who kissed each other on the mouth and held hands during the meditation. His grandmother grimaced to herself and told Marko that what they did was wrong.

"What they do by themselves is their business," she'd said. "But it's just wrong to do it in front of everybody in public and create a scene." Marko had been younger then and he didn't understand what she meant by creating a scene. They looked like regular people to him. But she told him not to look at them, so he didn't. And he believed her that what they were doing was wrong. That it should be a secret, and one that they should be ashamed of.

After about fifteen repetitions, his arms were tired again and he had to stop. He put the weights in his lap, but his mom put them back in his hands.

"Come on, ten more, then you can rest," she said.

"My arms are 91 percent exhausted," he said, complaining.

"Then let's use that last 9 percent," she said and smiled. Marko counted out ten more, really straining with the last three, and then dropped the weights on the floor. They thunked loudly and rolled into his wheels.

"Whoa, don't drop them that far, you'll break the floor!"

"Sorry. Mom?"

She picked up the weights and stood up. He wanted to say something that would keep her there, keep her talking to him. She started walking away.

"Mom!"

"What?" She turned around, irritated.

"I'm sorry I dropped the weights," he said.

"It's okay," she said and turned away again.

"I think I might have strong feelings for Malik," he said, calling after her. She came back to him, leaned down, and took his face in her hands.

"That's nothing to be ashamed of. That mean girl is just jealous. Ignore her or be nice to her, but don't let her get to you," she said. She kissed his cheek and walked away. Marko sat and felt the burning in his arms. He looked at his reflection again in the mirror. He flexed his muscles and was sure they looked bigger already.

19. Sometime in 1987: Sofia, Bulgaria

Todor had been away for most of his children's lives, so when he came home after serving time in a Thai prison and being discharged from his duties as Trade Ambassador to find that they were already twelve and thirteen years old, they were strangers to him. Marko was tall for twelve, and such a beautiful boy. His youthful face reminded Todor of Emil's face, his lean and strong legs of Emil's legs. Todor tried not to look at his son at all for fear he would see Emil instead and reveal a forbidden desire he knew he felt and was ashamed of. But ignoring the boy seemed to make him pursue his father's attention all the harder.

It was a Monday afternoon when Marko came home from school early and surprised Todor in his study. Todor heard someone enter the house and climb the narrow, spiral stairs to the second floor. There was some light shuffling, then the sound of bare feet descending the stairs and slapping through the living room's hardwood floor to Todor's study.

Marko walked in almost naked, dressed only in tight, small underwear, holding a camera. He handed the camera to Todor and asked him to take photos.

"I want to be an underwear model, like the boys on the billboards," he said.

Todor was frozen in his seat. The camera fell from his hand and thunked on the desk. He picked it up. Todor tried to stand but quickly fell back into his seat. He felt lightheaded and heavy-bodied. He held the camera out to his son helplessly. "I can't . . ."

"Please, papa. I need you to do this. We won't tell Mother."

The boy had never called him Papa before. Only Father. Todor's chest burned with a strange mix of fatherly love and animal lust. His son was long-limbed and narrow. Todor raised the camera to his face and regarded Marko through the lens. Marko draped his body over the corner chair and glared at the camera with a serious expression on his face. His lips, slightly parted, glistened pink. Todor realized his son had applied some of his wife's pale pink lipstick. Todor snapped a photo, then advanced the film and snapped another. Marko shifted his body on the chair into a different seductive pose for each consecutive photo. After several on the chair, Marko stood and removed his underwear.

"Let's take some like this," he said. Todor continued taking photos, trying hard not to think about what this meant, trying hard not to see his son so objectively. He conjured images of Marko as a baby, wholly asexual, completely nonthreatening. The boys in Grafton, the young diplomats in training, they were a risk to his career and even his freedom. But his son, his own son—he was a risk to Todor's life. If he touched his adolescent son the way he now knew he might want to, he would not be able to live with himself.

The roll of film ran out and Todor dropped the camera from his face. Without the barrier of the lens, he felt too close to his son's nakedness. The erection in his pants ached. Marko's penis was flaccid. Todor was relieved that his son didn't seem to notice the bulge in his pants. The boy's intentions were innocent. He trusted his father as a safe person to take nude photos of him that he would keep for himself. A normal experiment of boyhood. Todor's chest burned with disgrace.

Marko replaced his underwear and took the camera back from his father.

"Thanks," he said. "I'll mail them off to be developed but I won't show anybody. I just want to see what they look like." Todor nodded. Marko left, closing the door behind him.

Todor fell back into his chair. Slowly, with sadness and a sense of defeat, Todor slid his hand down his pants and relieved himself of his shameful desire.

It should have occurred to Todor that such an incident would inevitably be found out. For Marko to have such photographs, he would have to have them in the house. And any item in the house was eventually found by Lydia, especially if it was deliberately hidden. So when he found her standing by their bed, stone-faced, clutching the nude photographs of the boy, he couldn't say exactly why he was shocked. A part of him was actually relieved to be caught. Just as Lydia found every hidden object in their house and brought it to the light, so she did with him and all he contained. This part of himself would now be known to her, in its darkest, most twisted manifestation.

"I can explain," he said.

"There is no explanation for this. I know everything already and anything you say to me now will only make it worse."

Todor sat on the bed and lowered his head into his hands. His fingers were calloused from all the manual labor he'd done as a boy. They scratched the tender skin around his eyes. He remembered one of the young men commenting about the roughness of his hands.

"I'm sending the children to my mother's," she said.

"Why?" He sat up and looked at her, pleadingly.

"They are not safe here. With you."

"I would never—"

"Stop!" She silenced him.

20. February 13, 2015: Cambridge, MA

At first, Kali thought she couldn't track when the change happened. She felt it had been like a slow fade from one way of being into another. She went from the dragon-like power of maternal ferocity to the walled off numbness of yearning to get out, get away, to not have the relentless responsibility and grief. But then she realized that there was, in fact, a specific day when the change started, when it distinctly occurred. It was a Monday morning and Kali was getting Marko ready for school. He was in his second month or so of McKinley and he was exhausted from all the mental activity and effort. His days were long, between the lengthy commute, the day of school, and the after-school program Kali enrolled him in. He got on the bus at 7 a.m. and she picked him up from the bus at 6 p.m.

He was grumpy and glowering that morning, refusing to eat almond butter ever again. Kali had been packing toasted AB and J's in his lunches for as long as he'd been going to school. Organic, sprouted-grain bread, raw almond butter, and fresh apple preserves. She felt the need to feed him only organic, preferably raw and whole, clean foods. There was so little of his health she could improve or control, and it was the one domain in which she could make choices that mattered, regardless of the expense.

"I hate that shitty almond butter. It tastes like nothing," he said. Kali's sigh was involuntary and poorly timed, overlapping with the tail end of his complaint, accompanied by a flippant gesture of plopping the freshly bagged sandwich on the counter dejectedly. Marko wheeled forward, crashed the chair against the bottom cupboards, reached up on the counter to grab the sandwich, and threw it against the wall. Then he glared at Kali. It wasn't the first tantrum he'd had, and she knew it wouldn't be the last. He was ravaged by hormones, overfilled with emotions, over-stimulated mentally, challenged maybe too much, severely limited in strength and physical ability, incontinent. And now he was starting to deal with sexual desire, which threatened him and which he didn't understand or know how to navigate. It was very understandable that he would behave that way. Still, looking at the wasted sandwich on the floor, the smear of organic raw almond butter on the wall, Kali felt contempt. One jar of that almond butter cost her $16.99. She had to work two hours at her job to make the money for one jar.

And then she felt worse than contempt: cold nothingness. Numb. The kind of numb, she thought, that prisoners must feel when they know they'll never see the outside of their prison again for the rest of their lives. There was a time when Kali thought that Zach was her prison, and if she could find her way free of him, somehow get out of that marriage, she would be emancipated. But that was not the case. When Zach lived with them, he ate the expensive organic strawberries that Kali bought for Marko. Kali thought that was bad—and it was. They didn't have any money. They couldn't afford those berries and they were for Marko. They were for his son whose body was ravaged with dis-ease. Dis-ability. They were not for Zach's strong, able body to consume like it consumed everything else. But in that moment, in the kitchen before school, Kali would have rather watched Zach eat the sandwich worth its weight in gold than see Marko not only refuse it but also throw it across the room, against the wall, on the floor.

Kali said nothing. Marko glared at her and she glared back. He must have seen it in her eyes: the coldness, the numbness. He must have registered it as rejection, as not being wanted, because he burst into sobs. He went from stone-hard anger to wet, hot anguish in one split second. He covered his face with his hands for the first minute or so, then, having received no response, reached his arms up to Kali. His red face and pleading eyes did not move her, and she did not do what she knew any half-decent mother should and would do in that situation. Instead of melting the ice around her heart, Marko's display reinforced the sense of her imprisonment. It was the closing and locking of her cell door, the securing of shackles and chains around her ankles, the hardness of the steel bars. Her responsibilities as his mother were the terms of her sentence and there was no escaping that. No parole board. No chance of getting out early for good behavior.

Kali retrieved the sandwich from the floor and pieced it back together inside the baggie, then placed it gently into his lunch box. He wailed even louder. She walked past him, out of the kitchen, and into the bathroom, where she closed and locked the door. She turned on the faucet full blast to mute the sound of his wailing and then stepped into the dry coolness of the empty bathtub. She squatted down there, pulled her knees up to her chest, hugged them, lowered her head, and rocked gently side to side. Kali started chanting, under her breath at first, then louder as the sounds of Marko's agony persisted to assault her ears through the rooms of the apartment, through the closed door, over the rushing water in the faucet. She plugged her ears with her fingers and chanted louder:

"ADI SHAKTI, ADI SHAKTI, ADI SHAKTI, NAMO NAMO,
SARAB SHAKTI, SARAB SHAKTI, SARAB SHAKTI, NAMO NAMO,
PRITHUM BHAGVATI, PRITHUM BHAGVATI, PRITHUM BHAGVATI,
NAMO NAMO,
KUNDALINI, MATA SHAKTI, MATA SHAKTI, NAMO, NAMO . . ."

Rhythmically, Kali repeated the chant for five minutes. Then, she removed her fingers from her ears and closed her voice. She stood up from the tub, stepped out, and turned off the faucet.

Silence.

She opened the bathroom door and stepped out. From the short passageway outside the bathroom that connected their two bedrooms and the rest of the apartment, Kali saw Marko in the living room with his back to her. She approached him. He was sitting quietly, waiting.

His lunchbox was in his lap and his coat was on. He was ready to go to school. Without speaking or looking him in the face, Kali retrieved her jacket from the coat closet, her keys from the kitchen counter, and pushed his chair out to the car.

She looked at his face when she leaned to lift him from his chair. His eyes were unfocused and cast down, his expression unreadable, strangely adult. He looked more like Zach than ever before.

21. February 15, 2015: Cambridge, MA

At night, Marko lay awake reading his mother's diary.

The chronic itch in my back preceded Marko. I traced the first time I felt it to my first night in America. Window guards were installed in the high-rise hotel room I stayed in during my first night in America. I know because I tried to open the window and feel the breeze. When it would barely open I tried removing the guards, but I didn't have the proper tools. I should have known from the look on the receptionist's face when I checked in that suicide would be prevalent here. So prevalent that the expense of window guards was justified, because hotel guests were likely enough to fling themselves out the windows.

I looked across the narrow street to the neighboring building, people stacked on top of people. All that weight. I'd never seen the like of it. I stared at the building for a long time, scanning the exterior for falling bodies. Surely, one must fall soon. Statistically, for a city this big, packed so densely with serious, well-dressed people, there should be a suicide occurring every few minutes. I watched and thought of the brother I had named Marko.

I didn't sleep that first night, drawn to the window as I was. The outside brightness at night exceeded that of day. There was a concrete dullness to the days. The buildings that scraped the sky blocked the sun.

Everyone below was left to scramble around in shadows with coffee. Everyone got buried in a haze of automobile smog. Exhaust from pipes mixed with exhaustion and scowls to build tension, winding people so taut that one pluck would burst them.

At that hotel window in the bright night, I was cracked wide open. Even long after I was exhausted and my eyes were stinging with the effort of staying open—even with the dark, warm pocket of the surrounding room, even with the blanketed bed behind me like a black cat rubbing against my leg, purring, beckoning—I couldn't yield to sleep.

Here was New York. Manhattan. Not on a glowing television screen but alive, right outside my window. So close I could feel its skin against mine. Far more amusing than the myths and legends about it suggested. I watched out the window relentlessly, hoping to make at least the slice of terrain I could witness less alien, less perilous. But what I felt was less than the unbearable anxiety I expected.

At some point, perhaps because I was delirious with no sleep, I started talking. The city was a patient listener, but hardly passive. It sat erect, eyes wide, prickling with attentiveness, as though it hadn't heard thousands of stories just like mine before. Every so often, it interrupted with a brief question, or with a signal that it was still with me (like the flicker of a streetlight or the wink of light reflected in a puddle) no matter how tedious my tale. I talked at length about my father, complained about his alcoholism, his depression after his imprisonment, his withdrawal from us. I talked about my brother and how my parents abandoned him. I talked about my mother and her affair, the man she loved and took as a lover for decades behind my father's back. I listened to the disdain in my voice when talking about it—not for the fact that she had been an adulterer, but for her inability to leave my father. Not for his benefit, not to set him free, but for herself and her lover. She chose instead to stay in the self-imposed prison of my father's gloom and her own failed expectations of what a life with him could be. The city listened and listened. But then, in the very dim first lights of dawn, when gray started to encroach on the bright night lights, it startled me into new awareness by asking me, "Who would you be if not your father's daughter? Your mother's daughter?"

The question was, at least at that time in my life, unanswerable. But it wasn't beyond pondering. The city's direct question that night, uttered in a high, hard voice nothing like my own, could not be ignored.

Who would I be if not my father's daughter? My mother's daughter? They are in me, like a tumor or a cancer. Not a clean tumor that can be sliced out by a deft surgeon. They are lesions, sclerotic patches woven throughout tissues and the membranous linings of organs. They are like arterial plaque throughout my brain and spinal cord—the necessary places where it can never be safely removed. They are integrated into my central nervous system just as thoroughly as the information it has received from my environment. In this way, they are a part of the coordination of the activity of all parts of my body, all its peripheral systems. The actions of my parents—no, the consequences of my parents' actions and inactions—have pervaded every region of my existence.

With this new awareness, Manhattan revealed to me with its first dawning the revelation that I had come to America primarily to disregard, deny, or disguise: the fact that my parents would always be with me. They remained inside me, contaminating me in an irreparable, powerful way.

Marko fell asleep with this image of his young mother in a New York hotel on her first night in the States and woke up several hours later knowing what he had to do. Just as she wanted to be free of her parents, he wanted to be free of the dark body. Everyone felt imprisoned by something, he realized. Most people have the choice to free themselves from it. Up until now, Marko had never thought he could have that choice. But then he found the dream bed.

While he listened, waiting for his mom to wake up, he opened the novel, *The Unbearable Lightness of Being,* and started reading again where he'd left off. His eyes were drawn to an underlined part:

> The days she walked through the streets looking danger in the face were the best of her life. She now knew there were conditions under which she could feel strong and fulfilled, and she longed to go off into the world and seek those conditions somewhere else.

This made him think of the dream bed and what it had felt like to be someone else, somewhere else. Not feeling that vast darkness so close, ready to swallow him. He didn't care if there was danger there. In fact, he realized he wanted danger. All at once, he ached to go back, to *seek those conditions somewhere else.*

Later, in the dream bed, he waited in the claustrophobic place for something to happen. He closed his eyes and tried to relax. It wasn't until he was almost asleep that he heard the voice of a man asking him what was wrong, if he was okay. Then he was there, on the floor in the bathroom. The bases of pedestal sinks along the tiled wall. The stalls and urinals opposite them. The cold floor, the smell of the able body. He breathed it in and sat up.

"Let me help," the man said. Marko gripped the man's hand and arms and pulled himself to his feet, which were still sore. The shoes he had cast off were there on the floor.

"I must have passed out," Marko said.

"I need to get you to the clinic," the man said.

"No, please don't, I'll be fine. Just give me a moment." Marko bent and retrieved his shoes, then walked back to the man's office. The nameplate on the door read: Ambassador Antonov. Marko stopped midstride and nearly fell. Antonov was his mother's last name.

The Ambassador grabbed his arm and braced him, leading him into the office and closing the door behind them. Marko sat in the chair and looked at the door. It was heavy and wooden with a window covered over on the inside with a poster of soldiers and the caption: "The Bulgarian Army Ranks." Marko put his shoes on, a much easier task in this body than in his own. Just feeling the chair against his backside, the cloth of his pants against his legs, the ache in his feet as he tied the laces—it was like journeying in a foreign country, but not as a tourist. The man, Ambassador Antonov, was standing near the bookshelves with a furrowed look of concern.

"Ambassador, thank you for helping me."

The Ambassador took a deep sigh and removed his glasses. He rubbed his eyes with the heels of his palms and then looked at Marko. In that spectacles-free face, Marko saw something familiar. The man's close-set eyes were rounder and darker than they looked through the lenses. The plane of his forehead when smooth looked taller. His hairline was straight across, giving way to thick, black hair combed back in waves. Marko's gaze lingered on the Ambassador's hair and then traveled down to his collarbone before landing again on his eyes.

"What is it?" the Ambassador asked. He replaced his glasses.

"Oh, sorry, Ambassador. Without your glasses on, you reminded me of someone." It was true, he reminded Marko of someone or something, or at least evoked a sense of familiarity in him, but he couldn't place it.

The Ambassador grinned and said, "Todor. Please call me Todor."

"Todor, thank you for helping me."

"Don't thank me yet. It seems there's more wrong with you than this problem with your feet. If you're going to be passing out too, I can't make a strong case for you to stay here." The Ambassador walked to the chair opposite Marko's and sat. "And why do you want to stay? Don't you miss your family in Bulgaria? Your young wife, perhaps? What's so great about Thailand?"

Thailand! Marko looked around the room. There was a very old-fashioned phone on the desk and a few other objects that looked old and that Marko didn't recognize.

"What year is it again?" Marko asked.

The Ambassador scowled. "It's 1985."

Marko nodded. He swallowed. Marko wasn't born until 2000. Here he was, fifteen years before his birth, in Thailand. He looked out the window. Before it was just a drab office, like the offices at school. Just bushes and trees outside the window. Everything seemed different and more exotic now.

"I've never been to Thailand," he said. Unwilled and automatic, he felt the smile stretch his face. Here he was with a pair of working legs, in a different time, and in Thailand. Consumed by the desire to explore, he stood.

Todor stood and frowned. "Let me help you," he said, reaching out and taking Marko's hand. The touch set off a wave of goosebumps up Marko's arms. He pulled his hand away.

"I'm okay, I'm much better now, thank you," Marko said.

Todor took a step back and rubbed his hands together slowly. Then he shoved them in the pockets of his trousers and thrust them forward. His face reddened. "Let me walk you back then," he said. There was something in his eyes, but Marko didn't know what it was. It made him feel nervous, but to his surprise, he didn't recognize the feeling. He suddenly realized why: his synesthesia didn't exist here. Without shape and color, his emotions were unknown to him.

He opened his mouth to refuse the offer, but said instead, "That would be fine, thank you." Marko realized he didn't know where he was going. He would need the Ambassador to guide him.

They walked out of the building into the road, which amounted to a clearing of the brush with muddy ruts where tires and tanks had passed. The foliage was thick and green. The air smelled sweet and felt soft against his skin. The sun was shining, and while it wasn't too hot yet, Marko sensed it would be soon. Marko walked alongside the Ambassador, limping a bit. His feet hurt. Each step sent a shock of pain up into his legs. Worse than the pain though, he was unpracticed at walking. It wasn't what he expected, what he'd dreamed about for so many years. In his imagination, walking was effortless, like floating. But in reality, legs were heavy things! There were hundreds of muscles working together to choreograph just one step, and it was exhausting. Add to that the tenderness at the base of those heavy legs, where his feet connected all of the weight of his body with the surface below, and it was amplified exponentially. Marko didn't know by what exponent because he didn't have the math, and everything seemed to require so much more attention and work without the math.

"Who do I remind you of?"

Marko looked at the Ambassador, whose walking did look effortless in comparison, and was confused.

"Back in my office you gave me a strange look. I asked you what and you said I reminded you of someone with my glasses off." The Ambassador removed his glasses again, folded them up, and slipped them into his pocket. He smiled. His teeth were stained a pale yellow and one of his two front teeth had a small chip on the inside. Marko had to look away and concentrate on walking.

"Oh, someone I used to know back home," he said, "a friend." Marko decided it was better to make something up than try to explain what it was he'd really felt.

"What kind of friend, exactly?" The Ambassador winked. Marko was again confused.

"Oh, just a friend I went to school with. His name is Malik." Marko thought of the real Malik and how he didn't remind him of the Ambassador at all.

"Did you and Malik do things together? Intimate things?"

Marko felt the nervous feeling again. They had emerged from the rutted road to a courtyard among several buildings. Marko was trying to hang back and follow the Ambassador, and the result was that the two men kept slowing down. The Ambassador stopped and touched Marko's forearm. Marko felt the shock and the goosebumps again.

"You don't have to be afraid to tell me, son. I'm that way, too. I have some friends here in Grafton and it's all very discreet. I can be discreet," he said and let his hand drop. He went on walking and Marko followed. They arrived at a building and walked through several corridors past many identical gray metal doors with numbers on them. Todor stopped at one and faced Marko.

"This is the one, yes?"

Marko nodded. He reached for the door handle and found it locked. The Ambassador patted Marko's pocket.

"You'll need the key, son," he said and smiled. Marko reached in his pocket and found the key. He unlocked the door and swung it open. Inside was a small space with a cot and a desk. A shelf was attached to the wall and several books were stacked high on it. Paper and a pen sat on the desk. The Ambassador took a step toward the room.

"There you are!"

Both men were startled. A young woman appeared. She was dressed in uniform and her hair was up in a tight bun. Her face was a soft oval but her eyes were hard. Marko again had a sense of familiarity that he couldn't quite place.

"Very well, son, we'll talk again soon. I'll look into the braces. Come by my office in a few days for an update. Ma'am." The Ambassador nodded at the young woman and walked away. Marko watched him take his glasses out of his pocket and put them back on.

"Emil, what was that?" the woman asked. Marko looked behind him down the hall but nobody was there. Then he realized that she was speaking to him. *His* name was Emil.

"What was what?"

"What were you doing with the Ambassador here in the dormitory?"

"He was just walking me back. I went to talk to him about something."

"Oh right, your braces. Are you okay? You look pale. Are your feet hurting?"

"Yes, they hurt."

"Well, let's get you off them."

She pushed him inside the room and onto the cot. She knelt down and removed his shoes, then lifted his feet onto the cot so he was reclined. She undid his pants and pulled them off, and then removed his underwear. Marko felt the erection and instinctively covered it with his hands. She stood and took off her clothes, too. The expression on her face was very matter-of-fact. Alarm bells were sounding in Marko's head. He opened his mouth to say something, to warn her that he'd never done this, but words wouldn't form.

She grabbed his hands, pinned them down over his head, and mounted him. She let out a groan of pleasure and Marko was disappointed that he didn't feel anything. Aside from the butterflies in his stomach and the intense nervous energy, he felt nothing. He looked down, and there was the penis—his penis—inside her. She moved up and down on it, yet it remained numb. A lot of time passed during which she sat astride him doing the same motion.

Marko looked at her face and watched it turn so red it was almost purple. A vein appeared on her forehead, zagging down like a lightning bolt. Her eyes seemed to bulge as she stared at the wall behind him. Then she screamed and convulsed, collapsing against him. Marko closed his eyes and felt the numbness spread across his entire body until it consumed him and he wasn't there anymore. He wasn't anywhere. He was in the formless place.

The sound of his mother's voice broke through and brought him heavily back into the dream bed and into Marko. The sensation was like squishing into a dark, wet, spongy place filled with troubling pains and sensations. He was so disappointed to be back, he might have cried, but confusion and fear that his mom was there capsized his despair. He pushed open the hinged side and slid his top half out. There was his mom, standing overhead, glaring down at him

"Mom?" Marko said, and his mom dropped down to her hands and knees in front of him. Her face was red with rage. She held a hammer.

"Mom, what are you doing?"

She grabbed Marko under the arms and lifted him into his chair. She got back on the floor and pulled the dream bed out from under her bed and struck it once with the hammer. Marko heard it crack.

"No, get away from it!" Marko pulled at his mom's shirt.

"You've been using this behind my back! You can't do this anymore, Marko, it's hurting you!"

"I wasn't! It's not!" Marko shouted. That was it. He was caught. He'd never get back to Thailand and Emil now. His hands were flying and he was rocking back and forth in his chair so hard that it was starting to inch forward on the carpet. Then he thought of something.

"It's a place where I like to go to meditate. It's fine. It calms me down," he said.

His mom looked at him, stunned.

"That's it? It calms you down?"

Marko's relief was a flat white. He stopped rocking but kept his hands moving. Would she let him keep using it?

"What's going on? What is that? Kali, why do you have a hammer?"

It was Marko's grandma. Marko quickly put it together: his grandma had come to get him off to school so his mom could go to work early. His mom must have come back unexpectedly. His grandma must have been late arriving.

Marko's grandma began pulling his chair back, away from his mom.

"It's fine, Mom, it's a box I made. I was just fixing it."

"It looks like a coffin," his grandma said. Marko craned his neck to look up at her behind his chair. She was grimacing with disgust.

"It's not a coffin," his mom said, and pushed it back under the bed. His grandma pushed Marko out into the living room and his mother followed.

"Marko, you're coming with Grandma, yes?" Lydia said. Marko looked around wildly for his mom. He thought his mom would be taking him to the bus. He couldn't leave her alone in the house now, not when she had just found him in the dream bed and might go destroy it.

Marko's mom went to his room and came out again with his backpack and handed it to him. "I have to go to work early, I forgot to mention. Grandma will take you to the bus," she said and kissed the top of his head.

"What? Why? Why didn't you tell me?" The prickly anxiety started getting stronger. Marko yanked open the zipper on his backpack and checked to see that his book and iPad were in there.

"I thought I told you, I'm sorry," his mom replied lightly. "Have fun, I love you!"

"Okay, let's go, Marko. Say bye to Mom," his grandmother said, pushing Marko toward the door. Marko looked back at his mom. She was leaning against the wall looking exhausted. He thought he saw fear in her eyes.

22. July 7, 1994: Sofia, Bulgaria

Dear Lydia:

When you read this letter, I will be gone. My plan is to dispose of my life as efficiently and neatly as possible. The last thing I want is to burden you with my lifeless body the way it burdened you while vital.

I need you to know, though, that it is a matter of brute physiology, this proclivity of mine towards young men. I am writing you this letter because there are some things about me that I want you to understand. Perhaps, in understanding, you will find forgiveness. Not for my sake, but for your own. I see the effect of the anger that you carry toward me on your face. It ages you far more than time. Your small, wiry body takes energy from it, I know. It's a slow-burning fire that propels you forward through life. Always doing, never being. If you find forgiveness, you can perhaps just be.

My father, as you know, was a military officer. He served in both the First and Second Balkan Wars. His time in the military was challenging. War hardened him. It made him worse than unhappy. It made him mean. He was rarely home, but when he did come home, he would inevitably find some aspect of my two sisters and me that fell short of his expectations. Punishment would be swift and firm. He made us strip down naked and bend over the side of his bed, whereupon he would whip our backsides with a leather belt. My sisters would scream and cry while I would remain silent and resolute. This would make him beat me far longer and harder than my sisters.

Once, after a beating, my oldest sister told me that I should scream and cry also when he beat me. That way, he would show me mercy the way he did them. She assumed that I did not cry because I was too proud. She was mistaken. I did not cry because I enjoyed it. What I kept hidden from all three of them was my arousal. When he was done, I fell to the floor and waited for him to leave the room before I stood up and got dressed. He and my sisters thought I fell to the floor face-first because I was in so much pain, I couldn't stand. While that might have been true, the real reason I did this was to hide my erection.

My arousal wasn't based on what you might be thinking. I wasn't aroused by my father or his violence. What aroused me was my older sisters and their naked bodies. The way they thrashed and heaved beside me, bent over the bed. My very first sexual attraction being toward my own sisters and tied to violence unsurprisingly resulted in shame and dysfunction. Going through puberty, I dreamt of being my father and beating a young boy with a belt. Only in the dreams, I would also be naked, and sex would follow the beatings.

Lydia, I know this must be disturbing for you to read. And maybe I will never even give you this letter. It is selfish, after all, to unburden myself of these shameful secrets only to burden you with them after I am dead.

When I met you, I was attracted to your mind more than anything. I had never met a woman so brilliant. You were smarter than me and most men I'd known. What I still don't understand is what attracted *you* to me. I know that after our courtship, it was your parents who pressured you into a marriage with me. But something drew you to me in the first place. What was it? It couldn't have been my wealth; you had money of your own and the means to support yourself. It couldn't have been my looks; you were beautiful and could have had a beautiful man. Perhaps it was my mind. The conversations we had when we met were works of art. We explored every topic in depth and introduced new topics seamlessly. They stretched hours that felt like mere minutes.

In those conversations—whole worlds—I fell in love with you. But after we married, we stopped talking.

I did not stop loving you. Not even after I started having affairs.

You never seemed to enjoy sleeping with me. And when you stopped sleeping with me, after several rejected advances, you invited me to take my appetites elsewhere. I don't state this to place blame; my sexual deviations were never your fault. But I do want to remind you of that invitation you made me.

I know that you likewise found an outlet for your own appetites, though I suspect it amounted to more than that. I suspect you fell in love with another man. Every time I came home, I half expected you to be gone, having run away with him. But you stayed. Even though you were never in love with me the way I was with you, and even though you were likely in love with another man, you chose to stay with me. I don't know whether to be grateful or resentful of that. I think I feel both at the same time.

Lydia, this isn't the life I wanted for either of us. I never wanted to be anybody's prison. Just as I'm sure you never wanted to be trapped. Nor did I want to be a man who exploits his position of power for sexual satisfaction from younger men. Nor did I want to be a father whom you judge as unsafe for his children, for his son. And because you will not leave me to make a life for yourself that will permit your happiness, I will remove myself from the world and free you. And free our children. I know you think I have taken my freedom and withheld yours. And perhaps that's true, at least physiologically: my body has had what it wants.

But real freedom, I think, is a state of mind. Thus, I have always been trapped.

Love forever,

Your T.

23. February 21, 2015: Cambridge, MA

The mentor program through Harvard had been going on for two years by the time Marko was thirteen. One month before his fourteenth birthday, he and Kali had an appointment to go meet another mentor. Kali went with low expectations. Every mentor Marko had been paired with so far—five, in total—had been a college student who was doing his or her degree in special education or some other field working with kids with disabilities, and for whom the mentor program fulfilled a requirement. Each one of them seemed detached and disinterested, even rude. One guy just took Marko to Friendly's every Saturday. Kali had to give up her Saturday to go with Marko and this kid. He always ordered onion rings and bought Marko a milkshake. Then they would sit there in silence. Kali had to think up things to say, encourage Marko to ask the kid questions, which he would answer in one or two words.

Another girl couldn't even remember Marko's name. She kept calling him Robert or something else that didn't sound anything like his name. Just outrageous errors. Kali started to get angry when she'd correct her.

"It's *Marko*," she'd snap, and the girl would look at her surprised and nervous.

So when it came time to go meet yet another mentor for Marko at a coffee shop downtown, Kali was resentful of the time it took to get on the train and ride there, navigating all the stairs and curbs and obstacles with Marko in his wheelchair.

And then they met her, and Jen was more perfect for Marko than anyone Kali could have designed herself.

Jen hadn't volunteered for the mentor program to fulfill a requirement for her degree. In fact, she was completing her degree when she volunteered and it had nothing to do with kids—she was a pre-med student. She had asked to mentor a kid in a wheelchair. Marko was the only one to meet that requirement at the time. Marko and Kali loved her from the beginning.

What Kali noticed about Jen right away was her lightness and her smile. Jen shone with confidence, sitting with shoulders back and head high in her wheelchair, as if she were standing taller than anyone. The effect was an air of having made a decision, like she was able to choose whether or not to position herself in a wheelchair without the use of her legs. Of course she wasn't, and she didn't, but her demeanor made it seem as though she had chosen to sit for the sake of advocacy—a gesture of solidarity.

It was only natural that Marko, along with anyone else whose body might have robbed him of certain abilities—such essential abilities that they effectively rob him of part of his identity too—should mind their condition, mourn it as a comparative loss. But Jen, who hadn't been born with disabilities but rather acquired them in an accident at a young age, wrenching her from abled to dis-abled, hadn't given herself over to strife. She seemed to transcend the rough edges trauma often leaves—shifting to match the bounded and boundless world as she met it all around her.

24. February 21, 2015: Cambridge, MA

Marko never had any siblings, but if he had, he imagined it would have been a sister and that having her would feel like how it felt to be with Jen, his mentor. She had been in a car accident when she was only five years old. She emerged paralyzed from the waist down. Like Marko, Jen grew up in a wheelchair. When Marko met her, she was twenty-one and had just graduated from college. She was applying to graduate schools. Marko hoped she would not leave Boston. Even though Marko loved to be around Jen, he didn't ever know what to say to her. One day, in the car on the way to pick up Jen, Marko's mom tried to coach him, prepping him with socially appropriate things to say.

"Act interested," she said. "Ask questions about her. She went to New York last week, so make sure to ask about her trip." Marko felt nervous. He didn't know how to have conversations with people. It was a challenge at school, and it was a challenge with Jen. He could talk to his mom and to his grandma, but everyone else made him nervous. He didn't want to say the wrong thing and be laughed at. Nobody had ever actually laughed at Marko for saying the wrong thing, but sometimes, when he heard people laugh, he believed they were laughing at him.

They arrived at Jen's house to find her waiting in the driveway with a bag and two sled hockey sticks across her lap. She was going with

Marko to hockey for the first time. "She has her own stick," Marko said as they pulled up.

"Yes, it looks like she does," his mom said, her voice smiling. Marko didn't know why, but this made him even more nervous.

Marko watched his mom get out of the car and take Jen's bag and hockey stick. His mom hugged Jen and he saw them both smiling. This made Marko smile but it also made him feel nervous. When his mom helped Jen into the car next to Marko in the back seat, Jen said, "Hi, Marko!" Marko tried to say hi back, but it came out a hoarse whisper.

"Say hi, honey," his mom said. He said it again, louder this time, and too loud. He shouted it. An awkward silence followed while Kali loaded Jen's wheelchair in the back of the Subaru. When she got back into the driver's seat and pulled away, Marko felt her eyes bore into him by way of the rearview mirror. He took a shallow breath.

"How was your trip to New York?" Marko asked Jen, turning away from his mom's stare. His heart beat so fast it vibrated.

"Oh, it was really nice. I love New York," Jen said.

A few moments passed in silence and then Marko's mom asked, "Were you looking at graduate schools there?"

"Yes," Jen said, "I interviewed at NYU. It went really well." Marko felt sick with dread. He looked wildly at his mom in the rearview, and her calming gaze was there to meet him. She shushed him with her eyes.

"Well that's great, how exciting! Of course, Marko and I would hate to lose you, but you wouldn't be too far away if you ended up in New York."

Marko blurted, "Yeah, we would hate that if you left."

Jen smiled and said, "I would hate to leave you guys, too! But yes, it's close. And also, Harvard is my first choice, so if they let me in there, I'll be here in Boston for at least five more years."

Marko was awash with relief. Of course they would let her in. As though reading his mind, Marko's mom said: "Of course they'll let you in!"

Marko wished he had said it, so he added, "Yeah, of course they'll let you in."

Jen laughed and said, "Hope so."

"What's that you're doing?" Jen asked Marko, pointing to his arms. They'd been doing their nervous dance again. Marko felt a rush of feeling number fourteen, embarrassment, burn his face with its red heat.

"Oh, I can't help it, it just happens," he said. "It's unconscious," he added, which his mom had called it before.

Jen said, "It's pretty; I like it. Do you mind if I do it, too?" Marko said he didn't mind. Jen began to move her arms in a similar wave-like pattern out in front of her face. She also bobbed her head, as if to a beat.

Marko said, "It's actually a move that my mom does in yoga. She says it takes the kundalini, or life energy, and moves it up the spine to the higher chakras."

"That's right! Marko has a lot of life energy to move," Kali said. Marko glared at her in the rearview but she wasn't looking.

Then Kali put in a CD and played a yoga song. She drove with one hand and moved her free arm in the same motion. The rhythm of the music gave them a pace to move to, and Marko discovered that he was doing it consciously now, moving in time with the music.

When they arrived at the hockey building, the music was blasting from the windows and all three of them were dancing to it with arms in the air.

The car rolled by other kids in wheelchairs, who stared into the windows with confused smiles. Kali parked and got the chairs from the back. Marko, who had been feeling so good just moments before, was now filled with anxiety again. He didn't want other kids in chairs to be there. He didn't want Jen to pay attention to them and not him. He had been picturing going to hockey with just Jen and his mom, and now they were all here and Marko would be left alone and forgotten in a crowd of kids. Without being able to stop it from happening, Marko was gone inside the dark body when his mom lifted him from the car and put him into his wheelchair.

"What's wrong, buddy?" his mom asked. But Marko couldn't hear her. His eyes were glazed over and he was crying. Kali watched as he rapidly pummeled his face and head with his fists while he screamed. But inside the dark body, Marko was still and holding his breath. He knew if he breathed in, the dark body would rush into his lungs like soot and he would choke. Being in the dark body was like being held under water—quiet and calm and weightless, but also smothering and airless. If he held his breath long enough, the dark body would let him go. Just when his lungs started to convulse, he surfaced, gasping for air.

His mom's face was very close to his and he heard her steadying voice in his ear: "Calm down, honey, take a deep breath, everything is fine, just breathe . . ." He took deep breaths the way his mom had taught him: counting to ten in, counting to ten out. He opened his eyes and wiped the tears from his face. There they were surrounding him: Jen, his mom, and a few other kids and adults. They all looked sad and expectant.

"Sorry," Marko said, because he couldn't think of what else to say or do. They all tittered and smiled and shrugged, excusing him, and then they made their way toward the entrance together.

Marko hung his head, embarrassed. He had never been able to control these episodes. And they were unpredictable, even to him. At the slightest provocation, he might fall too close to despair, where the sucking quicksand dark body would quickly consume him. He could not begin to articulate its real source. It came over him like ice water every time. At first, it was always shocking. But then it subsided and it was just cold, merely tempering.

He knew he sometimes hit himself when he fell in, but he couldn't stop it. It wasn't as though he didn't care. He cared very much, both in terms of how others saw him and the well-being of his own psyche. But the way that he was supposed to be, a way that was intended for the consumption of others, in a manner that was consciously entertaining, conspicuously user-friendly—it wasn't something he could always do. It was performing. He could do it sometimes, maybe most of the time, but the despair was always nearby. When he slipped inside the dark body, he didn't know what he looked like from the outside, but he could feel in his body that it was different. It was uncontrolled, untethered to any responsibility for pleasing others.

Once inside the building, Marko kept his eye on Jen, wanting to see her reaction to the team. A small crowd of kids moved from wheelchairs to skate platforms, donned shoulder pads, pulled on jerseys. The space was tight, glutted with gear and parents and kids and coaches, but it started clearing out rapidly as kids were lifted and carried onto the ice. Jen took it all in quickly and then fell in among them, moving herself from her wheelchair to the floor deftly, and gracefully accepting help being hoisted onto a skate platform that fit her. She secured her own straps and pulled on the gloves. She gripped her two hockey sticks, which were used to maneuver on the ice as well as push around the puck.

Jen was ready to go and was carried off before Marko was even out of his chair. His mom was having trouble finding gear his size. All of the other kids had gotten there first, leaving little to work with. Eventually, his mom found him a platform and some gloves just a little too big for him. Marko thought this was fine at first, but once he was out on the ice, he quickly realized he was having a hard time holding onto his sticks with the oversized gloves. When he dropped one stick on the ice, he wasn't able to pick it up with his gloved hand. Just when he was about to pull off the glove to pick up his stick, Jen appeared.

"Can I pick that up for you?"

Marko nodded and blushed and Jen picked up his stick. He took it from her and smiled. "Thanks," he said.

"Follow me," Jen said, and she skated off to the side of the rink. Marko followed, but couldn't keep up with her speed. The platform was heavy and his gloves were cumbersome. All the other kids were skating around warming up and a few of them moved into his path. When he made it to Jen, she was laughing. Marko's stomach burned. Was she laughing at him?

"This is so fun," she said. Marko tried to smile but couldn't. He was too nervous. He wanted too much for her to like him.

"When you push yourself forward on the ice," Jen said, "start with your sticks here, not up here." She demonstrated what she meant, placing her sticks at an angle to the ice and a bit behind her hips. Marko saw how this provided more leverage to push the weight forward with force. He tried it and followed her in a circle a few times. He found he was able to move faster when he copied her techniques. Then she showed him how to turn and stop quickly. Marko had a bit of a harder time with this because it involved some hip movements that he wasn't capable of. Still, he was happy to be moving faster.

When a game started, Jen proved herself a quality athlete. She was easily the most skilled player on the ice, moving fast and keeping command of the puck at all times. When she passed it off to others, she positioned herself near the goal where someone could pass it back and she could shoot it into the net. This happened several times before the other team could score even one goal.

Marko couldn't keep up with them. Although he was moving faster than he had been, he was still the slowest one. After a few times pushing himself across the rink after the group, his arms were aching. Just as he was about to move off for a rest, he heard Jen call out to him. He lifted his head. She passed the puck directly to him; it stopped against his stick. He scooted it a few inches before someone from the opposite team swiped it cleanly away from him. He gave Jen a worried, apologetic look, but Jen only winked and shrugged and then flashed him a reassuring smile. Marko moved off to the side where he rested for the remainder of the game.

⮃

Later, when Marko was alone with his mom again, she asked him to talk about what had happened in the parking lot and why he cried. "I don't know," Marko said, "I just cried."

His mom sat in front of him on the floor and leaned close. He thought the brown and orange in her eyes looked melty, like she was about to cry and if she did, the tears would leave watercolor streaks on her face. But she didn't cry. She wouldn't. She always held it together. Marko worried that his mom was secretly ashamed of him for not being able to always hold it together, too. "Okay, I won't press you," she said and leaned back. Marko sensed that she was about to look away, about to get up and do something else, and he scrambled for something to tell her that would keep her there.

"I like Jen," he said.

His mom smiled, but it was a sad smile. "I like Jen a lot, too," she said. Then she got up and walked out of the room. There wasn't anything else Marko could think of to say at the last second that might hold her attention. He looked around on the floor. There wasn't anything within reach for him to occupy himself with. His chair was in the dining room or entryway, and he needed help to get back into it. He dragged himself to his room and closed the door.

Inside his room, he found a pencil and a pen. He wrote: "Dear Mom," paused, and then wrote a letter explaining, as best he could, why he had cried that day in the parking lot. He wrote about the dark body, how it was like an open doorway that was always close, and how at any moment he was capable of stumbling into it without warning. He wrote his worst fear: that his mom really wished she had a normal son who could walk and act normal. Just writing it down nearly made the dark body close over him. When he finished the letter, he folded it up and put it in his pocket.

Later that day, with his mom, Marko asked if he could burn some paper outside. His mom looked surprised. "What paper?"

"It's something I wrote down, just some sad feelings I was having. I thought if I burned it, they would go away."

His mom made a face like a frown, but Marko could tell she was not unhappy. She was surprised, proud, and a little sad all at the same time. Marko saw it all in the clear window of her face. In certain unexpected moments, Marko's mom was transparent. "I think that's a great idea, honey. I've done things like that before, myself. Hey, how about if we do it together? I'll go write down a few things that I'm sad about and we'll burn the papers together. How does that sound?

"It sounds okay," Marko said, "but I don't want you to read my paper."

"Deal," his mom said and smiled. She patted Marko's shoulder, then went away to write her sadness down. Marko knew what she would write, that it would be about his dad leaving, and about her own father leaving.

Marko's mom came back with her paper along with a bowl and a lighter. She gave these things to Marko and then pushed him out to the front patio. There, she placed the metal bowl on the small square table and put her folded paper inside. She looked at Marko and raised her eyebrows. Marko pulled his letter to his mom out of his pocket and put it in the bowl.

She lit the papers in the bowl and they were suddenly ablaze. Pieces of paper ash floated hotly up in the breeze and suspended for a moment before falling, leaf-like, to the ground. By the time they touched the ground they had disintegrated completely. Black ash scattered along the porch floor and off onto the stairs and into the bushes. The fire in the bowl died down and was gone. The bowl itself was charred brown and black and held most of the paper ash still inside it. Marko looked up at his mom to see her smiling. Marko smiled back, but he didn't feel any better. In fact, he felt 27 percent worse. The feelings he had written down and addressed to his mom seemed to burn hotter inside him and to push him further away from her.

"Wow, I feel great! How do you feel?"

Marko gave a weak nod and then wheeled away to the edge of the patio. He looked out at the street: a chain of cars lining each side, people walking dogs, a person riding a bike. A little farther down, he saw what looked to be a mother and a son. The son was tall, almost as tall as the mom, but had the skinny body and ambling gait of a kid Marko's age. They brushed hands as they walked and turned their faces toward each other from time to time. Marko strained his ears and heard the muffled sounds of their conversation. He watched their backs as they moved away and as they walked, their legs.

25. March 14, 2015: Millis, MA

Marko was at the Ashram for the night with his grandma. While he lay in bed, Marko read passages in *The Unbearable Lightness of Being* about Tereza's memory of her childhood, which seemed vivid as she replayed it in her mind.

When Marko looked down at his life at age thirteen, he saw his parents finally splitting up. They had been warily circling each other for years—his whole existence, every bit of which he could remember. Marko didn't realize until he turned fourteen that his ability to form and hold memories was superior to most people's. He had thought everybody could turn and look at any event in their history as easily as he could. It wasn't a literal "look," as with the eyes, but a subconscious look. There he was at two, floating in his mother's arms, the math in his mind telling him the shape of his lower half and where it collided with her body, her arms, assuring him that his weight was supported even though it felt like floating, or like the ground had risen. He remembered wanting always to be held when he was little, to get that elevated vantage.

He remembered his father yelling at his mother: "I've been displaced in this family by your mother! Your mother is now Marko's father! This family is now you, her, and him!" He remembered her responding in a quiet, eerily calm voice that this fact was his fault, his doing, and if he wanted to be a father, he should be one. And it was true, Marko knew; for those years his father had rarely been there. All Marko knew of him was a deep frown, a muscled torso, and strong, hairy arms. Then he moved out. Moved to California to have a new wife and a better, more normal son. And Marko knew nothing of him anymore.

Marko remembered the last time his mom had sent him away to his grandma's. "At noon, your grandma will be here to pick you up," she had said. Hours of the day are arranged in Marko's mind in a wide arc from left to right, with 10:00 p.m. at the top and 8:00 a.m. at the bottom. It had been 9:30 a.m. when Marko's mom said this, and Marko remembered looking over at noon and feeling a lot of number six, which is dread. He felt tired, and the climb to noon seemed impossible. He had wanted to stay with his mom then, too, just like he had today.

He had heard her that morning on the phone with his grandma negotiating some extra time away from him in the coming weeks. She said she had to make some trips for work. He didn't believe her. He knew she wanted to get away from him, that he was a burden to her, and this made him feel twice as heavy as he actually was. He didn't realize he was hitting himself until his mom picked him up from the floor and held his arms down. She sat on the couch with him and hugged him, pinning his arms. He remembered how he relaxed and nuzzled his head into her chest and tried to resist the gravity of the dark body. He knew that being sad made it harder for her to be with him. He could feel that she was sad, too, and that made him sadder, and they kept weighing each other down in this way.

When Marko looked down at seven years old, he saw his parents deciding to tear the wallpaper out of the bathroom and paint the walls yellow. Marko's favorite color was yellow, so they decided to do this in both the bathroom and Marko's room. Marko rolled around on his scoot (the platform with wheels he had used) back and forth in the short hallway in front of the bathroom, and listened to them arguing. He wasn't paying attention to their words, only the sound of their voices, which grew louder and harsher by the minute. Tuning out their words when they argued was a skill Marko had honed years prior. He hummed while he paced, rolling tight circles back and forth, back and forth. Abruptly, Marko felt himself snatched up from his scoot. It was his father—he held Marko tight to his chest and yelled, "I'm taking Marko and we're leaving!"

Marko was too stunned to cry. He looked into the red face of his father and went rigid. The math was speeding in his head, calculating the points in space where his unfeeling body met his father's body.

"Don't you dare," Kali said, following them. Zach ripped Marko's coat out of the closet and stuffed one of his arms through. "Zach!" Kali yelled. When he turned, she slapped him hard across the face. The loud *thwack* startled Marko out of his trance and he screamed. He felt 50 percent scared and 50 percent sad. Kali grabbed him and pulled him, but Zach pulled back. They played tug of war with his body until Zach pried Kali's hands off of Marko and pulled him free, spinning away and running for the door. Marko was jostled in his arms, screaming now. He closed his eyes and the math with shapes and colors slowed. He saw the dimensions of his body there in the numbers, a grid-like cast of his shape.

When Zach reached the car and placed Marko in his seat, his mother was there again, trying to get to Marko. Zach blocked her then pushed and held her back, twisting up her shirt in his hand with one arm while he attempted to buckle Marko in with the other. Marko reached for his mother and screamed. She pulled back, slipped quickly out of her shirt, and shot forward to snatch Marko from his seat in the car. She pulled him into her arms and turned quickly. Walking back toward the house, Marko saw neighbors and others gathering around and staring. Marko looked at his father. He stood motionless by the car, breathing heavily, red-faced and frowning. His mother, wearing only a bra, carried him quickly inside and closed the door. From inside, Marko heard the car start and the tires squeal as it sped away.

Kali carried Marko to his room and sat him down on his bed. Calmness came over him, and he sat stoically staring at the wall.

"Are you okay?" Kali asked. He nodded. He looked her in the eye.

"Did Dad take house keys with him?"

"I don't think so."

"Go lock the door," he said. She looked at him for a moment and was silent. He thought she looked afraid. He expected her to ask why, but she didn't. She got up and walked out of the room. He listened carefully for the deadbolt and the chain lock at the back door. Moments later he heard the side door lock. She returned to his room and sat down next to him on his bed.

"If Dad comes home, you have to leave. You two can't be here together," he said. She frowned, then set her face to neutral and nodded. She bowed down and wrapped her arms around his slight frame. She rested the side of her face on his shoulder.

"Okay," she said, calmly. Then, "I'm so sorry, sweetie." Marko wished she would say more or feel more, either explain or cry, but she did neither. But Marko knew what she didn't have to explain. It was obvious when she looked at him. Her eyes were like a huge sign that read: I AM MISSING MY LIFE! THE MARRIAGE I SHOULD HAVE HAD! THE SON I SHOULD HAVE HAD!

"Maybe you can take a relaxing bath," Marko suggested.

She sat up. She moved stray hair out of her eyes. "I love you," she said.

"I love you, too, Mom," he said. She placed her hand on his cheek, stroked the side of his face twice, and forced a smile. She kissed him, stood up, and walked out.

"Try to nap," she said, pulling his door closed. Marko hadn't napped in years. But when he lay back in his bed, he realized he was very tired. In the bathroom next to his room, he heard the sounds of tearing wallpaper again. Tearing and scraping, tearing and scraping. It made a rhythm and Marko closed his eyes to hear it. He counted the beats. Behind and around this noise, he heard muffled voices outside. A few times, he thought he heard someone speaking his mom's name. They were talking about them, he thought. He felt scared and angry. He hoped the police wouldn't come again. He kept counting. Each time he heard a car pull into the parking lot, he stiffened with the anticipation of hearing angry pounding on the door. But it didn't come. Marko's mind began to drift when he got to number 500 and he realized the tear and scrape weren't happening anymore. He counted on anyway, hearing the sounds in his mind and keeping time just beneath the surface of consciousness. Above the depths where sleep would claim him, he saw the outlines of people. They were glowing, yellow, and smiling at him. He fell into sleep knowing he was safe.

Now, seven years later, Marko had trouble falling asleep, even though he knew he was safe.

26. March 14, 2015: Cambridge, MA

"So you mentioned that you had abortions. Tell me more about that."

Kali settled deeper into the IKEA loveseat and glanced at the obligatory box of tissues. She thought about the cemetery. That's where she went to think about the lost babies. It was there, at the cemetery, where she found the nearest thing to privacy she had ever known. When Kali first found it—years ago, before Marko—she had just had an abortion. The air was softer then, because summer had just begun. The pain in her womb was, in its tangibility, a relief. It wasn't the first abortion she'd had—it was the fourth. And yet, her youthful indifference was gone. At twenty-six, youth and all its benefits had long since left Kali. She had spent it fast and hard. Sometimes, ignorance can be the best protection.

Kali told the shrink about the cemetery and its secret green pond where the dragonflies were born.

"More die than are born, and maybe that's why I always go there to think about this," she said.

The scum on the surface of the pond was bright green and luminescent, as though illuminated from within. At dusk its glow turned paranormal, intensified by the hundreds of dead bodies surrounding it. In fact, Kali knew, the bodies must have made the grounds richly fertile, as all the foliage of the cemetery was unmistakably brighter and lusher.

"Now it's been fifteen years since I first went to the cemetery. Fifteen years since I had the abortion that destroyed my marriage. To fix our unfixable mistake, we got pregnant again. And for a while, we were happy. Filled with hope for the future."

Young and invincible and in love. Their combined income was seventeen thousand dollars each year. They didn't have any money, but they didn't need it. They only needed their attic apartment and their love.

"When the baby was born, the hole that had always been inside me was transferred to his body. I remember the midwife looking between my legs like she was watching a car wreck. She wouldn't look at me. 'Where is the baby? Let me have him,' I said."

The easy smile on Kali's face was still there but the feeling rising inside her no longer matched it. She felt herself going back to that moment, the moment when everything changed.

"There's something wrong with the baby."

"What's wrong with the baby? Let me have him, give him to me!" The midwife cut the silent gray cord connecting his body to Kali's and lifted him away from her. She swaddled him and mumbled rushed words tinged with panic to the hospital nurse. They began to take him out and Kali screamed.

"GIVE ME MY BABY!"

The midwife stopped. She looked at Kali with bloodshot eyes and a bloodless face.

"The baby has a hole in his back."

"I won't touch his back." Kali said it calmer than she felt. The midwife didn't move. Zach, who had been paralyzed and useless at Kali's side, finally spoke.

"Our religious beliefs dictate that she has to hold the baby before you take him anywhere."

The midwife handed Kali the baby at once. Kali looked at Zach and was more grateful than she'd ever been. It was the exact right thing to say—legally, they could not refuse the couple's request after that. They had no such religious beliefs. Kali held him for exactly three minutes.

It was early in the morning. The baby was taken away from Kali. It felt like hours they were gone. She was left alone in the room. She delivered the placenta and lay there. Finally, she got up, even though she wasn't supposed to. She had to find her baby and hold him. She made it to the hall and saw five people in white coats coming toward her. As soon as they approached, she collapsed. She fell against the wall and slid down to the floor. She stayed there while they told her everything that was wrong. It wasn't just one thing. It was five or six things.

In his first six months of life, he had major spinal, brain, and heart surgeries. He was on methadone for morphine withdrawal.

The nurses hated Kali, but she didn't mind. It was when she first learned to get comfortable sitting with people who were actively contemptuous toward her. They wanted her to leave like the rest of them but she couldn't. The only time she was able to take her eyes off of Marko was when she looked around at the other babies. All around her were tiny bodies in sterile glass bubbles. Rows of babies that had no one. Inside one of the bubbles, Kali saw a baby opened up and pulled apart: a cracked chest with unhinged ribs and the little lungs pulled out, resting on the platform beside it. There was saran wrap over the sternum. Kali learned later, after seeing it many times, that when babies have open-heart surgery the doctors have to wait for the swelling to go down before they can put the baby back together. The chests are so small, they can't just stuff everything back in and close it up.

For the first few months after Marko was born, the sights and smells of the NICU would give Kali the urge to scream and wail. Combined with the throbbing pain in her genitals and the black blood that fell out of her, the open babies in sterile bubbles and the corresponding smell (like hand sanitizer) were too much. The urge would come on so strong, and at such frequent intervals, that Kali would start to sweat with the effort not to fall apart. Her back muscles would tighten so hard that she would be sore later. Only the most dedicated act of concentration would keep her in one piece. To focus, Kali would watch the clock. She would imagine it surrounded by other hidden clocks, each set at a different *time. In this way, the unfamiliar and terrifying became, gradually, the familiar and almost comforting. The ticking became her most precious companion. Even after she took Marko home, frequent trips back to the hospital were anticipated with joy. Kali's actual home became the place to escape, while the hospital became what felt like home.*

"You've told me this story before," the shrink said.

Kali stared at her. Her mouse-brown hair suddenly looked ugly.

"In your first session, in fact, using many of the same words, you told me about when Marko was born."

"Good memory you have." Kali felt offended and was ready to get up and walk out.

"I only mention it because I know it's a story you've told only me, which means you've told yourself many times. I'd guess every day for fourteen years?"

Kali blinked. She glanced again at the tissues. A lump was forming tight and heavy in her chest.

"And I'd also guess that you tell yourself the story every day because back then, when Marko was brand new and so fragile, you showed up with everything you had to take care of him. And now, fourteen years later, you find yourself with a son almost just as fragile as he was then. But you can't show up like that anymore and you feel guilty about it."

"I'm supposed to feel excited about it?" Kali shouted. She slapped the tissue box off the end table and stood up. "Of course I feel guilty! My bones, my organs, all my cells are saturated with guilt! I'm paying you to tell me what I already know now?"

"You're angry."

"Another brilliant observation!"

"Kali, please sit down."

Kali walked out.

27. March 15, 2015: Cambridge, MA

When Marko woke the next morning, he waited for his grandma to wake up and catheterize him. To pass the time, he read a passage in his mom's diary.

So-called privacy has never been mine. When I was a child, my mother had all the doors in our house removed—to my room, to the bathroom, to the closets. Even the shower doors were clear glass. Sometimes, they would fog up and become opaque. It was the closest thing I had to privacy and because of it, I showered more than necessary.

Apart from privacy, my mother also disliked the construct of time. Every clock in our house was set to a different time. Each day was incalculably long—a mess of divergent hours and overlapping circles from ignorant clock faces looking down on me. Ticking away my life. Ticking carelessly, aimlessly. It wasn't until I noticed how the sun climbs through the sky that I learned the true nature of time—that it marks different points along that endless, boundless repetition. It counts its recurrences, letting us know we're growing older and moving closer to death. One day, I thought it important to set all the clocks the same and let them agree; whether the current time was accurate or not didn't seem important. In fact, the starting point being 12 and ending in 12 made no sense— it seemed absolutely arbitrary—so I decided to start at 1. But it didn't work, because my mother scuttled behind me, setting them all back to their different times with her lips fused together in a surprised and uneasy line.

I was a very sensual and sexual person from a very young age. Sensual, because I was fascinated with the experiences afforded by the senses and by the distinctions between the types of experience each sense facilitates. The way something smells, for example, is a wholly other thing from the way it feels against my bare skin. And the nuanced variation among the full range of experience from any one of these senses is outrageous.

Sexual, because I loved having orgasms. I found my first orgasm by accident. The showerhead had broken and I had only a hose emitting a firm column of water. When I washed my genitals, I felt the most peculiar sensation, which at first I found almost unpleasant. Yet, I couldn't stop. I couldn't move the spigot from my genitals. It reminded me of appetite, but concentrated and multiplying—demanding to be sated. My hips started gyrating, unwilled. Then it happened. It was small and shallow but absolute. I had no idea what it was—I worried something had just gone very wrong in my body. But I couldn't stop thinking about it and I couldn't wait to try it again.

Lacking privacy, I had to learn to masturbate without anyone knowing. I did it in the bathroom while sitting on the toilet. The way my body was positioned on the toilet allowed most of my lower torso to stay hidden behind the sink pedestal, so I could discreetly place my hand over my genitals and slowly, slowly move it. My facial expression never changed. I learned to orgasm imperceptibly. And I found I could achieve it easily, sometimes with barely the slightest movement. Most of the activity lived in my mind—in the scenes I imagined—where my mother could never look. There were enough images in my mind to provide a lifetime of orgasms, and I knew I would need them all. Because each one loosed something previously condensed. Kind of like the way two single cells contain a future, whole person: a birth, a life, a death, and all of the time that takes and all of the senses and experiences afforded by that time. Each small orgasm contains a glimpse into something that big—something that transcendent.

If Marko had read that before he masturbated and had sex as Emil, he would have been feeling thirty-seven (confused) and maybe fourteen (embarrassed). But after he himself had had an orgasm, experienced its physical and chemical effects, he understood. He had also watched the girl on top of him have one, and it looked to Marko like her head was going to blow off. Marko was in the bed at his grandma's apartment. He looked down at his crotch and put his hand there. He thought about the girl on top of him. He thought about Malik. He thought about Jen. Then, he thought about the Ambassador. He felt a funny feeling in his middle, like his stomach had wings and was flapping them rapidly. The math gave him the position of his lower half against his bed and he could almost feel it. He was almost Emil.

"Marko?"

Marko jerked his hand back and looked up. It was his grandma.

"Don't you knock?"

His grandma took a step back out the door and knocked on the doorframe.

"What?"

She poked her head in. "Your mom's coming. She's on her way, so get your stuff together." Marko sat up. That was the best news he'd heard in a while! Now he could go back in the dream bed. He could go back to Emil, to Thailand, to the Ambassador.

28. 1984, Thailand

Todor couldn't stop thinking of Emil. He decided that the next time the boy came to him, he would make a move. The thought scared him because it was very risky. He'd told Emil that he had been with other young men in Grafton, but it wasn't true. He had never allowed himself to be so careless. Still, his draw to Emil was powerful enough to overcome his fear. And he sensed that Emil would be discreet. He sensed that what he felt was mutual.

But several days passed and Emil didn't return. Todor had gotten Emil's braces and they had been delivered to him, so he was sure the boy would come around to say thanks. When he did not, Todor's desire for Emil drove him to purchase the company of a young male prostitute in Bangkok. It wasn't the first time he'd done it, but it was the first time he would do it with the intention of pretending it was Emil. He had already spent hours in his office, staring at the door, waiting for Emil to walk through it. He had tried to take his appetites out on Lydia, but she wouldn't let him near her. It was an irresistible urge that couldn't be quelled any other way. Maybe that was why, for the first time and the last, he wasn't extremely careful.

The young man looked nothing like Emil, but that didn't matter to Todor. He had a powerful imagination. All he needed was a warm body, preferably male and young, as the blank canvas he would use to paint his vivid and complete picture. Glow, the club he'd gone to the first time, was closed. The doors were locked and the lights were off. This should have alerted Todor to a problem he would find out about too late: that a police crackdown on gay prostitution was underway in Bangkok. Because Glow was the hub, it had been raided and fined out of business. When Todor had gone there the first time, he had lurked outside in the shadows until he saw the right fit—a tall, lanky boy walking toward the door wearing tight pants. Then, drawing his hood up around his face, he'd strode past quickly, grabbing the boy's arm and pulling him into the alley. This was all to avoid being seen and recognized in the vicinity of Glow. After paying him, the boy had told Todor of another, lower profile spot in Bangkok, so, this time, finding Glow closed, he headed there.

It was a public toilet below street level. Todor got lost looking for it, wandering the blocks around it and finding nothing until he stopped and peered into every doorway. Finally, he came upon an unmarked door that led to one flight of concrete stairs going down. Todor descended the dark, damp staircase into what smelled like sewer and sex. A wave of fear and repulsion came over him and he very nearly turned back, but he caught the outline of someone down there, a slender figure. Todor entered the dim room. There were two stalls and two sinks in the cramped space. The ceiling was low and the floor was wet with semen. The young man stood at one of the sinks and faced Todor as he entered. Todor pulled his wallet from his pocket and opened it. The boy opened his pants. Todor approached and turned the boy around, gently pushing him against the wall.

Before he could take his pants down, Todor was grabbed from behind and dragged back up the stairs. In the street, he faced three officers wearing tall hats with badges on the front. He was handcuffed and arrested. The satisfaction in their faces enraged Todor. He writhed and kicked as he was forced into the back of a truck. The doors closed and he found himself with three other men. They stared up at him and then dropped their gazes to the floor.

His first thought was of Lydia and how ashamed she would be. When the truck stopped and the doors swung open, Todor immediately began talking about his ambassadorship and how he was a protected representative of the Bulgarian government. He asserted that he was not engaging the young man for sex but rather attempting to capture him and turn him into the police. The Thai police didn't appear to care. Todor was aware of the way they hated the foreign government officials infesting their town and looked for any reason possible to arrest them. He'd advocated for several young recruits arrested by Thai police for engaging female prostitutes. There had been three of them, and all of them were dishonorably discharged after serving a mitigated sentence in a Thai jail.

Todor was detained for three days before he was able to contact anyone. He called Lydia and urged her to take the kids and return to their home in Bulgaria. He said he had been arrested on trumped-up charges and that it would be a lengthy process that she should not be pulled into. It was another three days before he could contact his superiors. A week later, he was released.

29. March 14, 2015: Cambridge, MA

It seemed to Kali it was always, always winter. No warm spring in the middle. Just light and dusty snow, or light and plump snow, or heavy and wet snow and gray and cold. Every day, the bottoms of her jeans dragging on cold concrete—being short, pant legs were often too long on her—and getting stuck under her heels. No plucky young women scantily clad. No strapping shirtless men. Just a metallic sky and frozen, unused playgrounds. The light draining out of the day as early as four in the afternoon. Then it would still be dark in the morning, like coffee spilled on the sun.

Without the sun to warm her, she needed very hot coffee. Her hair, glossy and black, would steam in the frigid apartment air after every hot shower, so she started taking cold showers again. She had found a method for taking cold showers that worked well: First, stick your hands under. Next, each foot, one at a time. Then each arm, followed by each leg. When her extremities were bright red and burning cold, Kali could step under and turn her face up into the icy blast. While under the water, she rubbed and rubbed every inch of her body vigorously.

By the time she was done, when she turned off the water, Kali would be shivering so violently that her teeth would clatter even when she tried to clench them closed. But stepping out into the apartment and wrapping herself in a white, fluffy towel, she felt warm. Those few minutes after the cold showers were the only times Kali felt warm.

Before walking anywhere, she put on seven layers of clothes and a hat and a scarf and gloves. Kali had to prepare for war out there. As she went to see a shrink after years of having it suggested to her, the sky wasn't metallic for a change: it was like marble, all gray and gold.

The last experience with the shrink had left her feeling lonely and needing to feel wanted, so Kali planned to meet a woman she had been sleeping with. When she saw the sky, she stopped and looked up at it for a long while. It was almost enough to make her cancel her plans and go back home, because the surprise of a beautiful sky reminded her that she could never share something like that with the woman she was going to see. But she looked back at the icy sidewalk and kept walking.

Kali was always hungry that inexhaustible winter. It was precisely that which drove her out of the apartment that day in pursuit of something that wasn't going to sate her: an older woman she'd slept with on and off since her separation from Zach. It wasn't just sex she was hungry for; it was that bigger thing of which sex is sometimes a small part. She wanted mystery. She wanted knowledge, but not knowledge for its own sake and not the kind that can be taught. Kali wanted the kind of knowledge that can only be obtained through living, an experiential knowledge that comes like a gift on a wave of wild, raw life.

She was hungry to leave her skin, to leave gravity, to go bounding in something more massive than the ocean and just as violent. The urge was toward something that would change her so radically that she would become what she did not know. What she'd never even seen.

Whatever it was that Kali wanted, whatever unutterable, vague thing, she held onto anticipation for it, a hope that was so strong it made her fingers ache. It woke her in the night. It thinned the air so that she could never get a good breath. It wilted her a little with sadness.

Kali walked into the café and saw her. She looked at Kali with cold eyes. Slightly less cold than Kali's, but still without warmth. Half of the already small amount of desire Kali had for being with her drained. By the time she sat across from her, the other half was gone. She began talking immediately, incessantly about something Kali couldn't understand: an investment she made that went sour, all the particulars of the transaction. Usually, Kali could muster a smile and feign interest, take her hand and lean toward her across the table; but on this night she couldn't offer even that much. The idea of being alone was turning less painful than the idea of sitting there with her for one more minute.

"I have to go to the bathroom," Kali said, then stood up and walked away before the woman finished her sentence. Kali yanked her coat off the chair so hard it clattered, nearly fell over. She put it on as she walked past the bathroom and back down the street the way she'd come, not looking back.

Kali passed a dark, slumped figure on a bench and had the fleeting instinct to stop and find out if the person was okay. But this was Central Square and there was a slumped figure on every bench. Kali walked on and thought about the person she had just passed. She guessed she was a woman. Kali also guessed that the woman was intensely lonely, felt overburdened by obligation and commitment, and had no faith in relationships. This last because she had tried to be in them many times and each time, despite her purest, highest intentions and most earnest efforts, she watched them degrade and corrode before her eyes. Even as she railed against it, whether quietly inside herself or outwardly to the intimate partner or to the world outside, it turned indifferently bad. She likened it to standing before a lovely sculpture of fine metals—iron and chrome and aluminum and steel—and wishing for it not to rust. But because it is in the air and exposed to both moisture and oxygen on a daily basis, it rusts. Slowly but surely, its beauty turns to ugliness.

Crying would have felt better than anything right then. Kali wanted to cry hard and wretchedly. But instead, she felt a dull, mute wall of pain that gave way to nothing. It was a strong wall, after all, and it held everything fast behind it.

30. March 15, 2015: Cambridge, MA

Back at home, Marko could see that his mom was in a bad mood. She didn't talk much and kept staring off while Marko tried to talk to her. He asked her if she wanted to watch some baseball with him and she said sure. But then Marko was watching baseball by himself on his iPad and she was sitting next to him staring at the wall. After a while, Marko paused the game he was watching.

"You okay?" he asked her. She looked at him and didn't say anything.

"Do you want to use the dream bed?" she asked.

Marko nodded, stunned.

"You'd rather use the dream bed than watch baseball?"

Marko was unsure how to proceed. He wanted to use the dream bed more than anything. But he didn't want to act too eager either. Usually, nothing could be more desirable than baseball on the iPad.

"What kind of dreams have you had in there?" his mom asked. Marko shrugged. He couldn't decide what to tell her.

"I apologize for what happened when I caught you in there. I wanted to destroy the thing. It's just those headaches you've been having and a superstition someone told me about that thing and how it could possibly even do harm. There's that risk. Anyway, I wish you would have asked first."

"Sorry."

"I built it with the help of a woman I met at the ashram. She's a shaman. She gave me the directions to build it and gave me the materials, which she blessed. She told me it would do one of two things, either past life regression or what's called shamanic journeying. The latter is what has happened to me. It's basically a state of vivid, lucid dreaming that reveals something important to me about myself. Each time has been pretty intense for me. That's why I'm very curious to know what it's been like for you."

Marko wondered if he were dreaming right then. The quality of what she just shared with him was 73 percent more personal than anything she'd ever shared before. "I don't know. It just relaxes me," he said. She squinted at him.

"I've had dreams of being someone else. Someone older who can walk." Marko exhaled. He hadn't realized he'd been holding his breath. Her eyes widened and filled with fear. She leaned forward and grabbed his arm.

"Are you regressing? If it's a past life, people you encounter there would possibly look familiar to you. You would come back with knowledge from your past life that could be dangerous."

"Why dangerous?"

"She told me that regressing takes a toll, whether physically or emotionally. She told me that there was a man she made a dream bed for who started having chest pains after he came back from a regression. He came back knowing what his past self knew, she said, and it aged his heart. The man started coughing all the time. He went to the doctor and they did a scan and found out that his heart was enlarged and leaking fluid into his lungs. He had been totally healthy! So they put him on medication. He got better for a while. But then he went back in the dream bed and had a heart attack!"

Marko's hands were going.

"There are other stories, Marko. A woman who went mad. Another woman who got very depressed then just disappeared. It's not a joke."

Marko didn't realize he'd been smiling. It wasn't the sad stories about the people that pleased him. It was his mom's deep and palpable concern for him.

"Have you noticed anything? Any new pain in your body after going in? Any depression or dark thoughts?"

There was the fear in her eyes again. Now he understood. She was worried about what the dream bed was taking from him in exchange for what it gave. Marko thought of the dark body and how it seemed to get more powerful and closer to him each time he travelled to Emil. Also, he'd been having headaches a lot, especially when he read.

"No, nothing like that," he said. She looked relieved and he knew he'd said the right thing. "Can I go in there now?"

His mom was calm when she answered, which surprised him. "Yes, but I should tell you that your grandmother knows about the dream bed now. She saw it that day and even though I put her off, she knew what it was. The shaman who gave me the plans lives at the Ashram with Grandma and they know each other. Grandma knows the stories. Now, she's threatening to try to get custody of you because she says I left you alone and allowed you to put yourself in danger. She doesn't believe in what the shaman does, she calls it nonsense, yet it seems it scares her to know you're doing it."

Marko leaned closer to his mom and grabbed her arm and clung to it. It worried him very much to think of having to be with his grandma 100 percent of the time. Dark green cubes of fear clunked painfully through his head.

"It'll be okay," his mom said, seeing that she'd scared him. "She won't follow through with this. The only thing is, now that she's started this, we're going to have to go through it. Grandma told me she knows a counselor that she wants to have you talk to. So that might happen, a counselor might come over and ask you questions and ask me questions."

Marko gripped her arm harder.

"All you have to do is tell the truth. I won't ask you to say anything you don't think is true," she said.

"What do I have to say to stay with you?" he asked. She smiled and pushed his hair back from his forehead.

"The truth," she said. He could tell she was lying.

Marko decided to go into the dream bed one last time, then ask her to get rid of it. If it were there when the counselor person came, they wouldn't be able to deny its existence, which is what Marko knew he had to do. He got in his chair and wheeled into her room. He locked the wheels. He looked behind him, but she wasn't coming. She disappeared into the kitchen. He closed the door to her bedroom and climbed to the floor.

He woke in Emil's body, knowing it right away by the sore feet. He was in the cot in his small room in the dormitory and he was alone. On the small desk was the novel, *The Unbearable Lightness of Being*. The Ambassador had given it to him. He opened it and fanned the pages. The same dog-eared pages and underlined passages were there as the ones he knew from his mom's copy of the book. He placed the book back on the desk and sat on the bed. On the floor, tucked under the bed and peeking out, were metal contraptions. He pulled them out and saw that they were flexible braces for his feet and ankles. He fit his feet into them and put his shoes on over them, marveling again at the ease of doing this. He stood and walked out of the room. With the braces on, he found his feet hurt less. The braces held his feet in place, not allowing them to turn in and walk on the sorest places. He walked through the corridor and out into the sunlit courtyard. The air was humid and hot. Before he completed ten paces, he was already sweating.

He eventually found the rutted road and followed it, but it ended abruptly, giving way to a footpath into the forest. Even though he knew it wasn't the way back to the Ambassador's office, he had the urge to explore it, so he went. The path reminded him of a time he had gone camping with his mother and grandmother. They stayed in a cabin, one of a dozen or so, clustered around a corner of a lake. Many times a day, whenever his mom went out looking for kindling, or off to the deer blind, or down to the dock or to the beach, she took Marko along, pushing his off-road wheelchair over the dirt paths, rough with rocks and roots, that wound around the camp.

Now here he was in Thailand as Emil, walking with a stiff-legged gait along a similar path, having a memory of Marko's life that would take place in the future.

A stream ran to the right of him. The path curved close to the water, then climbed above it. In places it rose steeply. He had to pick his way across rocks and over fallen limbs. Sometimes the trail became less than obvious, and he'd have to decide whether to go this way or that. When he'd gone about a mile he realized he didn't know what he'd do if he fell and couldn't go on. But compared to how impossible this hike would have been for him as Marko, he felt invincible as Emil. He went on, sweating and with throbbing feet.

He was high above the stream by the time the path looped around, turning back the way he had come. He felt better knowing he'd begun closing the distance between himself and Grafton. If he began to fall, he doubted he'd be able to catch himself. He gave himself up to what might happen. He noticed his worries, just as his mom had taught him, and did not let them take over. As Emil, he saw—as he never had seen as Marko—that doing so only robbed himself of the pleasure his experience might otherwise offer. It was as though his mother were there with him as Emil, leading all three of them through the forest.

He finished his walk and it was lovely: the rushing stream, the little mushrooms as orange as salamanders, the mistiness of the woods. When he emerged, he found himself back where he started, drenched in sweat. Unsure of which way to turn, he returned to his room to rest and cool off.

As he was walking up the narrow hallway toward his door, Marko saw him. The Ambassador. He was flanked by two other men. As he got closer he saw that they were police officers, and he knew that the Ambassador was in trouble.

"Emil, I just came to tell you that I'll be leaving soon. I wanted to make sure you got your braces and I see that you have." There was his mouth, his chipped tooth. Marko felt a shiver go through him and he hugged himself. The Ambassador's eyes were pleading, heavy. Marko couldn't make sense of it.

"What happened? Where are you going?"

The Ambassador didn't answer. He just dropped his gaze to the floor and turned away. Marko wanted to grab him and pull him back. He had the same sense that he had when his mom walked away from him while he wanted her attention. Frantically, he looked for a way to keep him there. He saw the novel on his desk and picked it up.

"Ambassador," he called and walked after Todor and the officers. The Ambassador stopped and turned. He looked ten years older than he had just a moment ago. The skin around his mouth and chin seemed to sag with new weight. Marko handed him the book. He took it and smiled. Even his smile was a frown. Then he was gone.

A sharp pain shot through Marko's head and he fell to the floor. He woke up screaming in the dream bed, his head so full of pressure he was sure it would explode. He felt himself being dragged out. He tried to open his eyes but his head hurt too much. Under the sound of his own cries, he heard his grandmother's voice, and then his mom's. They were yelling. He heard a loud crack and opened his eyes. Another bolt of pain shot through his head as he saw his mom, in a rage, smashing the dream bed apart with the hammer. The dark body swallowed him and he was gone.

31. March 15, 2015: Cambridge, MA

The doctor told Marko that the shunt in his head had malfunctioned and the cerebral spinal fluid was accumulating around his brain. They needed to admit him to surgery immediately and replace the shunt. Marko had had many surgeries. While the doctor spoke, Marko listened for every utterance of "the," "it," and "now." The doctor prefaced almost every sentence with "now." After every second "it" that Marko heard, he lifted his hands alongside his face. After every fourth "it," Marko cut his field of vision in half with his hands. After every fifth "now," Marko cut back the other direction and lowered his hands. In doing this, Marko found a calming rhythm in the doctor's speech. He couldn't remember the last surgery he'd had near his brain because he had been a baby. His heart surgery had scared him a little. But this surgery scared him a lot. Marko was afraid that all he was, everything about him, was concentrated in his brain. If they messed that up, he would disappear forever. But if he counted words and marked the rhythms, maybe he'd be safe.

Marko's hydrocephalus required the insertion of a tube inside his body. The tube, a catheter, had a shunt and a valve on one end. The shunt end was in his head, just under his skull where the excessive cerebral spinal fluid formed. The valve ensured a one-way, regulated flow of the fluid through the tube. The tube drained in his abdominal cavity.

His first tube required a second surgery when he was three years old to replace it as he outgrew it. The second required a third surgery to replace it when he outgrew that one. The third tube was meant to grow with him, as it was coiled up in his abdominal cavity. As he grew, the tube would uncoil, and he would never need to have it replaced. Unless it got infected or obstructed, which of course it did.

After the doctor left, Marko sat in a shared hospital room with his mom, waiting for someone to come and take him in for surgery. Behind the closed curtain separating Marko from his roommate, he could hear small sobs. Another voice was there, making soothing murmurs, but also sniffling. Marko could smell the fear in the room. He asked his mom to help him into his chair. Without telling her what he was thinking, he wheeled slowly across the room to the curtain partition. He glanced back at his mom, then peeled back the curtain. Marko found a boy in there, at first laying with his back to Marko.

"I've been through plenty of surgeries and there's nothing to be afraid of," Marko said. Marko's mom fell in behind him and pulled the boy's mother aside and into the hall to talk with her.

Marko turned to the boy. He looked very young, curled in the bed like a pill bug. "I'm Marko. What's your name?"

"Matt."

"What is your surgery for?"

"My appendix. What's yours?"

"My brain."

Matt's red eyes widened. "Oh no, that's serious. Are you scared?"

"A little, but I've been through this before and it always comes out okay. I have hydrocephalous. There's something called a shunt in my head that drains fluid from around my brain to other parts of my body where it can be absorbed and expelled. Something went wrong with the shunt they put in when I was a baby, so they have to go back in and replace it now."

Matt shook his head slowly and frowned. "How old are you?"

"Fourteen. You?"

"Eleven." Matt's expression reminded Marko of an owl—wide-eyed and curious.

"You'll be okay, Matt."

Matt leaned back against the pillow propped up behind his back. He wrung his hands. "What happens when they put you to sleep? Do you dream?"

"No, you just skip time. One second you're in a room, the next you're waking up in another room."

Matt blinked, then sighed. "And you don't feel any pain? Even when you wake up?"

"No, you don't feel a thing. When you wake up, you'll be a little out of it and spacey but you won't feel any pain. You might be confused about where you are and what's going on, but that doesn't last very long."

Matt laughed and said, "That's funny."

Marko smiled. He worried that he was lying to Matt, because maybe he would be in pain when he woke up. Marko had always been in at least a little pain, so his frame of reference was skewed. Still, he wanted to make Matt feel better and he had accomplished that. Matt was smiling when the nurse came to take him away. He gave Marko a high five on his way out. Marko saw his mom hugging Matt's mom in the hall. She broke away and followed Matt's bed when it passed, then turned back and said, "Kali, thank you so much!"

Marko wheeled out to his mom. "Can we go talk to other people who might be scared?"

Kali smiled and nodded. She went to the nurse's station and asked the desk nurse for permission to talk to other patients who might be scared. Marko didn't hear what the reply was, but it must have been yes because Kali came back and pushed him over to the next room. On the bed was a bald child who could have been either a boy or a girl; Marko couldn't tell at first. He realized she was a girl when she turned her face to look up at her mom. Her features were delicate and soft.

Kali spoke to the girl and her mother. "Hi, I'm Kali and this is Marko. We'd like to talk to you if you don't mind."

Each looked skeptical but accepted the invitation. Kali ushered the girl's mother into the hall while Marko wheeled up beside the bed and offered to talk if she was scared. The girl had stomach cancer and this wasn't her first surgery, either. Her name was Amanda and she was sixteen years old.

"It seems like you have more experience than I do with this stuff," she said. Marko was struck by her voice; it had poise and a maturity that didn't fit her age. She was very smart, he could tell. This made him nervous. He didn't want to say anything for fear she would think him stupid. Marko was suddenly mute, which was fine because Amanda had a lot to say.

"My parents are getting a divorce. They fight all the time. My mom already has a new boyfriend. She hasn't told me but I know about him. She started dating him a long time ago, so she cheated on my dad."

Marko wanted to tell her about his parents and how they used to fight and that his dad left and had a new wife. But he couldn't get himself to say anything.

A nurse came in to get Amanda and take her to surgery.

"Well, it was nice talking to you, Marko," she said. Marko still hadn't said anything. He wanted to say something to her, but not just anything—he wanted what he said to be perfect. He wanted to say something she would remember forever. He ached with the desire to deliver just the right words to Amanda. Something about her face, her very round face with red lips and eyes more closely set than average, made him want to make a lasting impression. But more than that, he wanted to know her and he wanted her to know him.

But then she was leaving, and Marko would never see her again. Panicked, he stuttered as her bed was being wheeled out and said, "I—I—It—It's gonna be okay. You'll see." Amanda smiled wide at him and winked, and then, to Marko's astonishment, she blew him a kiss. Marko felt the immediate reddening of his face. Was he supposed to do it back? He couldn't react fast enough, so he gave her an awkward wave as she rolled out of sight.

Kali walked back into the room smiling, looking dreamy. She bent double to hug Marko hard; his face smushed between her muscled arm and her head. Her thick black hair threaded with gray smelled like lavender, her scented shampoo. Her skin didn't have a scent, but it smelled like her—the olfactory signature of her essence. He inhaled it and felt secure. She leaned back and held him by the shoulders, out in front of her like a painting she was admiring. Her eyes darted back and forth between his two eyes. He wondered if his were doing the same. His head hurt.

"You're the bravest soul."

Marko was more pleased with this approval and attention than he could adequately express.

"Thanks, Mom, you're brave, too." He knew that compliments were to be traded, never just accepted. He'd learned this from his dad, who had always immediately reciprocated every compliment, usually in kind.

Marko had collected many examples of the kinds of compliments people traded. For instance:

"You have a great smile."

"Thanks, you have a wonderful smile yourself!"

From a woman:

"That's a handsome tie."

"Thank you, your dress is stunning."

Marko couldn't remember when he first realized that most things said and done between people are transactions, but it was something he solidly understood by now. His mom, perhaps the only exception to this rule, laughed at his response. "Honey, you can just take that I'm proud of you, really take it in. You don't have to always say the same things back to me."

This criticism made red heat of fourteen creep into Marko's cheeks again as he felt flustered and embarrassed. Everything he thought he knew about the world and how to be in it seemingly never applied to his mom. She always wanted him to be "himself," but Marko didn't know who himself was. Nor did he know how to act like he knew and that he was being it. He wished he could tell her this, but he didn't want to spoil the moment. So he forced a smile and nodded.

By the time the surgeons were ready for Marko, he and his mom had had the opportunity to speak with two more kids awaiting surgery, the only remaining two on the floor at that time. The two experiences were much the same as the others—Marko spoke with the child while

Kali spoke with the child's parents—but Marko couldn't stop thinking about Amanda and what he would have said to her. Both the kids he talked to last were boys and both surgeries were minor. But they were both still scared and wanted to talk to Marko about their fears. During the last visit, the boy Marko was listening to asked him a question while he was spaced out thinking about Amanda. Marko tuned in to see the boy looking expectantly at him, waiting for his answer. Not wanting to admit that he hadn't heard the question, Marko shrugged and said, "Uh, I'm not real sure." The boy's forehead wrinkled in confusion and then turned to sympathy. He probably thought Marko was slow. Marko started to say that he didn't actually hear the kid's question, but it was too late; they came to collect this boy, too.

It was a long while before they came to get Marko. When they finally did, the sun outside the windows was already low in the sky.

32. March 15, 2015: Cambridge, MA

When Marko went into surgery, Kali went home to get a shower and change of clothes before heading back to spend the night. When she arrived home, Lydia was there waiting for her. The shards of smashed wood that had been the dream bed were sticking up from a box she'd put them in. The box sat by the door.

"I told you not to let him in that thing," Lydia said. Kali sighed and dropped her bag on the floor. She sat in a chair across the table from her mom and glared at her.

"If I want your advice, I'll let you know, Mom."

Lydia stood up and walked into the kitchen. She started doing dishes. She looked up from the sink at Kali and said: "Hot water and chemicals must have caused it." Her eyes were a blaze of revelation and devastation. It was the kind of epiphany that kicks you in the kidneys.

"Yeah?" Kali challenged, her voice as sharp as a blade. She stood up. "Well, Mom, it could have been that. It could have been chlorine. I even drank coffee, Mom. I didn't know I was already pregnant and I was tired and I drank about a half a pot of coffee for the first time in my life." She watched the blaze in Lydia's eyes turn to ice instantly. Her mouth turned down and she stood up straight, correcting her slant, a horrified poise.

"I always wondered why I felt nothing when I chugged all that coffee and now I know it must have been because the little fetus in my womb absorbed it all, straight into his unformed spine. Straight into his unformed heart. And the unfinished business of a body in formation was permanently marred and it was my fault." Kali moved across the room as she spoke, closer to Lydia. Lydia backed away, and Kali raised her voice. Her mother turned from horrified to frightened. The turning was seamless, like a ripening.

"There is no way you can make me feel guilty, Mom. You know why? Because you can't pour more water into an overflowing cup. There's no room for more guilt inside me, Mom. It's already oozing out of my every pore. Yes, I sat in hot tubs filled with chemicals for the entire length of my pregnancy. The nurses already told me that the elevated temperature for long periods of time could have harmed my baby. Do you know when they told me that? While he was having his first surgery, in the first twenty-four hours of his life. While they were closing the hole in his back over his spine."

Lydia was crying, like she always did, and Kali backed her to the wall where she couldn't retreat any further. Anger and fear burnt in Kali's gut, right at the center point of her body, so hot that she swore she could smell smoke.

"And then two months later, when the first shunt they put in his head to drain the cerebrospinal fluid failed and they had to replace it, cut him open again, do you know what the nurses asked me again for the tenth time in two months? Do you know, Mom?"

"Please, stop," Lydia blubbered, howling into her palms covering her face. She closed her eyes.

"Mom! Look at me, Mom!" Lydia opened her eyes.

"Did I take any fucking folic acid! That's what they asked me, Mom."

Kali picked up the closest thing to her, a lidded tin can filled with notepaper and a little pencil, and hurled it at the side wall in the kitchen. It burst on contact and bits of paper bloomed out. They seemed suspended for a long moment before raining down. The clatter of the pencil and the can hitting the floor were so satisfying that Kali had to have more, and louder. She grabbed the edge of the kitchen table and upended it.

"No I didn't fucking take any fucking folic acid and yes I sat in hot tubs and guess what, everybody? While I'm on trial you might as well know that I fucking ate sushi, too!"

The table and chairs seemed to tremble at the sound of her fierce, ragged scream. The sight and the silence left in the wake of her fury formed a tableau of pain, so white hot it was molten. The devastated table and chairs. Everything that had been stationary and peaceful was shattered and strewn. Lydia crouched and curled tight on the floor against the wall, snot and tears covering her long hands, which were stretched across her face. Too frightened to make a sound.

33. March 16, 2015:Cambridge, MA

When Marko woke, it was the next day. The surgery had taken thirteen hours. It took another few hours for Marko to wake up fully. Marko was shocked: what could possibly be happening for thirteen hours? But the surgery was a success, they said, and Marko would be fine. After the initial pain of healing wore off, he should have no more headaches. "Should" was a word Marko distrusted. But then, as his mom always told him, there are never any guarantees.

In the days following that surgery, Marko recovered at home. There were times when his mother couldn't be there with him, so his grandmother was there. His mom and his grandmother had settled on an agreement that his grandmother would drop the counselor assessment idea if his mom agreed never to leave Marko alone and to dispose of what was leftover of the dream bed. But Marko felt lonely with just his grandmother and sad at the loss of the dream bed. His grandmother doted on him every minute—could she get him this, could she get him that? A drink, something to eat, a sweater, a cold washcloth, some more pain medication, anything at all? Marko politely declined most of her offers, but he did accept a few. Not because he actually wanted anything, but because she seemed hurt that he didn't need her help. In this way, she was more of a drain on Marko than a help. If he couldn't be with his mom, he would have preferred to be alone. He would have preferred to be Emil.

To soothe himself, he watched baseball. When his grandma went to the bathroom, he took a break from baseball to read his mom's diary. It was an account of one of her shamanic journeys in the dream bed.

I had a dream that I'd been shot through the middle of my body with a cannonball. It didn't hurt but to ache and make me feel hollow. Walking down the street, I felt the wind blow right through me. It was the most unbearable feeling—the yearning to be whole was overpowering.

I went into a restaurant and ordered everything on the menu. I ate until I was sick but the hole was still there. I went into the restroom and masturbated until my genitals were numb but the hole was still there. I went to a bank and robbed it so that I had enough money to buy anything at all that I wanted. I went and bought a car and drove it around. Many people noticed me in my new car. But the hole was still there and the longing was worse than ever. I picked up a handsome man and had sex with him in the car. After that, a woman. Several men and women followed, but no matter how much sex I had, the hole remained.

I bought a beautiful dress and hid the hole, but when the wind blew hard enough, the dress billowed into my hollow.

I loved and was loved; the hole remained.

I made small miracles with my talents and was revered and admired; the hole remained.

Perhaps if I gave the rest of the money back, the hole would get a little smaller. But I couldn't find the bank and was instead in a new and unfamiliar neighborhood. I gave the rest of the money to a person walking by who seemed homeless. The man was dirty and stinking with weary eyes and stained clothes. He received the money skeptically, asking me what I wanted in return. "Nothing at all," I said and he smiled. His teeth were yellow and brown, his gums, gray. The man hugged me and I felt my hole widen against his coat. I pulled away and ran off.

Then I had an idea. I went to a library and checked out two hardcover novels of the right size and shape. Next I went to a hardware store and found what I needed: glue, bubble wrap, Styrofoam, tape. Carefully,

*I taped over the hole in my back, glued the two books together vertical-
ly, then aligned their spines with the broken cross sections of my backbone. I fortified that with a ballast of Styrofoam and then added tightly
packed bubble wrap. Finally, I taped over the front of the hole, securing
the whole contraption. After I walked out of the store, I realized I had
not paid for anything. I thought about going back, but I didn't have any
money. So I kept walking, no longer feeling the wind blow through me.*

*I could feel the stories inside me and they made me cautiously hope-
ful. Cautious because the stories were too formulaic, like neat equations,
as though anything in life were solved that way, as though anything were
ever that ordered.*

*As I walked, the tape in the front began to bulge. I placed my hand
on it and felt movement underneath. I pushed down and felt a twinge of
pain inside, which meant I was whole again, or at least growing whole.
This made me happy and so relieved but the pain kept getting worse and
the bulge grew bigger. I sat down on the sidewalk and breathed deeply. I
got up and squatted and pushed; something was coming out.*

*That's when I woke up, but not into real life. I woke into another
dream. I was back in the delivery room giving birth to Marko. Zach was
there and the nurses, those wretched nurses. There I was, the younger me,
so naive and unsuspecting. I watched the scene from the vantage of the
ceiling and I noticed new details I never could have noticed then. One of
the nurses was staring at Zach with a sinister look, her eyes darting back
between my legs whenever he caught her staring. Zach was close to my
face, bent over me, whispering something. I was screaming and drooling
and growling. The nurse delivering Marko was elbow-deep inside me,
her face flushed, her bangs pasted to her forehead with sweat.*

*"He's crowning," the nurse said and smiled, revealing strange, pointy
teeth. The smile was clownish, almost maniacal, and her face was so
dark red it was nearly purple. The baby slid into her arms. She frowned
deeply and peered closely at the baby. She looked at the other nurse, who
was also frowning at the baby. Zach, positioned at the foot of the table
between my legs now, did not frown, nor did he look happy. His expression was frozen in a state of shock and awe. I was speaking, telling them
I was hungry, asking after the baby. The two nurses got busy separating*

him from my body. They cleaned him carefully and swaddled him. They were too quiet and did not answer my questions. I started to raise my voice. The nurse walked toward the door with Marko. I screamed at her. She turned around and said, "He has a hole in his back."

I woke up. The inside of the dream bed was damp. I'd been sweating. I got out and rubbed the spot on my back, which was actually itching. It wasn't burning or feeling slimy like usual; it was itching deep below the surface where I could never reach. The room was dark and cold. I shivered and heard my teeth clatter. I got off the floor and took off my damp clothes. Through the window, the dreary winter morning was just breaking. Images from my dream stayed with me as I dressed in dry clothes and went to the living room to start my morning yoga. The dream had seemed too long for only one session in the dream bed. The end, where Marko was being born, had seemed different than it was in reality—spooky. The pointy teeth and the sinister look. Then, as I was warming up with spinal flexes, I realized I had woken up before the nurse gave me Marko to hold. For some reason, this bothered me and I had to go check on Marko in his bed.

He was there, sound asleep, breathing rhythmically in the dark. I sat beside him and watched him, the side of his face so peaceful just then. I wondered what he was dreaming about and hoped it was a good dream. Then it hit me: did Marko dream about walking like I sometimes dreamed of being in a wheelchair? Did he dream about being whole when I dreamed about having a hole through the middle of my body? The spot deep down itched again and I scratched at the surface far above it, sating it not at all.

34. March 17, 2015: Cambridge, MA

Marko needed to walk. He tried many ways but couldn't get his grandmother to leave. Then, he had an idea. He saw her yawning a lot and suggested they both take a nap. He claimed he had slept badly and was tired, too. Marko went to his room and she lay on the couch in the living room. He waited until he heard her snoring and then he went to his mom's room. The dream bed was gone, as he had known it would be. There was nothing but empty space under her bed. Marko slid under. He lay there with his eyes closed. Maybe the surface where the dream bed had touched would have retained some of its magic. Maybe he could still go back. He lay a long time before he fell asleep.

Marko woke, and he was Emil again. He was back in Thailand but he was standing in front of an abandoned building. He felt his legs beneath him and looked down. He was wearing uniform pants. They didn't look like Emil's legs. But maybe they were. He took off his pants and his underwear, his shoes and socks. His legs *were* Emil's, he could see now: strong and covered in dense, black hair. His penis and scrotum were Emil's, too: nestled in a shock of black hair, a perfectly shaped phallus growing longer and firm under his observation. He took a tentative step, then another. He walked, then ran, then sprinted, barefoot, toward the building.

It was Emil's dormitory, overgrown with weeds and ivy and moss. The jungle had encroached on the grounds; the place was empty and untended. It was as though Emil had returned to the place but behind time. Time had moved on, carrying all the people with it, leaving this version of Emil behind in the emptiness.

The heavy double doors to the dormitory were ajar. Emil pulled them open and stepped through. The hallway smelled of mildew and was covered in dirt and dried leaves and jungle debris. He felt cold with no pants on and his erection started to throb and ache. Emil walked the corridors until he found the space that had been his room. It was empty and the cot was upended, the thin mattress on the floor. Emil sat on the mattress and took the erection in his hands. Other than the sound of blood pumping in his ears, there was a pervasive silence spread over everything. No animal noises, no wind. The head of the penis was bone white and vulnerable, but sweet. The patches of skin on his inner thighs were hairless and untouched, taut, beautiful. He took a deep breath. He kept his eyes on his groin, not allowing himself look away or hide from his simultaneous reverence and revulsion. He thought of scaleless fish, but shut the image out of his mind. He thought of knives. He thought of the woman who had mounted him the last time he was in this room. In that moment, he could smell her. Her sex was still on him. Even alone, he felt shy but proud.

When he couldn't stand it anymore, he gave into the urge to penetrate something, anything, and thrust his erection into his closed hands, which he had lubricated with his saliva. He thrust without thinking about the scars on Marko's spine, without remembering the numbness in Marko's penis. He thrust knowing about the tyranny of appearance, of beauty, how it wasn't real. As Emil, with this body, with this sensation, he knew he'd found something real, as real as knives, as real as fish, and as real and natural as thunderclouds that never boomed, silently dropping rain.

35. March 17, 2015: Cambridge, MA

Kali came home that evening to find Lydia asleep on the couch and no sign of Marko. Dinner hadn't been made. Had she done his catheter? Kali went to Marko's room but found his bed empty. His chair was parked near the door. She knew where he would be. She could tell from the carpet that Marko had dragged himself into her room. She went in and found him asleep under her bed. He had removed his pants and diaper and was messy with bodily fluids. Kali went to the bathroom to get a washcloth and a bucket of soapy water and a new diaper and then returned to her son. Gently, she washed the urine and semen from his body, trying not to wake him, trying not to think about the regular fourteen-year-old boy he wasn't able to be.

Marko's hipbones protruded from the pale skin of his waist as he lay on his back. They reminded Kali of the protrusion on his back made by the pronounced curve in his spine. The incredible smallness and fragileness about him and his bones reminded her of something she couldn't at first place. Then she remembered: the river in Bulgaria at the foothills. The rhythm of it and how she used to sit and watch for hours. Water finding water, water finding more curves. Once, there was a dead pigeon with its bones sticking out. They looked fragile and fine, yet also strong, like they could be taken apart and then lashed together with willow branches and pine gum to make a raft. A strong raft.

Kali finished washing Marko and gently put the diaper on him. She pulled his legs into the pant holes and began to pull them up, but Marko stirred and started to wake, so she stopped. Looking at him, there in the half light of the room, on the floor just under her bed, all she could see in that moment were pigeon bones and a pair of pants.

36. March 18, 2015: Cambridge, MA

Marko woke in his own bed. It was very early morning. His body was sore but his head didn't hurt. For a moment, he thought he could still feel his legs and feet, but as soon as he looked down, the sensation faded and he was himself. The experience left him burning with questions and confusion. He felt agitated, impatient with his unruly body. With urgency, he called out to his mom. When she didn't appear right away, he called out to her even louder. He kept calling until she appeared with an alarmed, fearful expression. She sat down on the bed and peered at him with lines across her forehead.

"What is it, what's wrong?"

"Where did I come from?"

The lines deepened. She didn't understand.

"Where do we all come from?"

Her face relaxed, some but the lines remained. "Well, you have a spirit—"

"I know all that; you've told me, but how did all this happen? What came before this?"

"I'm trying to understand what you mean, Marko," his mom said slowly. "Did you have a bad dream? I found you under my bed last night and carried you in here. What happened?"

Marko thought about it. No, it wasn't a bad dream, but it had disturbed him greatly to wake up from it into his own life, his own body. He wanted to be Emil. Or anyone else.

"Where did the world come from?"

Kali slouched and her forehead turned smooth. The corners of her mouth lifted only a little. Marko was annoyed at her amused posture; this was s serious matter.

"Well, there's a theory that the whole universe is a kind of ordered debris from a big explosion out of nothing, called the Big Bang. It happened billions of years ago and the Earth and everything is just expanding out from that single point of spontaneous something."

Marko knew that already. His problem with it always was: how could something come out of nothing? But then, of course it can, because before he existed, he didn't exist, and so he was nothing, and then suddenly he did exist, becoming something.

"What about all of life? Evolution?"

"You can look it up. But from what I understand, the world started out as a ball of ice, mostly. Just a frozen planet exploding everywhere with volcanoes, which released a ton of water vapor, making oceans. The heat from the volcanoes warmed the earth and the lava brought out elements from deep inside, which reacted with other elements, which formed primitive life. The earliest life was said to develop out of this."

"Can I look it up now?" Marko was dying to know more. He reached his arms around his mom's neck and she lifted him from his bed into his chair. He rolled himself into the living room right to the computer. He looked up what he needed to know on the Internet. He read everything he could about volcanoes, how they helped to form life on earth and how they destroyed earth. There were so many different types of volcanoes, slow ones that gave warning when they were about to blow, and then instead of blowing, just oozing out the molten rock. Then there were hot, fast ones that exploded and covered everything instantly. In some cases, the covering happened so instantly that the lava preserved the life forms it obliterated, turning each into a perfect sculpture to be unearthed and studied and placed in museums eons later.

But the idea that everything in the universe, all the intricate nuances of life and all of the distinct groupings of the elements, came to be out of nothing, seemed to Marko impossible and borderline barbaric. Existence must mean something more. The questions of existence, the hows and the whys, pressed into Marko powerfully, almost strangling him.

He realized then that the questions were always there, present in every material thing, looming in the moments where everything turns heavy and meaningless. They were present also in moments where happiness was so spontaneous and whole that all of the objects around Marko seemed to be there for the very first time. And the questions were there, present in the in-between times, when everything just is, and is neither good nor bad.

Marko let his gaze rest in the computer screen. He unfocused his eyes, making the letters and words blur into broken horizontal lines of indistinct, arbitrary shapes. He looked down at his lap, then his legs, their unnatural flatness against the seat of the chair. He pressed down on his thighs, feeling the nothingness. He closed his eyes and tried to summon the math, but it wouldn't come. His position in space and in time was uncharted in that moment and he sensed its smallness, its impermanence. Billions of years, billions of miles, the unfathomable measurements of history and galaxies, and the insignificance of his struggling little self against it all with nothing but questions and a will to survive. But why? Yet another question.

It seemed to Marko that he was trapped—inside a body, inside time, inside his own limited mind and intellect, too small to determine what it all meant and where it all came from. He pressed the heels of his palms against his closed eyes and saw the spots of light, stars in the dark.

"You okay?"

It was his mom. Marko opened his eyes. He blinked away the stardust swirling around her bright face.

37. March 21, 2015: Cambridge, MA

Kali's shrink asked her to talk about her childhood—her parents
and her dead brother. Kali tried. She started talking about her
parents' relationship and how needy her father sometimes was,
but it made her remember how needy Zach sometimes was.

Marko was three. He had just recently become mobile. He had a
scooter board that he could drag himself on and off. It was early December, and Zach decided that they should get a Christmas tree. He
thought it was important for Marko to be able to get a tree and decorate it. Kali was dreading the task of getting the tree "as a family." Zach
and Kali decorated trees the first two years they were together like the
happy couple they were, but then after the first pregnancy and abortion, which was just before Christmas, they stopped. This would be the
first time since.

"Can we not call it a Christmas tree? How about a Winter Solstice
tree?" Kali said this dripping out of the shower, red from the cold water. Her voice shuddered when she spoke. She was not feeling well and
hadn't been for a week. She hadn't been able to do her yoga in three
days and her energy had bottomed out. She hoped that a cold shower
would shock her system and give her the energy to follow through with
Zach's plan for the day.

.

"Call it whatever you want to call it. It's a Christmas tree." With that, he walked out of the bathroom. Kali bent over double at the pain in her stomach. She crouched in front of the toilet but nothing came. The pain was still there, but her mouth wasn't watering. She wished that she would puke so she would feel better. Then, slowly, the pain went from sharp to dull and tolerable. She stood up, dried off, and wrapped herself in a white robe. She lifted the white towel she dried herself with and wrapped her hair. Kali walked into the living room and lay down on the couch. Marko came scooting in and reached for her.

"We're going to get a tree, honey, get your coat."

Zach walked in with his coat on and grabbed the car keys. "Do you want me to go get the tree by myself? Since you're not feeling well?"

He tried to make his voice sound sincere, as though it was a genuine offer out of care instead of a complaint. Still, Kali appreciated his acknowledgement that she wasn't feeling well.

"No, no. I'm coming. Let me get dressed."

She got up and moved fast to the bedroom. She grabbed whatever clothes she saw first and dressed hastily. She pulled the towel off her head and threw it into the dirty clothes hamper. Just after it landed, Zach came in and took it away. He went out the door of the apartment that led down to the basement where the laundry was. He often started doing chores obsessively when he was irritated. Marko called out to Kali.

"I'll be right there, baby, I'm getting dressed."

Kali heard his scooter sliding down the hall toward her. She tensed with the anticipation of seeing him. He appeared—a tiny blonde creature blinking up at her through thick-lensed glasses. Topless with pants on, still unbuttoned, Kali felt vulnerable in front of her son—a half-peeled banana. She quickly pulled a shirt over her head and turned to him.

"There. Mommy's ready. Is Marko ready?"

He just continued blinking at her. Sometimes, she wondered if he understood her. Zach banged back up from the basement.

At the store, there was only one Winter Solstice tree left and it was huge.

"It's too big," Kali said.

"Fine, I'll get a coffee," Zach said and went to stand in line. He held Marko, who reached for a box of candy canes on the shelf. Zach picked them up and handed them to him.

"He's had enough sugar today already," Kali said. Zach rolled his eyes.

"Fine," he said, "these aren't to eat, okay buddy? They're for decorating the tree."

Marko started wailing. Zach looked at Kali like it was her fault. Kali thought that it was his fault for giving Marko sugar but said nothing.

"You look terrible. Do you want to go wait in the car?"

Kali realized she was barely able to stand up and felt nauseated.

"Yes, I do, thanks," she said. She made her way slowly out of the store. In the car, she reclined the seat and closed her eyes. Again, she told herself, he had acknowledged her discomfort. He was trying. Kali wanted to try, too, but felt very weak. She thought about the guilt they had. Not just because they weren't good enough for a child, but also because that child came into the world so severely compromised. He spent the first two years of his life invaded in every way—cut open, pricked, threaded with tubes and sutures, handled and manipulated and moved by so many latex-covered hands. Neither of them understood the blatant injustice of that fact. Both of them wanted to somehow compensate for it, which proved so impossible that they mocked themselves by trying.

The back door opened and Zach put Marko's tiny body into the car seat. Marko was pushing his bottom lip out so far it looked swollen. The inside lenses of his glasses were wet with tears.

"What happened?"

"He wanted a candy cane!"

An accusation. Kali knew he meant that she was the one who had denied Marko the candy cane. Then, after denying him what he wanted, Kali had walked away, leaving Zach to deal with his tears. Kali started the car and drove it up the street to the grocery store.

"I'll just go get the tree if you want to wait here," Zach said, trying to make his voice sound considerate. Marko whined.

Kali got out of the car and walked to the trees lined up outside the store. There were two sizes, very small and pretty big. They chose the pretty big size, which cost fifty dollars. That was a lot of money for them and Kali didn't want to spend it.

"Do we really need this?" she asked.

Zach handed Marko to her and started carrying one of the trees off to the car. Kali went inside and paid for it. Marko started crying again.

"What's wrong, sweetie?"

He didn't answer. He couldn't articulate what was wrong, Kali thought, because neither could she.

Kali carried Marko back outside. She saw Zach across the parking lot struggling to put the tree in the car. Like heavy doll's legs, Marko's were swinging with Kali's gait and kicking into her thigh. She couldn't remember if she'd ever been conscious of this before—how his legs moved when she carried him—but it felt new. Kali put him in his seat and he cheered up because his face was close enough to the netted up pine tree to lean over and smell it. She got in behind the driver's seat and, smelling the pine, felt cheered, too. For a fraction of a moment, Kali had a visceral feeling that everything would be okay. *We are a family and will continue to be a family.* But as she drove the car home, a wave of sick hit her and Zach made one of his frequent, audible sighs. Kali noticed that the feeling was gone. Obliterated. Like it had never existed.

She pulled into the driveway and made the mistake of mentioning that they didn't have a saw and that they would need one to cut the bottom of the trunk off so that it would drink the water they gave it and live longer. It was a mistake because Zach used the comment as an excuse to complain that she was the one who had wanted to get the tree from the nearby store instead of from a tree farm where they would do all of that for you. Kali wasted a little time wondering why he was so bitter toward her.

Kali carried Marko into the house and Zach carried the tree. He left it on the porch, propped against the house, while he went to look for a saw. He didn't find one and this made him more bitter. He brought the tree in and Kali held it upright in the stand while he tightened the screws to hold it in place. Marko was on the couch, again asking for a candy cane.

"No more candy, sweetie, but you can have lunch. Do you want lunch?" Kali said.

This made him cry hard. It was heartbreaking to see him cry. It was almost painful enough to lead Kali to just give him a bowl full of high fructose corn syrup with a spoon.

"I'm sorry, baby, you'll have a candy cane, I promise. Just not right this second."

Zach, having tightened the screws in place around the tree trunk and secured it, got up and retrieved a candy cane from the box. He peeled off its plastic wrapping and handed it to Marko. He didn't look at Kali. Marko smiled through tears and sucked the candy cane. He didn't look at Kali either.

Kali opened her mouth then closed it. Not saying anything was better. It was important that she choose her battles, given Zach's wrath for her. Kali lay down on the couch and curled around Marko. She leaned over to the laptop on the coffee table and played some Christmas music. Zach was opening a string of white lights.

"Mind helping me with this?" he asked while looking at the lights. Kali got up and helped him wrap the string around from top to bottom. She lay back down while he adjusted it. It looked skimpy, and there was another string of lights in the box.

"Maybe we use both strings?" Kali said.

"I don't want too many lights."

Kali opened her mouth then, again, she closed it. She didn't care about the lights. Her stomach lurched with a stabbing pain and she groaned.

"Do you need to go lie down in the bedroom?" He barked it at her like a scolding.

"Would you like for me to go lay down in the bedroom?"

"Do what you want—you always do." He looked for the end of the string to plug it in. The plug side was at the top of the tree.

"Well, Marko, I have to do it over," he said irritably. "Daddy screwed up; I need this at the bottom." He heaved a sigh and started unraveling the string of lights.

"Or you could plug the other string in at the top and wrap that down and use both?"

He turned around half way, exposing the side of his face to her, and snapped, "I'm doing this myself, alright? Nobody's helping me!"

Kali got up and walked into the bedroom. She lay down in the bed under the covers and resisted the urge to rub the spot on her back, which burned and ached simultaneously. She thought about leaving the house. She felt sorry for herself and sorry for Marko, and angry with Zach. She berated him in her mind.

And then she heard a scream that sounded like someone being stabbed to death. It was high-pitch enough to not be able to tell the gender of the screamer. It sounded like it was coming from the apartment above them. Pounding footsteps, a slamming door, more pounding footsteps, then wailing. Kali looked up at the ceiling. Was the person up there being attacked? But the wailing sounded deep and ragged and familiar. And there was total, dead silence from the living room. Kali got up and walked into the living room. Marko was sitting on the couch, not moving, wide-eyed and shocked.

"What happened?"

He didn't respond or look at her. The door to the basement was closed. Kali opened it and went down the stairs, toward the crying. There was a person down there who looked like her husband only different—a grotesque grief caricature, his face bright red and shiny with wetness, his mouth contorted. As typically happens in a crisis, Kali got very calm. When she spoke, her voice was soft.

"What's going on?"

"All I wanted was for us to have a good time today, for Marko to have a good time! I haven't been excited for Christmas in so long and I finally was a little bit this year and I just wanted us to get a tree together and decorate it. Everything's ruined! You're miserable, Marko's fighting me—"

He went on yelling, bellowing complaints at Kali amidst more tears. Upstairs, Kali heard Marko crying. She turned around and headed up the stairs.

"Where are you going?"

Kali turned back around to face him at the bottom of the stairs. "Your son is crying. I'm going to go comfort him."

"I'm crying!" he screamed.

The expression on Kali's face must have registered her disbelief and disgust. She turned around and mounted another two stairs. He was yelling again and coming after her. Kali turned, put her hand up in a gesture of restraint and said, "Zach, I can't hear anything you're telling me right now. You'll have to tell me again later when you can speak respectfully to me and in a normal tone of voice."

She closed the door behind her at the top of the stairs. Marko had dragged himself off the couch and was struggling to get onto his scooter board. Kali went to him and picked him up.

"Where's my daddy?" he cried.

"Daddy isn't feeling well, sweetie. He'll be okay, he'll be back."

The door opened and Zach emerged, stone-faced and chilly. He crossed the room to the tree and started fucking with the lights again. Marko wiggled, wanting to go to him. Kali put Marko in his chair and walked out of the room, into the bathroom. She sat down on the toilet and hung her pounding head. Her body shook. She felt trapped and hopeless. She stayed in the bathroom a long while, trying to think of what to do next.

"Mommy, are you going to come decorate the tree with us?" Zach called out in a cloying voice from the living room. Kali didn't answer. Again, he called to her. His voice oozed.

"This is psychotic," she said to herself in the mirror. "We're both mental health workers. Zach is a therapist, a child psychologist who also works with adults. How is it possible that we're this sick? I have to go out there and play along for Marko's sake. He's just been traumatized." Kali splashed water on her face and dried off. She opened the door and walked out. She picked up some ornaments and hung them on the tree. Her fingers felt numb and as much as she tried, she couldn't fake a smile. Marko was decorating the bottom branches from where he sat on his scoot. He was smiling. All better.

"Marko, are you hungry for lunch?" Kali asked.

"Yes!"

"Okay, let's go," she said and he followed her into the kitchen. She heated him left-over brown rice and kale with tomatoes in the microwave, took him off of his scoot, and put him in his belted booster seat at the table. She walked back to where Zach was and said, "In your past relationships, did your girlfriends ever get sick?"

"That's not the issue," he whisper-yelled. "I understand that you're sick, but can you show me some appreciation for a change? All I need is a thank-you. When you lie on the couch all you need to do is say, 'gee, Zach, thank you for running around like crazy taking care of everything while I'm not feeling well. I really appreciate all that you do.' Is that too much to ask?"

As he spoke his voice grew louder, and Kali was certain Marko could hear every word. She walked away from him to the bedroom. He followed, barking, "Don't walk away from me!"

In the bedroom, Kali turned on him and said, "Zach, I don't like the way you treat me when I'm sick." It was the simplest, truest thing she could think of to say.

"Well I don't like that you don't appreciate me enough."

"You're not hearing what I'm saying. I want a partner who will be kind and loving to me when I'm sick."

"I want a partner who appreciates me."

"Okay, I'm leaving." Kali turned to the closet and pulled a few things out to put in a bag, not sure how long she'd be gone.

"So that's it? It's too much to ask? A simple thank-you?"

Kali was filled with so much disgust and judgment toward him that she couldn't open her mouth for fear of what would come out. The raging anger she'd expressed in the past had not served her well. And her anger was fast approaching rage. She walked out and he grabbed her arm, turning her around.

"Zach," she said, as quietly and calmly as she could, "I'm not fighting again in front of our son. When I feel appreciation for you, I tell you. When I was lying on the couch watching you fuck with the fucking tree, I didn't feel appreciative because what you were doing was unnecessary and annoying. I was trying to tolerate you but I'm done trying. Now I'm leaving."

Kali walked into the kitchen and he followed her.

"So you're taking a time-out, right? You'll be back later?"

He was referencing the rule from one of the latest relationship self-help books they had tried. Instead of storming out, Kali was supposed to request a "time-out" in a non-threatening way and announce that she'd be back later. Across the room Marko was turned around in his seat at the table, staring from Zach to Kali. He looked terrified.

"Yes, of course I'll be back later," she said in a singsong. She walked over and kissed Marko on the top of his head, rustled his hair, and walked out waving goodbye.

Talking to the shrink, Kali couldn't remember what happened next—where she'd gone or how it got resolved. The shrink asked her how she'd felt. That, Kali remembered vividly. She felt blown through the middle with a cannon ball, the edges ragged and bloody. She felt the ache and the emptiness.

38. March 21, 2015: Cambridge, MA

R ecovering from his surgery took so long, Marko was sure Malik
would have gotten a new friend to replace him by the time he
finally got back to school. He found a story that his mom wrote
in her diary about her first love. Marko wished he could have a first
love, too.

When I was a child, I felt it, that source of shame. Learning in the En-
glish-speaking school at the gated community in Thailand with all the
white children speaking English. I could never be one of them. These
things gave me away as a foreigner: my accent, my U-shaped scar, my
dark eyes and hair. They are some of the same things that give me away
as a foreigner to myself and to this planet. It's not all there is. This isn't
where I came from and it's not where I'm going!

I said as much to the little boy I fell in love with there when I was only
thirteen. He was nothing special at first. That's how it always starts—be-
fore somebody becomes crucial he or she is interchangeable with any
other interesting stranger.

I was sitting alone at a table by myself eating lunch and drawing in
my sketchbook. I still remember that my lunch was a bunch of grapes
on the vine and a hunk of sweet bread. I tore off small pieces of the
bread and tossed them on the ground to the birds. Then I plucked one

grape and popped it in my mouth. I alternated the two while drawing the belly of a whale trapping me inside of it. At some point, I felt his eyes on me and looked up. He sat a few tables away, also by himself, staring unabashedly at me over an untouched tray of food from the cafeteria. The lunch that the school dished out was usually some hot slop that the diplomats ate two rooms over. I started back at him, narrowing my eyes a little to look mean. He laughed at me and I gave him the middle finger. He looked at it with a puzzled expression. He had no idea what it meant, I could tell. I went back to my drawing and ate another grape.

One second later he was beside me.

"What's this?" He held up his middle finger in my face.

"It stands for a penis going into a woman's genitals." He blushed so immediately and so hard, his pink cheeks turned maroon. He giggled and brought his hand to his mouth and shifted on the seat. I had said it with no expression and I fought to keep my face expressionless, but I felt the involuntary heat rise and start to float up through the top of my head anyway. I had exaggerated my accent on purpose, and so anticipated his next question. He tried to ask it but was stuttering, which I instantly decided to love.

"I'm from Bulgaria. A city called Sofia. My name's Kali. What's yours?"

"Suh-suh-Sasha."

He had a small chip on the inside of his front tooth and a thin space between his two front teeth. The opening looked like a keyhole. It was the second thing I loved about him.

"Where are you from?"

It took him a while to tell me that he was from California, in America. A place called San Francisco. I realized that he didn't stutter when he had first approached me, so concluded that he must only stutter when he was very nervous. I made it my goal to make him as comfortable as possible so that he could speak easily to me. It didn't take me long to convince him to cut the rest of the day of school with me and go find something fun to do. We went to the community store and bought candy and soda then we left Grafton and went to the beach. The walk to the beach must have been an hour, and the heat in U-Tapao had backed off because it was a very cloudy day. During our walk, we didn't speak, and when thunder started to rumble, we both looked up and smiled at the very same moment. Seeing it, Sasha blushed again and that gave me chills. To affect someone so profoundly that it was visceral and visibly apparent was intoxicating to me.

By the time we made it to the beach, the rain had already started pouring from the sky and we were soaked. There was a tiki hut with a palm roof where we took shelter. We huddled together and watched the ocean. I focused my gaze on the line that separated the dark blue and gray tones of the sky and ocean. When I glanced over at Sasha, he seemed to be looking at the same thing. At some point while we sat there, he turned his face to mine and breathed on my ear. The softness of his breath got blown away with the violence of the storm winds before it could even land on my skin, but the closeness of his mouth made me sit very still. Then he touched his mouth to my scar. First, he brushed his dry lips across it three times; then he licked his lips and kissed it. When his tongue came out to lick his lips, it touched my face. This gave me more chills. I wanted to turn and kiss him on the mouth but I'd never kissed anyone before and I was scared.

I stood up and pulled him up beside me. I took my shoes off and ran out onto the shore where the waves came crashing up to my knees. I did star pose with my arms out to the sides and slightly raised, palms forward, and my legs spread apart. Sasha came too and did what I did. We stood side by side in five-pointed star pose facing the ocean. The wind whipped hard through and around us. The rain pelted our faces. I reached with my hands as far out as I could reach and thrust out my chest. I opened my mouth to catch the rain on my tongue and tasted salty sea spray. It felt like the elements washed my head and my brain and my mouth and teeth and hair and heart and guts and blood like they'd never been washed before.

When we retreated back to the hut and talked about it, Sasha said, "I feel cleaner now, somehow." That's when I fell madly in love with him all the rest of the way. I kissed and kissed him. It wasn't the first kiss that made me feel the chills again, but the tenth or twelfth, after we started getting it right. At first, it was just a mess of spit and tongues and bump-

ing noses and clicking teeth. Finally, we learned how to tilt our heads so they would fit together and how to move our mouths so it would make us feel good and want to keep doing it.

When we were walking back with soggy shoes and I was getting irritated with the blisters, I noticed that Sasha wasn't stuttering anymore. He was talking and talking nonstop, telling me everything about himself. He was the youngest of five kids and his dad was an Air Force sergeant. His mom was a doctor, and all she cared about were her patients. Neither of them was ever home and all his older siblings had busy social lives, so he spent a lot of time alone. He hadn't been there long—about six months—and he hadn't been able to make any friends yet until me because of his stutter. When I asked him if he'd ever kissed anyone before and he said yes, I felt bitter disappointment. He asked me if I had and I lied and said yes. He told me about his first kiss—behind the field house at the high school during a football game when he was eleven. He asked about mine and I described how it had felt with him those first few times.

"It was stupid and weird," I said. "It felt like a slimy little goldfish darting around inside my mouth."

"It wasn't stupid or weird with you," he said and blushed again. That's the first time I noticed that he had a pimple on the side of his face near his ear.

Later on that week when I developed a pimple on the end of my nose, I was convinced they were contagious and I had caught it from him. I stayed home from school that day and went to the pool with the nanny. Halfway through the day, I saw Sasha walk by the other side of the stone wall that divided the pool from the school area. There were square openings in the wall that revealed the profile of his face every half-second. It looked like he was walking with another girl. I was so jealous and mad that I refused to talk to him for a week. I didn't go to the cafeteria and I avoided him in the halls. One day, he was waiting at my house when I came home from school and demanded to know where I'd been and why I hadn't returned his calls.

"You gave me your pimple disease, first of all," I said, pointing to my nose tip, which was still red. "And you went off with some other girl last week that day I stayed home."

I spoke with such disgust and hate, he seemed to shrink in front of me. When he began to explain to me that it hadn't been a girl at all but a boy with long hair who he'd just made friends with, he stuttered so miserably that he could barely get the words out at all. While he was talking and sputtering, I remembered his head all dripping wet at the beach, his arms outstretched to the ocean, his smile. He stopped speaking and just looked at me. Each of his eyes contained a light, a small, illuminated scene like the kind on a full moon or in a marble. I spent the rest of the day in his sheets without any clothes on. The first time was not too different from the first kiss—bumbling and awkward as our bodies tried to fit together. Then we learned, with practice, what to do with our hands and limbs and mouths.

39. March 21, 2015: Cambridge, MA

That night, lying in bed, Kali wished she still had the dream bed so she could go into it. Deep down, though, she knew it was better that she didn't have that option. She didn't want to journey while she was remembering her ex-husband. Her mind needed to be clear for the dream bed. Otherwise, she would have a terrible dream about whatever occupied her mind. No, it was better that it was gone. Instead, she lay there and replayed their worst fight in her mind.

"Are you sexually attracted to me?" Zach stood in the doorway in a hat and coat, luggage strapped over his shoulder, just home after a week away at a conference.

"Excuse me?"

"I asked you a question," he said, laying down the words like bricks. Kali knew this was a setup, a foundation for a case he planned to build. But how could she lie?

"Can you close the door? The heat's on." It was the middle of winter and there was a snow emergency in Boston. Marko was ten. He was asleep in his room. Lydia was over, helping out in Zach's absence. But she too was already asleep.

"Are you sexually attracted to me?" He wielded the question like a loaded gun. Kali looked at him for several moments and gathered her courage.

"No."

Kali watched his eyes fill with tears. He dropped his bag on the floor, slammed the door closed, and stomped through the room, disappearing into the kitchen. Kali followed him. He ripped open drawers with a guttural sound coming from his throat. Kali was relieved that she'd earlier gathered up all the knives and put them in her bag to take them in for a sharpening. Not finding what he was looking for, he grabbed a ceramic mug from the drying rack and smashed it against his head with a desperate howl. The skin of his face broke open and bled into his eyes, dripping onto his shirt. Lydia appeared behind Kali.

"What's happening?" she asked, terrified. Both she and Kali had their hands over their mouths and stared incomprehensibly at Zach, who appeared subdued in the aftermath of his outburst. Red streaks snaked down his face and onto his yellow Cheerios tee shirt. His half-zipped puffy coat was black and hid whatever spilled on it. He looked down at his hands, which he held, palms up, at waist level.

Kali was the first one to break the trance-like stillness. She grabbed a dish towel, ran it under the tap, and then wrung it out. She handed it to Zach and told him to hold it against the cut on his forehead. Her voice was calm and even, and it felt that her head was disembodied when she spoke. Inside her head and body, screeching alarms were sounding.

"Let's get you to the hospital," Kali said. Zach didn't budge. Kali reached out for his elbow and he jumped away from her.

"Don't touch me," he snarled and walked out. Lydia still had her hand pressed to her mouth. She stood framed by the messy living room scene, with books and papers on the coffee table and floor and more clutter around the computer monitor on the desk beside the small couch. Kali had the sudden and overwhelming urge to clean it all up. Lydia let her hand drop and she peered at Kali wide-eyed. Kali looked warily toward the open door and the dark, freezing night beyond. The wind started a small snowdrift on the carpet inside the door.

"Can you watch over Marko?" Kali asked. Lydia nodded and frowned. Her eyes glossed up wetly. The expression on her face turned apologetic, and Kali had to walk away. Kali grabbed her scarf and hat and went outside, closing the door behind her and taking time to lock it as if there weren't an emergency in progress. Zach was waiting in the passenger seat of the car. Neither of them spoke for the first ten minutes or so as she drove them toward the hospital. Then, when they were almost there, he said, "We have to say that a flower pot fell on my head and broke, or something like that, okay?"

Kali didn't respond.

"I could lose my chance at a license," he said.

"Okay, a pot dropped on your head and broke," Kali said. He was scheduled to defend his thesis. He had almost all of the training hours he needed in mental health counseling and once he received his PhD, he would apply for licensure with the state to practice child psychology.

They waited in the emergency room for over an hour, then waited in the exam room for another hour before the doctor came in. They didn't speak to each other. Kali didn't dare look at him but stared at the wall or the floor. His anger was large and barely contained. It was a slowly inflating balloon. When the doctor left to prepare the suturing, Zach started to whine about the pain and the lack of topical anesthesia.

"I'll wait for you outside," Kali said and walked out. There was no part of her that could tolerate his whining. Guilt pressed against her sternum by the time she reached the waiting room, so she went to the vending machine that sells prepared food and bought him soup. She took pains to heat it in the microwave, track down napkins and a spoon, then find salt and pepper packets, too. By the time he came out of the exam room, the soup was cold again but Kali handed it to him anyway. At first he didn't take it, didn't even look at it or at Kali; he just looked straight ahead and walked straight ahead with an oblong X of tiny black stitches in his forehead. But then he abruptly stopped. He turned and took the soup from Kali with a look of such disgust on his face, the soup might have been a steaming turd. He threw it against the wall of the waiting room, where it exploded everywhere, barely missing people seated nearby. A collective gasp sounded from the strangers, but Zach kept walking. He didn't look back.

Feebly, Kali took the napkins she still had and dabbed the wall with them, mumbling apologies. The center of her back burned. The eyes on her were hot needles. She couldn't look at anybody; her face was bright red under the scrutiny. Looking around for more napkins and not finding any, she tossed the dripping handful she had in the trash and walked out, leaving the mess for someone else to clean.

In the car, Zach was again seated in the right-hand seat, waiting for Kali. She got in and started the car. Even before she pulled out of the garage, he began a stream of insults so horrible that their collective effect was numbing.

"You're a dirty gypsy Balkan that nobody wants. You think you'll find someone else? You'll get what you are, a frigid, cold, dried up, old bitch. I never should have let you name our son after your screwed up dead brother. You think your father was some big shot diplomat? He was a criminal and an alcoholic—"

"Get out of the car," Kali said and pulled over.

"I'm not going anywhere," he said and chuckled smugly.

"Then I'm getting out." And she got out. She started walking down the sidewalk. Behind her, she heard the car door slam and his footfalls on the concrete running after her. Kali started running but didn't get very far before he leapt on her back and tackled her. Her face smacked against the pavement and she felt her teeth cut into her top lip. Zach got off of her and she stood up. Her legs felt shaky. She swiped her tongue across her teeth to check for any that were broken or chipped but they all felt intact. She glared at Zach with her mouth throbbing. She felt the blood streaming from her lip and made no attempt to wipe it away. The taste was metallic on her tongue. He looked back at her as though he were stunned. He mumbled and reached for her, trying to apologize. Kali backed away. An approaching car pulled over and a man got out. He ran toward Kali.

"Are you okay?" he asked and stood between Zach and her. Kali nodded.

"Yes, I'm okay, everything's fine, it was an accident."

"It wasn't an accident, I saw the whole thing. Do you want to press charges? Because I'm going to the police right now and reporting what happened, whether you want to or not."

Zach's face collapsed into a clenched anguish. Kali found herself nodding, agreeing, and the stranger guided her toward his car. Kali got into his car and rode with him to the police station. Zach followed them. At the police station, Kali didn't press charges, but the state did. Zach was arrested.

How things had gotten so bad between them was a deep mystery to Kali. But she did know that it was she who ended it. She who pulled away. She who starved him of any affection. The more he pushed for it, the colder she turned. She wouldn't talk to him, either. Not about how she was feeling, not about the past, not about any hope of a future. He wanted to have more babies, siblings for Marko, but she was done. With him, she knew, she was done.

40. March 24, 2015: Cambridge, MA

The day Marko went back to school, he was saddened to find Malik gone. After school, he called Malik at home and found out that he was in Maine visiting his grandparents. Marko would have to wait another whole week to see him again.

The day after Marko went back to school, he went skiing with Jen. At school, he'd been picked to lead a discussion about a book in English Studies class. At first, Marko was 95 percent nervous because he was too shy to talk in front of the whole class. But when he wheeled up in front and looked at the small group of kids, most of whom were also in wheelchairs, all of whom he knew and felt familiar with and equal to, he wasn't as shy anymore. His nervousness decreased to 19 percent.

The story they had to read was Hemingway's *The Old Man and the Sea*. The kids in the class who actually read it thought it was about fishing. One girl said it was about a man's struggle with nature. But Marko had a different take: he thought it was a story about transcendence. When the old man goes with the marlin instead of fighting against it, he goes far off his path and holds on in spite of the pain. In doing so, he grows to revere the powerful marlin and judge it as his equal. More than that, Marko told the class, he feels grateful to the marlin for bringing out the best in him: all his strength and all his courage.

So when he arrived home from school to see Jen there with his mom in their apartment, he felt more confident than nervous. Especially because Jen had cut her hair short and, at first glance, Marko couldn't tell whether she looked male or female. Even knowing her gender, Marko didn't think it quite fit. It seemed apt that, like the circular nature of life and death depicted on the story—youth and age, creation and destruction—that this person he once thought he was in love with would transcend male and female, belonging to neither and also both.

Jen still sat quietly confident, radiating a self-sufficiency that was beyond the reach of other people's opinions. She looked relaxed and wore a slight smile. But there was something slightly off about her, too. Marko hadn't noticed it before and he couldn't say what it was, he couldn't prove it, but it was almost like Jen was a billboard on legs, just making the rounds. Marko imagined anywhere Jen went, people waved and blew kisses, or at least turned their heads in the direction of this great big sign. What the sign read was almost of no consequence; it read whatever the observer wanted to see. Jen seemed to also be burning with something, like regardless of what anybody saw on the billboard, she had yet to deliver its greatest message, but not even she knew what that message would be.

They left the apartment right away to drive the ninety minutes up to New Hampshire where they skied. They stayed in a condo that a friend of Marko's mom owned and let her use for free sometimes. Marko slept beside his mom on the futon and they gave Jen the bed. Marko had a hard time falling asleep that night, thinking about Jen in the other room. When he woke, he felt tired but well rested at the same time. The sum effect was what Marko imagined getting high might feel like.

When they went skiing, Kali left Jen alone with Marko at one point, and that was when Marko came to talk to Jen about something he never talked to anybody about: the math inside his head. It happened when Jen helped to transfer Marko from his chair to his sit ski. The math worked quickly in Marko's mind to show him that Jen was about to place him at an incorrect angle on the ski.

"The harness needs to be turned around," Marko said as Jen lowered him. In response, Jen lifted Marko, leaned over, and inspected the sit ski. Jen's arms were strong and easily held the part of Marko's weight left over from what he was supporting with his arms, which wasn't much. Jen's strength seemed to surpass his mother's and even his dad's. It was something Marko noticed right away: a strength combined with a lightness, like grace.

"Marko, how did you know that? There's no way you could have seen the harness from where you were."

Marko thought carefully about how to answer before he answered. He wasn't sure how to explain it, so he said, simply, "I just knew."

"But how? How did you know? Tell me."

Marko could see that Jen wasn't going to let it go. She was staring intently into Marko's eyes. Jen had turned the harness around with the other arm and paused, waiting for Marko's answer.

"The math, the numbers," Marko said. Jen's eyebrows rose. Marko said, "Sometimes, when people hold me, the numbers in my mind combine and make a kind of picture. Then I know where my body is and where other things are without having to look." Jen's eyes widened even bigger.

"So, you can see in your mind how your body is moving in space in relation to all other objects in space?"

"I guess so, yeah."

"Marko, that's amazing. I'm going to lower you to the sit ski again and I want you to tell me what position the harness is in when you're getting close."

Marko felt a little uncomfortable with this experiment, but he also felt excited under the intensity of Jen's attention. She lowered him slowly and Marko knew right away that the harness was ninety degrees off its correct position. "It's still off, needs another half turn," Marko said.

Jen burst out with a half laugh, half gasp. "Marko, that's incredible! Does your mom know about this ability?"

Marko thought about it. "She knows about the numbers," he said.

"She knows about how you can navigate space and time in your head with what's essentially calculus and n-dimensional manifolds on the fly?"

Marko felt anxiety. Jen was too excited and animated. Marko didn't want her to know this much and certainly didn't want her to talk about it to anyone else, especially his mom. "Don't tell her about it."

"Okay, I won't," Jen said. Marko looked closely at her. It was true. She would not tell. Marko felt relieved and more at ease but also a little on guard. Because now, and suddenly, the billboard that was Jen read: TRUST ME! TRUST ME! And instinctively, Marko didn't trust that.

41. March 28, 2015: Cambridge, MA

Marko willed himself to keep going: just one more thrust of his arms, just one more thrust. And one more now. His mom clapped and cheered him on and Marko knew she meant well, but he wanted to scream at her to shut up. Marko was tired and sweating. He was pushing his wheelchair around the track. One of his doctors, Doctor Chan, got Marko's mom all worked up about how important exercise and strength were going to be, especially as Marko grew. Since then, Marko's mom had kept on him about lifting his weights and exercising all the time. She was always taking pictures and videos and emailing them to Doctor Chan.

The air was cold but the sun was hot and Marko wore too many layers of clothes plus a ski hat. He stopped his progress and tore his hat off, swiping his forehead with it.

"Alright, buddy, shrug it off. Let's go!"

"Mom! Enough!"

Marko stopped altogether and leaned back in his chair. He tried to catch his breath. His heart was so rapid, he worried it would lift itself up into his neck and choke him.

"Okay, alright, take a break. " His mom trotted up to him and took her phone out of her pocket. She pointed it at Marko and said, "Say cheese for Doctor Chan!" Marko felt anger, orange and soft, squishy round, plugging up his throat, burning his chest. His hands started going, and his mom pushed them down, pinned them against Marko's stomach, getting them out of the way of the camera. Marko struggled to get a hand free and slapped the phone out of his mom's hand. It clattered to the ground. She reeled back and stared at the phone, then at Marko.

"Who cares about Doctor Chan! You had no right to break the dream bed! I thought you were dropping that crazy idea that it was hurting me. Don't you get it? I don't *want* to be in this body. I don't want to be me!"

Marko had never talked to his mom that way before and it felt good. He felt stronger for it. The flaming orange ball flattened and turned cool blue. His mom looked wounded. Marko's sense of power turned to guilt.

"I'm sorry—"

"Don't be sorry." His mom cut him off. She snatched his phone up off the ground and started walking away, sulking and angry. Marko wheeled after her.

"Mom," he called. But she didn't stop or turn around. She walked too fast for Marko to keep up and Marko was already tired. His wheels got caught in soft ground then and stopped him. "Mom!"

"What do you want from me, Marko?" His mom charged back and got in Marko's face. In her eyes, Marko saw a little girl. In response, he felt like a little boy, too.

"I want you to help keep me company when I'm feeling number eleven, I mean lonely," Marko said. He managed to say it without cracking, at least outwardly. Inside, he did crack, and the sadness became a stone-like lump in his throat. He knew if he said another word, he'd probably cry. But he didn't have to say anything more. His mom lowered her head.

"I understand, Marko. In the house I grew up in in Bulgaria, there was a small footlocker closet under the stairs. I don't know how, but it acted like a kind of dream bed for me when I was little. It was a portal to other worlds."

Marko felt his heart pick up pace again.

"I used to go in there and be alone and imagine I was a grown up in America and I had money and I had a car and I could go anywhere, do anything."

Marko didn't care about money and cars. He wanted legs. He wanted to feel the whole of his body. He wanted to be Emil.

"I know it's harder for you because of your spina bifida and everything else. But don't you see that's why you have to keep working hard, keep getting stronger? Your body is your body and it's up to you to make it the very best body it can be."

Marko gave his mom a quick nod and wheeled back to the track. He kept going, again around the track, fueled by the lump of sadness in his throat and the idea of another dream bed in Bulgaria. If there was one there, maybe he could get to it. Or maybe there were others. Maybe he could pick any enclosed space and make it work. Marko felt the lump of sadness slowly begin to melt as he pumped himself forward and heated up again. The cold, almost-dry sweat warmed against his skin and collided with the wind to provide the strangest sensation, almost like burning.

Marko reflected on what he'd said about number eleven, the loneliness, and wondered if his mom ever really could help to lessen that feeling. It was something he always felt, even when he was with other people, with a few exceptions. Jen. Malik. The Ambassador. But the Ambassador wasn't real without a dream bed. And Marko didn't know if he'd be able to find another one. And with Jen or Malik, it wasn't that he talked about much with either of them. In fact, Malik never said much of anything. But their company was dense with substance. Maybe it was understanding, empathy. But Marko suspected it was more than that, or maybe something altogether different. What he felt with Jen and Malik was the same thing he felt when he had briefly met that cancer patient at the hospital, Amanda. He felt a magnetism, a draw that was simple and compelling. He also felt connection.

Marko wondered if he was in love with Jen or Malik. He hoped not, because she was too old for him and he was a boy. She was twenty-one. Malik was Marko's age. But he didn't think that was it, because he didn't want to kiss them or anything. But sometimes when he was lying in his bed, he did think about cuddling with them. Not at the same time. He sometimes thought about cuddling with Jen, and other times, Malik. He imagined her or him behind him with their arms around him, holding him close. It was something he only ever did with his mom. And when she held him that way, he did feel less lonely. But not even that obliterated the loneliness altogether.

Before he knew it, Marko was all the way around the track and rounding it again for yet another lap. His mom was quiet; she'd stopped her cheering and was just standing and watching Marko with a weird expression on her face. Was it pride? Marko didn't know, but he didn't much care. He needed to complete one last lap and his arms were starting to scream and he was starting to pant and sweat was soaking his shirt. Just one more, now one more, he thought. But then he wondered if he should stop thinking about it and willing each arm to thrust, because it made him conscious of his exhaustion. When he hadn't thought about it at all, he had just sped around the track hardly noticing his effort. As soon as he became aware of it, it flared up to impossible proportions. It was nearly insurmountable, the fatigue. So he shifted his mind back to Jen, thinking of the next time he would see her and what he might say to her. Then he thought of Malik and when they would be alone together again. The thought of it made him nervous and powered him to the finish line. Back again at the starting point, which was also the end, Marko relaxed and sat back. His mom gave a loud whoop and high-fived him.

"Marko, you're amazing. Great job!"

Marko's mom pulled out the phone camera again and turned it on. Marko covered his face and said, "Not now, Mom." She peered at him over the phone, scowling, looking hurt. She let the phone fall and put it back in her pocket. Her mouth was a straight line and her face was still. She looked over Marko's head into the distance. Marko felt bad and wheeled closer to her. He lifted his hand for another high five, which his mom met after a brief hesitation. "Let's get out of here and hit the showers, okay?" Marko gave his mom a smile as genuine as he could muster. She smiled weakly back and nodded. Still a little distant, she pushed Marko back toward the car.

42. March 29, 2015: Cambridge, MA

Marko was going to have a date with Jen. It wasn't really a date, but he let himself think that it was because it was the closest thing to one he'd ever had. His mom was going to take them downtown to the movie theater and drop them off. They were going to see a movie by themselves, and then go get coffee before his mom picked them up again. The night before this event, Marko couldn't fall asleep. His whole body buzzed with anticipation, even the half he couldn't feel. He lay there in the dark and felt his heart beat heavier, faster, higher, as though it were close to his throat. He kept swallowing, trying to force it down.

Marko closed his eyes and tried not to imagine what it would feel like to kiss Jen. He didn't want to imagine that, because she was supposed to be like a big sister to him, and he knew that brothers and sisters aren't supposed to kiss or want to kiss. So instead he imagined kissing Malik. Each time though, Malik turned into Jen, and Marko stopped and started thinking about numbers to calm himself down. It was a new trick he'd started using. Different from the math that happened in his mind unwilled, this math was deliberate. When he learned in school about exponents and squares, it was like he already knew what they were teaching him. He was able to calculate the squares of numbers effortlessly and quickly, and when he heard a number, he recognized whether it was a square and could instantly identify its base. The trick he used to stop himself thinking of kissing was to think of a prime number and calculate if it left a remainder of one when divided by four. If it did, then the prime number should be the sum of two squares. Marko went through all the primes in turn, working them down, when they were the right kind, to their pair of squares, all the way to 193. His mind worked less rapidly on the higher numbers, so it took him a few seconds to determine whether 193 was the right kind of prime. Determining that it was, he quickly saw that it broke up into the squares 49 and 144.

By then he was calmer and tired and able to slip into sleep without further fantasy. Marko dreamed of a medieval setting where he was part of a crowd that had gathered in the very early morning to see someone hanged. He pushed his way to the front of the crowd to see the prisoner brought out. He had not even gone to bed the night before, but celebrated with people late into the night until it didn't make sense to go home and go to bed lest they risk missing the event in the square. He wasn't sure why he'd been celebrating or with whom, but he had a vague sense it was because this terrible prisoner had been caught and would be killed at long last. Two enormous men in armor led the prisoner. They were so enormous that they obscured the tiny body and face of the prisoner from Marko's view. He strained to see, and when he did, he felt all the blood drain from his face and almost fainted. It was his mother.

They were dragging her, lifting her periodically off the ground to untangle her feet, which kept twisting together like dangling strings. Her legs were mangled. The guards marched her straight ahead to where the gallows loomed. The sky turned dark and ominous. People cheered and clapped. His mom was so hysterical, he could hardly recognize her. Her face was contorted by grief, her eyes swollen shut, her mouth open and screaming. Marko screamed, too. How could he not? This must be a mistake, he thought; he had to save her. But when he looked down and saw that he had legs that worked and that he could feel, he recognized them as her legs. They were her legs on his body. He looked again at his mother and saw that the legs now on her body were his, only longer and emptied out, like a pair of threadbare pants dangling in the breeze.

His mother's clothes were gray and indistinguishable from the light. Her face was red from all the screaming. The crowd around him puffed with pleasure, eager to see her hang. Marko looked at the person standing next to him, smiling. It was his dad. "Why did you bring me here to see this?" Marko demanded, yelling. His dad didn't respond or even seem to hear him; he just kept smiling and laughing and clapping. Marko wanted to attack, but when he reached out to grab his dad's neck, it turned into a cloud of glistening splinters, sharp and dangerous. He pulled his hands back, stumbled, and fell into other clouds of splinters. Within moments, the bottom half of his body was shredded and bleeding. He lay on his side on the ground, dying, seeing his mother in the gallows, her legs back to normal again, swinging ominously above the ground.

Marko woke suddenly, ripped from sleep. His throat was dry and he had a headache. The vivid details of his nightmare were still with him, heavy in the room. He shook his head on the pillow, rubbed his hands over his face, and sat up. Light was dawning outside his window. He looked at his alarm clock and saw that it was just after 6 a.m. He reached for his wheelchair at the same moment his mom walked in, startling him.

"Sorry, did I scare you?" She smiled.

He looked at her legs. "I had a bad dream."

Marko opened his mouth to tell her the rest but he realized he couldn't. He stuttered and said, "Monsters that turned into splinters like razors cut me apart."

"Oh, honey, that's awful. It was just a dream." She rubbed one of his legs as she spoke. He watched her hand move and for a moment almost believed he felt it there, touching him.

"Are you excited for your movie today with Jen?"

Marko smiled as he remembered. He nodded and reached again for his chair, eager to get ready for the day.

↭

Marko followed Jen up the sidewalk after the movie. There was con-struction around one of the sidewalks when they crossed a street, and the ramped part of the curb wasn't accessible. Marko watched Jen ex-pertly pop her chair up over the curb, so fast that he didn't notice how she'd done it. He was stopped there before it, helpless. What had been so easy for her was insurmountable for him. The day was bright and cold, buzzing with activity.

"You have to come at it with momentum and then pop your front wheels up and push hard to bring the back wheels up. It's not easy. Do you want some help?" Jen faced Marko from up on the sidewalk. He looked at her and nodded. She always asked him if he wanted her help before she gave it. He realized that she was helping him learn how to ask for it himself. Not from her, but from others when he wasn't around her.

She bent forward and pulled Marko's front wheels up on the curb. Marko leaned dangerously back. He pushed forward with all his might and she pulled. He felt himself start to fall back. "Lean forward," Jen said, but Marko found that he couldn't.

He fell back and was caught. "Whoa, there," a male voice said be-hind him. His chair lifted onto the curb.

"Thank you," Jen said to the man.

"You okay?" he asked Marko, who was too stunned and embarrassed to say anything. Feeling the red in his face, he nodded and wheeled forward. Jen followed Marko and although he didn't know where he was going, he liked knowing she was behind him, coming with. After about a block, Marko's bare hands were so cold they were numb and a little painful. Just when he was about to stop and bury them into his pockets, Jen said, "Here we are, Marko."

He turned and saw her waiting in front of a door to a coffee shop. He wheeled toward her. She wheeled to where she could open the door, then used her chair to push it open wider. She held it open for Marko and he passed through. He turned to watch her come the rest of the way in but she was already there, bumping into him. "Sorry," she said and laughed. Marko was astonished at her ease navigating the world on her own. He rolled himself back, clearing the way for her to go forward. She messed his hair at the top of his head when she passed by, winking and smiling. Marko smiled and blushed.

He tried fixing his hair before following her to the counter, finger-combing it back in place. The gesture made him feel a strange mix of things: half pleasure (number thirteen) at the attention and her company, and the other half frustration (number twenty-seven) at more confirmation that she saw him as a child, cute and little. When she had bought them both tickets for a G-rated cartoon movie, he acted excited to make her feel good about it, but he wished she'd picked a movie that she might see with one of her peers. At least a PG-13 movie. At the counter in the coffee shop, she ordered a hot chocolate and looked expectantly at Marko. He remembered his mom had given him money.

"Oh, let me pay," he said and rolled forward.

"No no—just tell him what you want, I got it," she said, physically blocking him from coming near the register.

"I'll have a hot chocolate," he said. He pulled a ten out of his coat and thrust it toward Jen. She waved him off, paid, and rolled toward the bank of tables. One of the workers rushed ahead of them and cleared two chairs away from a table. Jen smiled and said, "Thank you," and Marko echoed her. He saw that she always thanked people. She had very good manners. When he faced her across the table, he spontaneously asked, "Do you ever get mad?"

She laughed and said, "Of course."

He faked laughter. "I can't imagine you being angry is all. You're so nice all the time."

"Well, I'm nice when I'm around you. Sometimes I get mad and I'm not so nice. I try to always be respectful though."

The drinks came. Marko sipped his hot chocolate and tried to imagine Jen angry. His mom told him that everybody contained both darkness and light. It was when the darkness got bigger than the light that people turned to violence. Even the universe had dark matter.

"Did you know that the center of the galaxy is a giant black hole whose gravity is so strong that nothing, not even light, can escape it?"

Jen smiled, "I know, yes. But how do we know what black holes are? They could be doorways to other universes. They could be anything. A black hole is a thing with mass and gravity that can't be seen. There's something to that."

"But it can be seen," Marko said.

"Well, we can see a black hole, but a hole doesn't have mass and gravity. What we can observe is something that looks to us like a void in space. So that's what we say it is. It consumes stars and produces stars. It's a creative and destructive mechanism in the universe. It's fascinating, really."

Marko was used to always knowing more about space than most people, because he'd read so much about it. Realizing that Jen's knowledge exceeded his made him both excited and jealous. "How do you know so much?"

"I don't know anything. I just learned about this stuff in science classes, just like you, and then thought a lot about it. Plus I read the news in *National Geographic* and from NASA. I like the pictures from the satellites. It makes me feel better to remember how small I am and the world is."

"I know! I feel that way too!" Now Marko was 100 percent certain that Jen was his soul mate. He wanted to tell her that he loved her. But when she smiled and messed up his hair and then told him his hot chocolate was getting cold, he felt like a little boy again and his heart broke. He sipped his lukewarm chocolate and wished it were hot. Its lack of heat made him feel cold. Several moments passed in silence during which Marko was uncomfortable and trying to think of something to say. But he could tell that Jen was not uncomfortable with silence. She was completely at ease.

"Do you ever dream that you can walk?" Jen asked.

"Yes, often. You?"

"Sometimes. When you dream that you can walk, do you feel your legs?"

"Yes. Sometimes even when I'm not dreaming, I feel my legs. At least I think I do. But I think that's because I can remember feeling my legs.

At least that's what my brother tells me. He says he can't remember feeling his legs. He was only two when we had the accident. I was five."

"Do you remember the accident?"

"No. But I remember the day of the accident, right up until around the time we got in the car to drive home, which was when we crashed. Sometimes, I dream about the crash and then I have what feels like memories of it, but I'm really only remembering my dreams of it."

Marko wanted to hear more, but was afraid to ask. He had never heard Jen talk about the accident before. He knew that her father had been driving and her mother did not survive, but he didn't know how it happened. Had their father walked away unharmed?

"What about you? Can you feel your legs in your walking dreams?"

"Oh." Marko was startled at the question. He'd forgotten that's what he'd asked her originally. He was thinking about the accident, making up details, imagining a big, blue, square car with all four of them in it rolling off of a cliff.

"I think so, kind of, actually yes. I actually visited a past life where I had legs, but bad feet," he said. Jen squinted at him and he felt the heat rise to his face. He hadn't meant to say that. What was it about Jen that made him blurt his secrets out to her?

"Oh, that's interesting. How did you do that?"

Marko was shy to answer. He was trapped now into telling her more. "Actually no, that's not what happened. I just have dreams, that's all. And when I wake up, I sometimes think I can still feel all the way down." The truth was, he could feel his lower stomach but not his lower back and not either of his hips. He looked down at his lap and the atrophied, flat thighs. He felt his face redden.

"Your mom is so great, isn't she?" Jen asked. Marko looked up at her.

"Yeah, I guess. I mean, I don't know."

"What don't you know?"

"Well, sometimes I feel like I don't know her very well. But I know a lot of people do like her. A lot of people take her yoga classes and call her and want to talk to her and stuff."

"But you feel like you don't know her very well?"

"Sometimes."

"Tell me more about that."

Marko felt anxious. How had they gotten on this topic of his mom and him feeling like he didn't know her?

"I don't know. I guess I don't really know what I mean. She's a quiet person and she's always acting happy. But I know she isn't always happy. You know?"

"Well, sure, but it's her job as your mom to keep a good attitude and be a good example for you. I think that's brave of her to always act happy even when she might not feel that way."

Marko realized that Jen's mother had died and that maybe she was jealous. At least Marko still had his mom. He felt guilty for what probably sounded like complaining about her.

"No you're right. She is really great. I don't know why I said that, I just wasn't thinking I guess."

"It's fine for you to say whatever you feel and whatever is true for you," Jen said. "Maybe, if you feel like you don't know her well enough, you should tell her that. Share with her what you just shared with me and tell her that you want to know her better. I'm sure she'd be receptive to that."

But when Marko got home that night and his mom asked him how it went, he said it went fine and found he couldn't go further than that. Nor could he confess his need to know her better. Nor could he ask her for anything. It was as though he could see in her eyes when she asked that she didn't really want to know. Just as she didn't want him to know how it was to be her.

43. March 30, 2015: Cambridge, MA

At the next shrink appointment, Kali found herself talking about when she'd first met Zach. Like she'd once been prone to do, before she turned jaded, Kali had fallen madly in love with him. What that meant was still a mystery to her. The retelling of the events that were a part of their meeting and courtship would fail to capture the thing itself or the reason why. Kali knew this because she had tried unsuccessfully many times. It was something irreducible that refused to come through in the summation.

She remembered there was an expansive feeling in her when she was with him, like her boundaries had been blown out and she was bigger than she'd ever been. The intellectual stimulation was also a draw—they talked about the topics nobody else would talk about, like how absurd it was to wake up, brush your teeth, go to work, go to sleep. Like how wild it was that people even exist, given the odds against it. Just the pure numbers with how many eggs a woman has versus how many she ovulates versus how many sperm a man has. That one of each of those would connect just so and at just the right time—it was the most impossible lottery. And the planet and the solar system and everything beyond and everything within, the infinite halving, how bodies moving in space affected one another, how they each found evidence that Confucianism was the belief system of dogs. Just the average household pet kind of dog, not the homeless gypsy dogs in Bulgaria—those ones were too concerned with finding the basic elements of survival like food and shelter to think about behavioral codes or bettering themselves.

Kali met him on South Green at her college campus on a spring morning. She had gotten into the habit of sitting in the grass in the morning and reading for a while with her coffee. She liked the bustle of activity. A fluffy white dog barreled up to her and attacked her with its tongue, its tail a blur, its front paws trying to climb to the highest point on her body while it licked her. She put her hands over her face and the dog licked her hands, her arms.

"Sherwin," a man's voice called, "get off her, get back here, where's your stick?"

The dog leapt off as quickly as it had come and bounded several feet away where it retrieved a large stick. The dog and its person proceeded to make a show of their playing, him lunging for the stick, the dog deftly avoiding him—a primal game of keep-away, a sure trick for artificially inflating the lure of a thing. The whole thing stunk of contrivance, which would typically annoy Kali, but in this case she found it endearing. Also, once she started, she couldn't look away from him. He was bulky and muscular but with the grace and agility of a dancer. He wore a faded tee shirt and jeans and his milk chocolate hair fell in his eyes in an intentionally messy way. Even though Kali stared, he didn't acknowledge her. Kali was certain he had intended to get her attention because she'd seen him before on the green with his dog and witnessed how smart and obedient the dog was. To jump all over her like it did, he must have dispatched it.

But he was definitely retreating, maybe losing his nerve, so Kali stood up, slid on her shoes, and started toward him.

"Hey, you, cute dog," she called. He looked up, tossing his hair from his eyes in a subtle nod. He smiled, which made Kali smile.

"I'm Zach," he said.

"Kalina." She stuck out her hand and he shook it.

"Lovely name." His teeth were white and he had a strong, prominent jawline. He was handsome in a very American way.

"Crow!" He pointed up to the branches of a nearby tree. Kali looked and saw the bird, which just then made a hoarse caw, like recognition of their attention. Even the dog stopped to look up. Kali kneeled down and buried her fingers in the dog's neck fluff.

"His name's Sherwin," Zach said.

"Is he some kind of poodle?"

"Yeah, a mix of that and other stuff."

"He's smart," Kali said.

"How do you know?"

"Because you can send him at will to accost any unsuspecting girl you want," she said.

A bright red crept instantly to his neck and face, blotchy like a rash.

"I don't know what you're talking about," he said, looking down and kicking the grass, smiling guiltily. He glanced at Kali and the red deepened.

"Look," he said and pointed again into the tree. Kali laughed and nodded.

"That's what I thought."

"Was I that obvious?"

Kali stood and swatted his arm playfully. "Maybe I'm just that smart."

He met her eyes then, shyly but squarely, and Kali saw everything she needed to know—he was searching and wounded. Kali ignored it and assumed her usual boldness.

"Let's do something," she said.

"Okay, what?"

"Something fun! Let's go to the beach. Do you have a car?" Kali started walking in the direction of the parking lot and he trotted to keep up. His car was a beat-up black Subaru that smelled like wet dog. When Kali first opened the heavy door and ducked in, she had déjà vu—the sight of him swiftly seated behind the wheel, his compact, muscled thighs, the profile of his serious face, the bulge of jaw muscle when he clenched his teeth, the car's smell—all of it together was a moment frozen in time. It was a living tableau she had seen before, and had known would happen. Kali had had such moments before but they were infrequent enough to still be weighty in significance. She decided it was a metaphysical signpost, alerting her that she was starting on a path she had always been meant to follow.

That sense of a beginning of something big stayed with her after that. It's what allowed her to overlook his messy apartment with dirty dishes stacked in the sink and dust-covered books stacked against the wall. Spartan in its furnishings, the place looked in transition, like somebody was in the midst of moving out.

"You're not interested in creature comforts I see."

"Sure I am, I just don't require much to be comfortable."

"Not much at all." Kali looked at the kitchen. The oven had been used—there were burned spills stuck to the top around the burners. Pots and pans were among the dishes in the sink.

"You cook?"

"All the time."

"Want to cook me something?"

"I thought you wanted to go to the beach? You want to stay here?"

They had only stopped to drop off the dog, which it turned out wasn't even his. He was dog-sitting for a friend. The beach would have gotten him too dirty, he'd said, so they needed to dump him off first. He'd had his outing for the day.

"I'm hungry, aren't you hungry?"

He smiled and nodded slowly, looking wide-eyed at her.

"Don't get any ideas. I'm not staying long."

"No, no, of course. No ideas at all."

He moved awkwardly past her and into the kitchen, where he turned on the faucet and started washing dishes. Kali followed him, picked up a dish towel from the plastic card table in the corner, and started drying, asking him where each thing went.

"Where are you from?"

"Bulgaria."

"Oh yeah, what part?"

"Sofia, the capital."

"What's that like?"

"I don't know, any city I guess. Where do you put your tall glasses?"

He leaned over her and opened a cupboard to her left. He turned his head mid-lean. His face was very close to hers.

44. March 30, 2015: Stowe, MA

At school, Marko had shut himself in every closet, stall, small room, and otherwise somewhat enclosed space he could find to see if it would act as a portal for him to get back to Emil. Nothing worked. Marko worried he would never get back to Emil again. He wanted to go just one more time. There was something unfinished with the Ambassador and Marko needed to finish it. After trying to make it happen on his own and failing, he started to give up hope. But in the back of his mind, he knew that he would have another chance if he could get to his mom's childhood home in Bulgaria and find the other dream bed there. The only thing that allowed Marko to stop obsessing about it was Malik's return.

When Malik was back in school finally, he and Marko went to their spot in the grass at the top of the hill again. It was colder that day and cloudy, but there wasn't any snow and the grass was dry, so they made a go of it. Once again, Malik lifted Marko from his chair and set him gently on the ground against the tree trunk. He sat next to him, shoulder to shoulder, hip to hip, and was still. Marko expected that he would reach for his lunch to start eating, but Malik stayed still next to him for what felt like a long time. Marko looked at Malik's forearm against his own. Thicker and darker, rougher-looking with the rashes, it made Marko's arm look smaller in comparison. Marko looked up to tell Malik this, but before he could say anything, Malik's mouth covered his and they were kissing.

Marko's stomach grew wings again and beat violently up his torso until it lodged in his throat and fluttered there. For the first several seconds, Marko simply held his mouth open while Malik's tongue moved around in there. Then, Marko reciprocated, moving his own tongue into Malik's mouth, tasting his mint gum. Abruptly, Malik stopped, pulling his head back and looking away. Marko swiped the saliva off his face with his sleeve and held his breath, waiting for what would happen next. Malik reached for his lunch bag.

"Are you all healed after your surgery?" Malik asked.

"I think so. My head still hurts sometimes but more from the incision than anything else. I don't get the pressure feeling anymore."

"That's good. Were you scared?

"A little."

"I was scared for you."

Malik took a bite of his sandwich and chewed for a while, then said, "I missed you."

"I missed you too."

"I started reading that book you told me about, the *Unbearable Lightness* one?"

"You did?"

"There's a lot of sex in it."

Marko laughed and said, "I think it's more about bodies than sex."

"Light bodies?" Malik asked. Marko thought of the yellow bodies of light he once saw during meditation.

"Bodies made of yellow light?" he asked. This time, Malik laughed.

"No, the light body, like weightless, and the heavy body, the one with weight. The light bodies are the soul? That's why it's called *The Unbearable Lightness*—"

"Yes!" Marko shouted, only just then seeing it. Tereza and Franz, the main characters in the novel, were interested in matters of the soul, the lightness of being, while simultaneously engaging in heavy emotions like guilt and fear. Tomas and Sabina were both all about the physical, practical body while being committed to a lightness of character. It was a paradox.

"Do you take any medications with black box warnings?" Marko asked.

"I think so," Malik said. "Why?"

"They're very heavy, I think, and they weigh me down. They make even my light body heavy."

"Oh, I don't know. I mean, how long have we been taking these medications? Our whole lives practically? And when did anything inside of that black box ever happen to you? Maybe think about the not-heavy stuff outside of the heavy black box, which is everything else, all the air, the empty space, the whole sky, and think of how light that is."

"Yes," Marko said again. He immediately felt lighter. He realized then that he was gripping Malik's thigh. He let go as if recoiling from a flame.

"Are you gay together?" It was Derekah. She rolled out from behind the tree, Mia pushing her wheelchair and Tia trailing behind. Malik scooted away from Marko and dropped a strawberry he'd been about to eat on the ground. Both boys stared after the strawberry as it rolled away in the grass toward Derekah's chair. She rolled forward, missing the strawberry by about three blades of grass. Marko watched the grass bending under her wheels, transfixed.

"Are you two gay lovers?"

The twins laughed and hugged each other. Marko looked at Malik, whose eyes were still trained on the strawberry.

"Mia and Tia," Marko said, "shouldn't you stay with the teacher?" The twins weren't supposed to wander off unsupervised, as they were mentally about four years old.

"That's not answering my question," Derekah snapped. But Marko's plan worked: Mia and Tia nervously retreated, worried they might be breaking a rule. Derekah lost her backup. Marko thought she would feel disempowered and perhaps be less intimidating on her own, but he was wrong. Instead, she shoved her wheel forward, rolled it with force over Marko's ankle, and parked it there. Marko closed his eyes and watched the thousands of tiny circles spinning, calculating, like a colossal system of congruous, toothless gears. He heard a thump and opened his eyes. Derekah was on the grass, her wheelchair toppled sideways. Malik stood over her mumbling something Marko couldn't hear.

"Help!" Derekah screamed. Her voice was surprisingly deep when she screamed. She sounded afraid.

"You hurt my friend you hurt my friend you hurt my friend . . ." Malik's mumbling grew louder and Marko heard the mantra.

"I'm okay, Malik, I'm okay," he said, although he wasn't sure that was true. His ankle had a dissymmetry to it that hadn't been there before.

45. March 30, 2015: Cambridge, MA

Marko found himself, once again, waiting to be seen by a doctor. He was taken to the emergency room, where he was told it would be a three-hour wait. Marko's mom was on her way, and he knew that she would do something to get him in quicker. Malik had wanted to come in the ambulance with Marko, which gave Marko feeling number 127, pink fuzz behind his belly button. To stop thinking about it, he read his mom's diary. But what he read didn't help him stop thinking about it.

I loved a woman once in a way that made everything burn—my hands, my thighs, the small spaces between us, time we spent together. Especially time we spent together. Our togetherness burned through time like an eighteen-wheeler burns fuel. The intervals I spent away from her sipped time with excruciating slowness. We loved each other that same burning way, and we knew it, but we never spoke of it and we never acted on it except to press close together in the innocent manner of cuddling little girls. But we were not little; we were bright, budding women and the searing wetness between my thighs when we pressed that way was anything but innocent. All I wanted was for her to touch there, or for me to touch her and find out if I was having the same effect on her.

We drifted apart as she became busy. She was a singer and a song-writer and she started to be recognized as talented. As the recognition widened, she gained success, and pulled away from me. I saw her play in bars, on stages, in videos, and I tried to forget her. I moved on, had boyfriends, eventually came to the States, met Zach, got married. Even with Marko and with my life at the happiest point in my marriage, even though I would not want to have missed it, I could not help regretting not fighting for her when I had the chance. Not telling her exactly how I felt, at the right time and place, when it might have worked. Not being patient and waiting for her to return to me from her distractions, which she always did. But instead, I left, I moved on with my life. I chose to leave her behind and forget her. All of that, if it happened, would have brought trouble and controversy anyway. That wasn't something I would have minded so much, but she would have.

There was a doctor I took Marko to in the city. His office was in a tall building, on the seventeenth floor. While Marko was inside, I sat in the lobby and stared out of a large window, looking down on everything. I saw the river from there and the Common, the tops of other buildings and the spires of churches. The people from that reference point were so tiny, so far away. When I saw a woman from that distance, I imagined it was her. I did this attempting to distance her from me still, make her a small, insignificant thing among small, insignificant things in the world. Just an insect. Just one small ant in so many ants. But imagining that a faraway woman was her, even from that window, even in my imagination, made me long for her even more. I realized it then, during that exercise: even if she were a star in the sky, impossibly far and unattainable forever, I would never gain the indifference toward her that I craved. And I would always believe that she had easily gained such indifference toward me. Because of course, on television and in magazines she looked glamorous and phenomenally happy. And wasn't I happy for her? Yes. Yes, of course I was when I really thought about it, separated my wants entirely from it. Then, just to think of her smile made me smile without willing it.

But if I thought of her happiness in spite of my absence—or worse, facilitated by my absence—I touched a despair so deep, it met the weariness of existence itself.

But what of that weariness of existence? Let it be there. Let it not carry so much weight. Let it be a light, nothing little detail. For people like me, who are used to getting everything they want and having pleasure and enjoying a healthy, functioning body and mind, that existential weariness comes as a total shock and dire disappointment when it inevitably surfaces in the lonely moments or the quiet moments or the long, slow days steeped in repetition. But for people like Marko, who live with it head-on like a face pressed against glass day in and day out, every day, well. It just is. Marko is as likely to complain about it as I am to complain about the effort it takes for my lungs to pull in and expel air all throughout every day. Or the effort it takes for my heart to beat. These things just occur almost as if behind the scenes, almost unnoticed. When Marko complains, it's about piercing and constant physical pain or about an inability to stand, an inability to walk. He doesn't think to complain about the simple fact that he was born and he exists and that this existence comes with a price he can't understand or measure. He doesn't question what makes it worth it.

And so I came back, always right back to the guilt. The shame of feeling badly for myself or of complaining about anything, ever. Because in comparison to my son, I have no business. And because for my son, I'm supposed to shine a light. That's my job and it's a simple job. The punishment I receive, directly or indirectly, for not being able to do it, will never be severe enough.

46. 1980s, Thailand

Todor never saw Emil again after that day when Emil gave him back the novel. He spent over two years in a Thai prison before being sent home. While in prison, he read and reread the novel, paying special attention to the parts Emil had marked. Through the novel, Todor fell in love with Emil. Rather, he fell in love with Emil's absence. His absence became more of a presence in Todor's life than his physical self had ever been. The markings he left in the novel were the flesh on the skeleton Todor had engineered from yearning. The relationship he had with Emil's absence was fueled by passionate dreams of frustrated desire. Todor never coupled with Emil in his dreams, but every night, he *almost* did. Each dream ended the same way: Todor knew that Emil wanted him too, yet there was no way they could find to be alone together. It was exquisite torture. It kept Todor going each day for seven hundred and seventy-nine days.

This was how Todor passed the days:
- Wake up
- Write the number of days out in his notebook in words rather than numerals
- Eat
- Read the novel
- Think about when and how to end his life

- Eat
- Write a letter
- Read the novel
- Talk with Emil's absence
- Eat
- Exercise
- Go to bed
- Dream of Emil

Each subsequent activity was a spoke on the wheel that was time in prison. One rotation of the wheel was one day. After the wheel turned seven hundred and seventy-nine times, Todor was released and travelled home to Lydia and his children.

When he was no longer a diplomat, he had to find another way to exist in the world. Before long, he became a spy for the Bulgarian government. Several years after travelling all over the world dealing in foreign government secrets, Todor found himself back in Thailand. He sought out the dormitory where Emil was last living and found the building gone, replaced with a train engine fueling station. It was so dirty that it alarmed him. There must have been an oil spill in the parking lot because it was swamped and permeated by a black luminousness. There was a man in the middle of a black puddle wearing dirty, oil-soaked overalls. They were too small, cutting into him at his crotch and underarms.

The man had several recruits around him, all greasy and soiled, bustling around, helping to clean up the oil. They looked happy to be together, despite the despicable task. Todor imagined that they lived together at the station that replaced the dormitory. There was a cement porch behind the filling station with dirty patio furniture. A rusted porch swing held a grubby, sleeping dog. The door to the station was pewter colored and ancient looking—tin, lead, and silver. It gleamed a bit against the bright glossy black.

Todor walked toward the group thinking he would ask about Emil, but then changed his mind at the last minute and left. Todor decided to use the resources at his disposal as a spy to track Emil down and go and see him. He sent word to his contacts and colleagues that he was tracking down the boy on behalf of a top-secret, high-paying client.

It was two months later, through a colleague spy, that he learned Emil had died only the year before from complications related to his disease. Todor was irrationally devastated. He had barely known the boy, but had built him up in his imagination to staggering proportions. He regretted knowing this information about the boy's death, because it killed Emil's absence for him—the most substantial presence in his life for a long time.

47. March 30, 2015: Cambridge, MA

At the hospital, a doctor reset Marko's ankle, which had been dislocated from Derekah parking her wheelchair on it. Prior to this, Marko was x-rayed extensively. The doctor treating Marko noticed a problem with Marko's bones completely unrelated to the ankle injury: the curvature of his spine. Marko had been told in the past that his poor posture resulted from a combination of his spinal injury being so low on his back and a bad case of congenital scoliosis. The consequence—that as he grew, he grew more bent over rather than taller—was life-threatening, according to this new doctor.

There was good news, bad news, and more bad news. The good news was that there was a surgery that might be able to correct his curving spine. The bad news: it was major spine surgery that was very risky and that he might not live through. And if he did live through it, there was a chance it either wouldn't work or that it could make him more paralyzed than he already was. The surgery consisted of cutting Marko open through the back and the chest and reinforcing his spine with metal rods to straighten it. The more bad news: he would die within a few years if he didn't have the surgery because the way he was growing would interfere with his circulation, his digestion, and his ability to breathe.

The silence in the room following the news was a quiet uproar. Marko brimmed with murky, colliding shapes and numbers, unable to make sense of the feelings. Sometimes, the signal of his own feelings was interrupted by his mom's feelings; then they all mixed and muddled together inside him. Finally the silence gave way to a barrage of questions from Kali. What kind of metal were the rods? Would it lead to more or less pain? Would Marko keep use of his arms? What about his heart? At one point during the questioning, his mom and grandma started arguing about getting a second opinion.

While Marko's mom and grandma argued and talked at length with the doctor, Marko felt eerily calm. Eventually, he asked if he could leave the room and let them talk. Instead, they left the room. Left alone with his iPad, Marko read his mom's diary.

Because my father was gone so often, my mom would take my brother and me and drop us off at her mother's house. My grandmother was not a warm woman. She did no parenting. She basically ignored us. If we sought attention from her, she put us to work on this or that chore— wash the dishes, sweep the floor, clean out the ice box, boil the potatoes, knead the dough. My younger brother was my passive playmate. He let me exercise my wildest imaginings on him. Because when I was young, I thought I would have wanted a younger sister much more than a younger brother, I would outfit Marko in wigs and dresses and put makeup on him and call him Ellie.

I remember one day, I dressed him this way at my grandmother's house. While we were playing, Marko grew tired and fell asleep in a chair. I left him there to go fix myself something to eat in the kitchen. When I came back with cheese and bread, my grandmother stood at the threshold to the attic room where Marko—dressed as Ellie—slept. Marko's hands were palms-up on his lap and his fingers were making slight movements, as if he were trying to grasp something in his sleep. His mouth was agape and his upturned face had the loudest snore emitting from it that it sounded like something motorized.

"What is this?" my grandmother asked when she saw me.

I took a bite of cheese and with my mouth full answered, "This is Ellie."

She scowled at me with her mouth open, a look that I'd imagine her giving me if I said every terrible curse word to her in a fast string. I stopped chewing and held the food in my mouth.

"What are you thinking, doing this to him?" she asked, the pitch of her voice spiking each word to barb me.

"He likes it."

Her face settled into resolute disgust then, like any hope or respect she had for me in her body had just been flushed out with three short syllables. I wanted to reach into the air and snatch the syllables back and swallow them and never say anything again. I swallowed the food in my mouth instead, which suddenly tasted sour. This was when I realized that speech can be as destructive as it is creative.

"Wake him up and undo this immediately. Get him dressed properly; then both of you get downstairs. I have work for you to do."

With that, she turned around and left. Her footsteps retreating down the wooden stairs, the clacking of her heels across the hard lower floor, and the lingering smell of her rose soap all combined to keep me frozen in place. It wasn't until I felt my heart beating in my throat that I realized I'd been holding my breath.

I woke Marko up and made him take everything off. I scrubbed the makeup off his face with a washcloth while he cried.

"Why are you crying?" I asked brusquely.

"Because I want to be Ellie," he said, whimpering. I felt irritated. I stopped scrubbing his face and looked at the red-stained washcloth and then at his face. His cheeks were ruddy without the rouge and his eyes were beginning to puff. I felt the hardness of my grandmother in me about to strike. I didn't want to be like that. My grandmother was brutality shrink-wrapped in skin. I gave him a hug and let him cry until he was finished.

"When is Mommy coming back?" he asked me.

"She should be back soon," I lied. But then I decided that she might be back soon, and that she would come back more quickly if we watched for her and wished it. So I got Marko dressed in his proper boy clothes and took him downstairs where we sat on the windowsill and stared out the window, waiting for my mother to come.

At some point I heard my grandmother walk into the room and I braced myself to reject her when she asked for something from us—some chore to perform. But she didn't ask. She simply retreated, more quietly than she had entered. Marko looked dejectedly out the window and showed no signs of comprehension. Eventually, we both fell asleep there. When I woke up, my arm was asleep, crushed under Marko's weight, and my neck was stiff. I dragged him upstairs and made him pee before getting into bed. We slept clinging to each other, back to front.

I could not have known that night while we slept, taking comfort in each other's company, that I would be taken from there by my parents to go to the Russian school, while Marko would be left behind with my grandmother to go to the boys' school near her. I didn't know that it would drain the life from him, those years. And I didn't know that at seventeen, Marko would have to get on a train to go to a military base where he would be trained for a war that would never come. I could not have known that sweet night that I would go to visit him by a six-hour train to that desert town to see him for a short, one-hour window of time that he was allowed visitors and that I would cry because he was malnourished with lice and skin lesions and scabies. They took my brother to this deprivation camp and held him prisoner for eighteen months because they thought the Americans were coming to invade Bulgaria. What would Americans want with us? We had no oil, no goods of any real value. They had already taken all of our finest minds. I knew they weren't coming. But even if they had, my brother would never have been of use to them for killing anybody. Once, my brother accidentally stepped on a small toad at night in my grandmother's driveway. When he lifted his shoe and found the carcass there, he sobbed. He fell to the ground and wailed. That hour I visited my brother in the desert was the last time I saw him alive.

48. March 31, 2015: Stowe, MA

The next day, Marko sat in the principal's office with his mom, Malik and both of Malik's parents, and Derekah and her mom. Marko had a cast on his foot. One of the school social workers, Miss Tate, was there to mediate. Malik's dad, a dark-skinned man with an accent that bent his English words into near-indecipherable sounds, spoke first.

"My son told me what happened. This girl has been harassing him and Marko for months. She came after the boys up there where they were having lunch and started harassing them again. She ran over Marko's ankle and Malik rushed to get her off of him, accidentally pushing her chair over in the process."

Marko looked at Malik, who was staring at the floor and gripping his hands together in his lap.

"That's not true," said Derekah.

Miss Tate asked, "What's your side of the story, Derekah?"

"His name is Derek," said Derekah's mom. Everyone looked at her.

"Mrs. Keating, we understand that your child wants to be identified as female and called by the name Derekah, not Derek," said Miss Tate.

"Wait, she's a boy?" asked Malik. Marko was confused; he looked at Derekah, whose face was red and angry. She stared at the floor.

"I'm not! I'm a girl!" Derekah shouted and then began to cry. She sat there weeping openly, her face covered with snot and tears immediately. Marko looked at his mom, who was giving him that *I told you so* face.

"Maybe we can do this another time?" Kali asked.

"Yes, I think Derekah and her mom should stay and talk with Miss Tate and we can convene another time," said Malik's dad.

Marko's confusion (thirty-seven) and anxiety (two) seemed to increase at the same rate as the volume of Derekah's weeping. If Derekah was really Derek, and Derek was a boy, was Derek gay? If Derek was gay, was Derekah not gay? Did Derekah's mom let her dress and act like a girl and then tell people she was really a boy so that she could make her life miserable? Where was Derek/Derekah's father?

While these questions piled up in Marko's head, Malik walked over to Derekah, leaned down, and gave her an awkward, one-armed hug. Derekah smacked him away and he stumbled back. He looked at her, shuffled his hands, looked at Marko, looked at the floor, and then walked out of the room.

49. January 7, 1975: Sofia, Bulgaria

Dear Kalina, my unborn daughter,
English will be your first language. You will escape this communist country and live and prosper in America. You won't be tied to Bulgaria the way I have been. You will live in a land where you can be anything you want to be and find acceptance for that. Your children, my grandchildren, will be born there, in America, and they will be free.

This idea of freedom—Kalina, it takes many forms. Many people think that wealth brings freedom but it doesn't. It brings power, and the more power one has, the less freedom, typically. When your mother gives birth to you within a few short weeks' time, I will be overseas in Thailand. As a Trade Ambassador for mine-building, I am at the mercy of my assignment. Once you are born, I will send for you and your mother and we will live there in a gated community in the suburbs of Bangkok in Thailand indefinitely. No doubt, we will end up back in Bulgaria one day, but you will already be on your way to America by then. And when you are established there, you can send for us, your parents, so that we might join you in our retirement and care for our grandchildren.

This is the inevitable path laid out before us. I can see it almost as clearly as I can see my own haggard reflection in the mirror. It brings me great joy to imagine a future like this for you and for us. But it's more than joy. It's a long-awaited exhale; a relaxation into all being right with the world. Your birth will be the beginning of everything I've ever wanted coming to me.

It is my hope that you will live a life free from the burdens and restrictions of real power. Instead, I hope you will live free in your mind and free in your body, honoring whatever you naturally are without judgment or shame.

And when your mother sees what a great father I will be to you, she might fall in love with me for the first time and finally let me in. She might finally grant me access to the deeper, sealed-away chambers of her heart. In her life as a woman and wife, I watch her go through many motions without internalizing any experiences. Once she becomes a mother, once she is turned inside out with labor and birth, once she holds you in her arms and feels your compact aliveness, your movement and breath, your heat—then she will be changed all the way through. She will be opened and that openness will be my way in.

And if this doesn't go all as planned, then Kalina, I hope one day you will know that I tried. I hope you will know that there is only one person I've deeply loved and that is your mother. Perhaps it's you, this whole person we made by coming together, who will make sense of it all. *It all* being where we come from, how we came together, and where we're going.

As I write you this letter, there is loud American music echoing through the house. Your mother is listening to it in the other room while she does her yogic practice. The lyrics include the phrase, "I need you until my dying day." This is what I mean by her going through the motions. She listens to music with powerful words and does a practice with the capacity for powerful transformation, yet she remains unaffected at her core. There is no one she needs until her dying day, least of all me, yet she listens to music that professes such a need.

Your mother has loved me. It is a love she made herself. It is love the weight of paper and the size of a pamphlet that fits in your back pocket. In the beginning of our courtship, we were enjoying chocolate drinks at the corner café while she talked rapidly through her knowledge of the biological system that is the body. It's all chemicals and impulses, you see. I knew then that what she was implying was that her love for me, and mine for her, could be reduced to chemical reactions originating between our ears. The amount of knowledge it takes to understand the physiology of love from this perspective would fit on a somewhat thick pamphlet. Its thickness would depend on the amount of detail it included.

Since then, I've done everything I can to that pamphlet of hers to help her see it differently—the way that I see it. I've cut it up into pieces and reformed it into a montage. I've retyped it, reprinted it, shrunk it, enlarged it, pasted it, punched holes in it, gnashed my teeth at it, decorated it with ink, crumpled it into a ball, torn it apart, and stitched it back up with linen thread. Because, if it's all there can be, I'll accept it over nothing at all.

So I keep her love for me in my back pocket, reassured by its meager weight, by its mere existence.

Meanwhile, my love for her might be able to be contained in volumes of thick-spined books in towering shelves sounding off across a great hall. Imagine the world's greatest library: every word of every book constantly changing, being written anew, so that every moment, each was a whole new book. This would go on endlessly, transcendent of time. That is what my love for her is. And its weight has been crushing us both. I try to relieve the pain of it by carrying on with other lovers. But somehow, all of the feelings conjured in those encounters serve only to multiply the volumes in the world's greatest library. Thus, adding to the weight of it all.

Love, your father, Todor.

50. April 6, 2015: Cambridge, MA

"Mom, I want to donate my body to research after I die." Marko said this while Kali was making his dinner. She didn't pause or look up from her activity of snapping the pile of peapods on the counter. Marko wondered for a moment if she'd heard him, but then he knew she had. This was just her way.

"What makes you think of that now?" She asked this feigning benign curiosity, but he heard the fear underneath and it pleased him. He was ashamed that it pleased him because he didn't want her to keep being afraid for him, but he knew it meant she loved him and that felt good.

"I had this talk with Malik about the light body and the heavy body and how one holds more meaning than the other while the other holds more weight. Anyway, what I realize is that my body, it's really the only thing that's mine. So I want to donate it after I die. If I die before my eighteenth birthday, I want you to make sure that it gets donated to science."

Kalina stopped what she was doing and looked down at him. She bent down and took his face in her hands. Her skin was damp and cold, making his skin feel hot. He could almost hear the hiss of extinguished fire.

"I will make sure of it. And you are so smart and grown up," she said. Her bright eyes darted back and forth from one of his eyes to the other. She kissed him fiercely on the cheek and returned to snapping the peas. Marko was wheeling away when she said, "But I'm not planning to outlive you, so don't die before I do."

Marko stopped and looked back. She knew as well as he that he would most likely die before she did. He felt the squishy, hot, orange anger and rolled back.

"I will die! And you know what? I want to do one thing before I die and I want you to care enough to give it to me!"

Kali stopped what she was doing and crouched in front of him. Her eyes glistened and the lump in her throat bobbed with the effort not to sob. This pleased Marko and also made him feel guilty. The two shapes crashed and combined, turned round and cool blue.

"Marko, I cannot operate as though you're going to die. I can't and I won't. Please understand." She squared her shoulders and the wetness in her eyes dried up. She was all strength, all composure.

"I want to go to Bulgaria. I want to meet my grandfather."

Kali gasped and laughed. "Where's that coming from?"

Marko couldn't tell her where it was really coming from, which was his desire to find the other dream bed she'd told him about in her childhood home.

"Grandma told me he's dying of cancer. I want to meet him before he dies." It was a half-truth. His grandmother was planning to go to "put their affairs in order" because he claimed, again, to be dying. She didn't believe that he had cancer.

"He always thinks he's dying," Kali said, shaking her head. Marko's sphere sank and darkened.

"But yes. I do want you to meet him and I want to take you there."

The sphere rebounded and rose, brightened, grew green blotches of excitement, began slowly turning so that it resembled the earth on its axis inside his chest.

51. April 7, 2015: Cambridge, MA

As Marko read more of *The Unbearable Lightness of Being*, he imagined Malik reading it too. One part caught his attention because it reminded him of a story from his mom's journal: When she lived at home, her mother forbade her to lock the bathroom door. What she meant by her injunction was: Your body is just like all other bodies; you have no right to shame; you have no reason to hide something that exists in millions of identical copies.

When Marko's mother was denied privacy as a child, she found a way to hide her true actions from her mother anyway. She did not want to hide her body from her mother because she felt ashamed of it; she wanted the privacy so that she could be uninhibited with herself. Being observed inhibits. Marko thought of the dark body and how it seemed at times to be a person, or at least a powerful thing with eyes, or with some apparatus for seeing, because he sensed it watching him always. Did that change his behavior? What would he be like, he wondered, without the watchfulness of the dark body?

He read on and found a passage that was bracketed and starred that nearly took his breath away. It seemed to have been written about the dark body itself:

No, vertigo is something other than fear of falling. It is the voice of the emptiness below us which tempts and lures us, it is the desire to fall, against which, terrified, we defend ourselves.

52. August 3, 2014: Sofia, Bulgaria

To my firstborn, Kalina,

Dearest daughter, I am writing you this letter because I plan to take my own life and I do not want to leave this world without first leaving you something of myself. We haven't talked much over the past decade, and I've never met your son, which saddens me. The state of my relationship with your mother has deteriorated more and more with the time and distance between us. I'm happy that she has been able to be there for you. I wish I could have been.

I plan to have you travel here with your son and your mother. I plan to accomplish this by telling you that I am dying of cancer. After you come and I see you and meet my grandson, I will sell this house that you and your brother grew up in and give you the money. Then I will die, but not from cancer, though this dark force in me might as well be cancer. It's not so much a thing as a place within me—a black hole of sorts—that sucks me in and holds me down. As long as I'm alive and tethered to this body and this mind, I will be imprisoned by this place. So my death should not be mourned, because I am setting myself free.

I fell in love with your mother because she took the end of my tie between thumb and finger and when I asked her what she was doing she said: feeling for smoothness. It was the most unique gesture and explanation for a gesture I had ever encountered. Most people I had dated came to me with a multitude of inane thoughts and words thrown together without discrimination. I myself had been artlessly rhetorical in 90 percent of the conversations I'd ever had. I gave more value to speech varied through phrases of eloquence than to the substance underlying that speech. Your mother had a diverse thought life and a simple way of sharing it without being condescending.

Another reason why I fell in love with your mother was her avoidance of my heavy eye contact. Her eye contact, the narrow gallery of her glance—it had perfect aim in its timing and intensity, and it always remained light. Or at least, not heavy. Her eye contact was like her speech: she would either speak most concisely or most fully. And there would be a good reason for either.

It wasn't just my eye contact that was heavy. Your mother tried but she could not bear the weight. In our early days together, I had this terrible habit of missing her even when I was with her. I thought it would be endearing but she experienced it as pressure. Instead of enjoying the moment, I was terrified of the moment's inevitable end and worried about when the next moment of our togetherness would be. Neither of us had a lot of free time. I thrived on that sense of constant anticipation. She was always present. Right with the moment. My preoccupation with the moment's end annoyed her.

Once, we were driving and I asked her what she was thinking about and she said: the lines that we drive on that carry us nowhere; the cracks of the pavement filled with battered moonlight.

Even the way her bad moods played out from the glittering arrangement of her brain was present and carved by the sharpness of her intellect.

You are this same way, Kalina. You are smarter than most people you meet and you know it and they know it. You won't give most people a chance and most people won't take a chance because your intelligence scares them. Don't make the same mistakes your mother made. Let people in. Your son, let him in. I don't know him and perhaps will never meet him but I suspect he is more like me than you. His absence of knowledge about you makes him want to know you all the more. It's more powerful than mere want; it feels to him as though his life depends upon knowing you. This was how I was with my own mother, which set in motion what I sought from women as an adult. And so the past repeats itself, plays itself out again and again in the next generation and the next.

There is something I want to confess to you. I have never told anyone, not even your mother.

When I was a child, between the ages of nine and twelve, we lived in India. We lived on a military base, but my mother worked outside of the base and dropped my sisters and me off at a village woman's house to be minded. The woman had three boys, all around my age. Most days, she would send her boys out to play with my sisters and keep me inside. She made me do chores like sweeping the floor and washing her clothes. At first, it seemed unfair, like she was singling me out to punish me. But after a few days, she made me take my clothes off to do the chores. Then after I washed her clothes, she made me wash her. She took her clothes off and sat in the washtub and gave me a cloth and a bar of soap and had me wash her body. She had large, brown breasts and a mass of black hair between her legs and under her arms.

When she had me do these things without my clothes on, I felt singled out because I was special, not because I was being punished. For many months, she never did anything beyond wanting me to do my chores naked and wash her body. But then one day, she made me do sexual things to her while she was in the washtub. She took my hand and put it on her vagina, pushed my fingers into her. She made me suckle her breasts. After weeks of doing these things only when she was in the washtub, we began doing them in her bed. And she would do sexual things to me as well. This went on for at least a year until one day I told her I wanted to be out of the house with the other kids instead. And so it abruptly stopped. She put me out of the house and did not let me back in. After it stopped, I spent my time running around with her boys, two younger and one just barely older. We connected with another group of boys in the village and we would all have sex with each other. It was a sort of game. We would chase after each other and wrestle, then clothes would come off and it would turn into sex. I think this is why, as I grew older, my attractions tended to be toward younger men and older women.

Or, maybe, one has nothing to do with the other. And maybe it doesn't matter.

Making excuses for my sadness doesn't lighten my burden. And it hasn't been all sadness, this life. There have been pockets of joy so profound that it felt more painful than the sadness. It was a sharp, satisfying pain—like a cramp in your side when you run too fast, too far.

Love, your father, Todor

53. April 11, 2015: Cambridge, MA

Marko's grandma came over late Saturday morning and Marko saw his mom getting ready to leave again. She'd been leaving every weekend for a couple of hours and it wasn't for yoga. She picked up her bag and started toward the door, then turned around and blew Marko a kiss.

"Mom, where are you going?"

"I'll be back soon," she said and left. Marko's grandma had gone into the bathroom. The front door was still open and slightly ajar, a side effect of a long-anticipated spring finally beginning to emerge. Marko didn't give it much thought before wheeling himself out the door to follow his mom. When he got out onto the sidewalk, he saw her turning left a couple of blocks up. Marko pumped his wheels as hard as he could to catch up. He made a left just in time to see her making a right. Wherever she was going, it was within walking distance. She wasn't going to her car. Marko kept pumping hard and started to sweat. He shot across the busy Massachusetts Avenue, making cars honk at him. He kept going, faster than he'd gone maybe ever, motivated by his mission to find her out.

When Marko made the right he had seen his mom make, he didn't see her. He kept going, looking left and right up every street as he passed. Finally, three blocks up, he spotted her again. She was standing on a porch punching numbers into a keypad. A buzzer sounded. She turned the knob and disappeared inside.

Marko wheeled to the house and bumped his wheels up against the first step up to the porch. There was a plaque on the door. He squinted and leaned forward to try to read it.

EILEEN LOTTERMAN, LSWA

Marko didn't know what those letters after the name meant. Was she seeing a lawyer? He decided to return home as fast as he could to look it up, and began to wheel himself back along the path he had come. When he approached his apartment complex, he saw his grandma out on the sidewalk hugging herself and looking worried. She spotted him coming and let out a groan of relief he could hear from two blocks away. She came trotting toward him.

"Marko, what on earth?" she demanded. She grabbed his hand and squeezed it and scowled at him. He yanked his hand away and kept going.

"Marko!"

Marko heard the patter of her feet behind him, chasing him.

"Leave me alone!" he yelled, and wheeled faster. He made it to the apartment and found the door closed and locked. His grandmother appeared moments later panting like a dog. She bent over and put her hands on her knees.

"What's going on?"

"Nothing, please just open the door and don't tell my mom."

"You know I have to tell your mother."

"No you don't," Marko said. His grandmother unlocked and opened the door and looked at him.

"Fine, tell her," he said and wheeled into the apartment. He went directly to his room, found his iPad, and opened up a browser window. He typed: "LSWA" and stared at the results.

"Can we talk about this? Where were you?" His grandma was standing in the doorway to his room, still catching her breath.

"Why is Mom going to visit a licensed social worker associate?"

"She's going to a therapist. Every week, sometimes more."

"Why?"

"Because your mother has some unresolved anger. She's trying to deal with it in different ways. This is one of the ways."

"Anger at me?"

Marko's grandma walked into his room and squatted in front of him. She took his hand again and squeezed it. "No, not at you. At the world. Your father. Her father."

"I don't understand. She was always leaving, every weekend, and not telling me anything about it," Marko said. "And it's because she's angry? Because she is going to a therapist? Well I'm angry!"

"I see that you are, and may we all be blessed with anger," his grandma said.

"What?"

"Do you remember when we went to DC? For President Obama? You were small, only six I think."

"I was seven. Yes, I remember." Marko was annoyed. His grandma always did this—changed the subject with some unrelated story. Also, he didn't want to be reminded of that trip because his parents had been fighting. Right before the inauguration ceremony, his dad stormed off and was gone for the whole time.

"Do you remember that church person who gave a speech? The gay Bishop? His name was Robbins or Robinson or something? He was hidden away from the news in favor of that big hotshot Warren who helped pass Proposition 8 in California banning gay marriage. I hated him. I hated that America had to be poisoned with the words of a man who believes in a small-minded god. I don't pretend to know about religion, but I know I cannot reconcile the idea of god with the idea of small-mindedness."

Marko remembered his mom booing that pastor. And he remembered her cheering the other one, but he didn't remember the words.

"Anyway, he said, 'bless us with anger,' because it helps us fight injustice in our lives and in the world. And he said, 'bless us with discomfort,' and when he said that, I couldn't help but to think of you and your mother, and the things you both understand."

Marko went into his room and got his iPad. He looked up Bishop Robinson's Speech at Obama inauguration and found the text:

Bless us with tears – for a world in which over a billion people exist on less than a dollar a day . . .

Bless us with anger – at discrimination, at home and abroad, against refugees and immigrants, women, people of color, gay, lesbian, bisexual and transgender people.

Marko felt a surge of love and pride for his grandma. He wheeled out to show her that he'd found the prayer but then stopped cold. There, at the door, was Malik.

54. April 11, 2015: Cambridge, MA

Kali sat on the IKEA couch and told her shrink that she would not be back after that day.

"Why's that?"

"Because I can't afford it, for one. I'm taking Marko to Bulgaria, I've decided, and I'm going into debt for it. But more because I'm fine. I don't need to talk and tell you stories anymore. I don't see how it's helping me. You never say much. So what am I doing here, really? Just escaping my son more?"

"You're coming here to escape him less. As you've been, you escape him even when you're with him."

Kali felt the urge to walk out again. But she sat still. She sensed a purpose to her visits to that IKEA couch. She didn't understand what was happening or why, but she felt her relationships with Marko and her mom starting to shift. To soften.

"You're pruning away the excess," the shrink said.

"Go on."

The shrink smiled just slightly, sighed, and put down the pad of paper she always held. She leaned forward toward Kali and said, "What you need to do, for your son, is to prune away those parts of yourself that obscure your true nature from him. Think of yourself as a Winter Solstice tree"—she winked—"that you pick out for its sparseness in the first place. Then, you get it home and work on it with a pair of pruners, thinning it further, so that it gradually loses the look of impenetrable, dense darkness and takes on the appearance of a cheerful, light waif. When you're satisfied that a person looking at the tree can also look sufficiently through the tree, so that you can imagine pausing in the heart of the tree, inside the world of it, then you proceed to the other kind of trimming. First stringing the lights, and then hanging the ornaments from the sparse branches, where they do not crowd one another but have ample room to dangle and shine. You will work to fashion a beautiful tree, and it will make all the people who see it happy, but none so happy, perhaps, as your son."

55. April 11, 2015: Cambridge, MA

"Malik, what are you doing here?"

"I wanted to come over and watch baseball," he said. Marko's grandma welcomed him inside and encouraged the boys to go into Marko's room. Marko closed the door and Malik picked up the iPad.

"Do you have music on here?" Malik asked.

"Some."

Malik tapped around on the iPad and Marko worried he'd find his porn links. Marko reached for it but Malik pulled it away. He said, "Hold on, I just found your KOL playlist."

The iPad sang out Kings of Leon and Marko sat back in his chair. Malik's head bobbed to the beat as he sat down on Marko's bed. "Sit here?" he asked, patting the spot on the bed beside him. Marko transferred himself from the chair to his bed and scooted over beside Malik. They sat close, shoulders and arms and thighs touching, looking forward and listening to the music. Marko closed his eyes and watched the math.

"Can you feel this?" Malik asked. Marko opened his eyes and followed the line of Malik's arm. His hand was on Marko's penis, which was erect. Marko was wearing a pull up instead of underwear and was terrified for a moment that it was wet with urine. He felt it and found it dry. He closed his hand over Malik's.

"In a way, I can," he said. Then Malik kissed him. The math was a tornado. Marko felt many feelings simultaneously, many colors and shapes. Marko reached for Malik's crotch while they kissed and fumbled at the waistband of his jeans. Malik undid his pants and guided Marko's hand. His breathing turned shallow and rapid against Marko's mouth. Marko remembered the way he moved his hand on Emil's penis and tried to replicate it on Malik's while also following the intermittent guidance of Malik's hand. Malik groaned quietly, and his body twitched and jerked. Marko's hand was wet.

"Sorry," Malik said and lifted Marko's hand away from his crotch. He held Marko's dripping hand aloft as though it were a fragile thing that might break. Marko grabbed the edge of his bedspread and wiped off his hand with it, then Malik's lap. Malik fastened his pants and Marko fastened his. They sat there in silence after the song ended for what felt like Marko to be a long time.

"Want to watch some baseball?" Malik asked.

56. May 13, 2015: Sofia, Bulgaria

Marko watched out the window of the airplane as it landed. He couldn't wait to get to the portal his mom had told him about and see if it worked to get him back to Emil. Because of this, he was overwhelmed with feeling number twelve (excitement). This was the first time he'd been to Sofia since he was a baby. The airport tarmac was overgrown with grass growing up through cracks. It wasn't even paved in some areas. Out in the grassy, unpaved parts, Marko saw old airplanes parked among the weeds like abandoned cars in the untidy yards of old people. The sight of the parked, old airplanes made him sad (three). There just wasn't any room in the world for old things that had outlived their usefulness. All the spaces were taken up with useful things. When something as big and heavy as a jet was too old and not working anymore, where could it go? Nowhere. So it sat there in the weeds, collecting dust. Rotting.

Marko's mom's cousin Aleks was there to greet them. He was thin and tall and vaguely resembled his mother. Marko's mom had told him about Aleks on the plane, explained that he would be picking them up and taking them to the house she grew up in, at least since her adolescence. He knew from their other long talks on the plane that she had moved around before then, spending many years in Thailand. As a little girl, she'd told him, she was fluent in Bulgarian, Thai, and English.

"Look at you!" his mom said and hugged Aleks very tight. Marko watched his face above his mother's shoulder and saw that he had his eyes closed. A few moments after they started hugging, though, Aleks opened his eyes and aimed them at Marko.

"Marko, this is my cousin, Aleks, who looks exactly like your uncle Marko who I named you after," Kali said. Marko stuck his hand out to shake but Aleks bent down and hugged Marko instead. It was an awkward, unreciprocated hug. Marko went tense and couldn't will his arms around the man's shoulders quickly enough. As a consequence of the delay, Marko's arms reached for Aleks only after he had already started to withdraw from the hug, which caused a moment's hesitation and confusion.

"You really do look just like my brother," Kali said.

"Your mother keeps telling me this," Aleks said with a thick accent. "How was your trip?" he asked Marko.

"Fine," Marko said. His hands were at work in front of his face, twisting up and down from the wrist, crossing his field of vision. He found that if he tucked his thumbs under the top pad of his palms and fanned out the remaining four fingers, his ability to concentrate on what was about to happen heightened. He saw it up and to the right, but not clearly. He was able to see shadows of unfolding events—kind of like what he imagined the shadows on Plato's cave wall looked like. He had read about Plato's Cave on the internet once. He found it by Googling the word *existence*. When he had read about the cave, he knew it was closer to the truth than anything else he'd found. Things, he'd realized, were more and different than what they seemed when you looked at them. There was a reality more real than what most people think is reality. What most people think is reality is actually only the shadows that the real reality casts upon the wall. And while you're alive in a body as a human, you don't have the ability to turn around. You can only stare at the wall. The shadows of unfolding events were like more wall space for Marko. He was able to scan the near future for anything ominous this way.

Unfortunately, Marko was aware of the way that Aleks and other strangers were looking at him—like he was very weird. He tried hard to act normal—to behave in a way that wouldn't attract undue attention—but even when he accomplished "normalcy," people still stared at him because he was in his wheelchair.

They made their way through the airport. Kali and Aleks walked ahead with their heads leaned in toward each other's, and Marko wheeled behind them. The floors in the airport were perfect for the chair. Marko could easily go fast, he found, and he was able to turn on a dime, which he enjoyed practicing. A few times, he raced ahead of his mom and Aleks and did a fast 180-degree turn to face them and then another fast 180-degree turn for a total of 360 degrees before he sped off again. He heard his mom laugh and clap and praise his moves, but when he smiled back at her, she had already resumed her conversation with Aleks.

Aleks drove them to his friend's to pick up a car that Kali could use while they were in town. The car was a small two-door and Marko was worried about maneuvering inside and also how it would fit his wheelchair. Kali quickly figured it out. She flattened forward one of the two back seats and opened the hatchback. She rolled Marko up against the back of the car and lifted his legs into the trunk. Then she stood back and asked Marko to scoot himself forward into the car.

Marko locked his wheels and pushed up on the arms of his chair. His hips lifted easily but he couldn't see a way to push himself forward over the ridge of the hatchback. He lowered himself again and looked up at Kali.

"Do you need help?"

Marko nodded. She leaned down and hugged him. He put his arms around her shoulders and she lifted him over the ridge and into the back of the car.

"There you go; now scoot into your seat, please."

Marko found that he was able to get from the trunk to the back seat of the car easily. He settled into the seat, buckled his seat belt, and smiled. His heart raced with a sense of pride in his accomplishment, his independence. Next time, he would try getting from the chair to the back of the car by himself. He turned to see his mom loading his chair into the trunk. It fit perfectly. She closed the hatchback and stood talking with her cousin again. Marko felt some of his good feeling drain away. The promise of independence seemed once again impossible when he realized there would be no way for him to get his own chair in the car.

His mom got in and sighed loudly.

"What? What's wrong?" Marko asked.

"Oh, nothing, everything's fine," she said. This made Marko feel frustrated. He knew everything wasn't fine and he also knew that his mom wouldn't tell him what was bothering her. She never told him the whole story, all of the truth. She didn't lie to him exactly, just told him about 10 to 15 percent of the truth instead of 100 percent.

"Where are we going next?" he asked. He decided that if he couldn't know what was wrong with her on the inside, he could at least know everything she was doing with him. She couldn't deny him that.

"To the house," she said.

"To see Grandpa?"

"Yes and your grandmother will be there too." Lydia had left for Bulgaria about two weeks before Marko and his mom, and had been staying in Sofia with his grandfather.

Marko watched out the window as they drove. He thought about his grandmother and something very interesting she told him before she left for Bulgaria. He had been thinking about what it must feel like for her to have her husband die. The closest thing Marko could do to imagine it was to think of what he would feel like if his mother died because she was the person Marko felt the closest to in the world. Just thinking about it made every part of him feel heavy.

"Are you sad about your husband dying?" he had asked her. They were sitting at the kitchen table eating soup for lunch.

"No." She frowned.

Marko looked at his grandmother's hands. One cupped the soup bowl and one held a spoon. Her hands reminded him of his mom's hands only older, more wrinkled and veined. He looked at his own hands, which were disproportionately large now from the growth hormones he'd been taking. He closed his eyes and pictured his mom's hands, which he had memorized, having seen them every day of his life on his body. Hands: his, his mother's, his grandmother's. Thinking of them made him realize how temporary and fleeting it was to have all three generations living and touching. He thought about the age of the universe (estimated at thirteen billion years) and the size of the sun (more than one million planet Earths could fit inside it) and how small that made him and them comparatively, how short it made their lives, each moment. Against such a colossal backdrop, they were microscopic insects blinking in and out of existence so rapidly that each life was hardly perceptible much less meaningful. But it meant something to him. And from his finite view, from his small and very limited body, he had a long life to live.

"What are you thinking about?" his grandmother asked.

Marko looked at her. She wasn't frowning anymore.

"It makes me feel better to think about the universe, how old and big it is, and how small and new we are, how much we don't know. Can't know."

His grandmother frowned again and then smiled.

"I think you're right, but then again, we know enough. And we feel a lot more than we know."

"What do you mean?"

"It's not something I can talk about. Because explaining it would require knowing and I don't know it; I experience it. But maybe I can give you an idea with a story."

Marko nodded. He was eager to hear it.

"In Bulgaria, I used to take your mother and your uncle to a place that I thought held some very special secrets. It was a rock face in the rough shape of a heart. Not the symbol heart we use on playing cards but the real shape of the heart, blobby with tubes and chambers. The heart rock was split down the middle and from it broke a flood of water. The water formed a pool and two rivers glanced off from the sides of that pool."

Marko imagined the scene surrounded by lush green, shining in the sun.

"On both sides, the right and the left, ribs of slate rock made cascades of the streams. They were rising and half clear so we could see the rock ribs underneath and the soft green moss that grew there on the surface. Once, when we went, I sat and stared at the streams while the kids ran around and played. I was taken by how, even in their constant state of movement, the streams looked smooth as glass, like a glass glaze over the slate. The illusion was so strong that I had to break it. I had to get in one of the streams and watch the water break around my ankles. So I took off my shoes and I stepped in, standing at the bottom of the slippery slate ribs where the water flooded up almost to my knees. I was wearing a summer dress, which I lifted up. The water was so cold it burned and my skin turned pink then red. The kids were so excited and they wanted to get in too. Your mom took off all her clothes and splashed into the stream behind me, screamed, and jumped back out. Your uncle dipped a toe in but, finding it too cold, decided to stay out. Then your mom stepped onto the slate slide, the ribs, and sat down. The water hit her back and splashed up around her. A few drops fell on my face and in my eyes. I could see that each drop contained a light, a small, illuminated scene, within which were racing images from some other place, some other reality altogether with different laws, different elements, faster movement, higher vibration. I blinked and lost it, but in that initial moment with the droplets in my eyes, I witnessed something important. Something that showed me definitively that there is much more to reality than what we can imagine. In fact, what we inhabit and sense is tiny in comparison and doesn't begin to represent the whole of what's going on right here, right around us, all the time. We have only a partial and distorted view."

Marko felt the truth of what his grandmother said deep down in his belly. He realized he was moving his hands in front of his face. As soon as he became aware of it, he stopped. He imagined the other, parallel realities tunneling out from the one he was in. Did they have different versions of him? Different versions of his mother and his grandmother? Were there other Markos that could walk?

"My point is," his grandmother said, "that you can take comfort in knowing that we are much more than these bodies, much more, even, than the consciousness we have now. Wherever your grandfather is going with his consciousness, he's going to stay alive through it. And I'll see him there after this life. I just know that."

Marko looked at his grandmother. She seemed to believe what she was saying, but also seemed to be afraid of what it meant. At least the last part. She seemed unhappy about seeing his grandfather there after this life. She said it in a way that sounded like she was dreading it rather than taking comfort in it.

57. May 13, 2015: Sofia, Bulgaria

When they arrived at the house, Marko saw his grandmother first, smiling and rushing toward the car. Marko felt the smile on his face widen and it made him realize his skin was dry. The big smile seemed to stretch and bunch and crack all the skin on his face and he wondered if he looked old too.

His grandmother opened his door and hugged him and then unbuckled his seat belt. She said something in Bulgarian but Marko didn't understand. He just said, "Hi, Grandma!" Marko's mom was busy unloading the car with their bags. She was struggling with the big one, Marko's, which was bigger than him and probably heavier. It carried everything Marko needed for a whole month away, the longest Marko had ever been away from home. Marko was shocked at how much space the catheter packs alone took up—thirty or forty of them filled half the cavernous space and a bunch more had to be shipped there.

Marko's grandmother scurried away to help his mom. She was never able to watch someone doing work without rising to help. Marko tried to think of the last time he had seen his grandmother sit down other than for meals. He could only think of times when he was still small enough to be held. Then she would sit and hold him and rock him. But that didn't count as sitting so much because she was still doing something. She never just did nothing. Marko wondered if she even slept at night.

He watched her face collapse into a grimace as she pulled items from the car. That was the other thing about her that Marko noticed—even though she always helped, she never seemed happy about it. Rather, she looked stressed while she helped.

Marko looked toward the house and saw his grandfather, who was an older version of Aleks. He stood in the doorway of the house and smiled. Marko was surprised to see him standing. He thought someone who was about to die would be permanently lying in bed. Marko waved and his grandfather waved back but didn't approach the car or move away from the doorway; he just stood there waving and smiling, bent forward a little. He looked tired.

Then, slowly, the old man approached the car. He crept closer with small, shuffling steps. His hands balled up in his pockets and he smiled. He was nodding continuously but just slightly. Marko saw that it was because he was shaking, trembling all over.

"You must be Marko," he said. His accent was thick like Aleks's. His face, closer up, was pocked and gaunt, a shadow of whiskers spread across his chin and the hollows of his cheeks. He resembled Marko's mom but also Marko's grandmother. They had the same slight frame and the same eyes, maybe even the same noses. They looked like they could have been siblings.

"You must be my grandfather," Marko said and smiled. The old man smiled wider. When he was close, almost upon Marko, he stretched out his arms like wing bones and descended for a hug. Marko reached up hesitantly, worried that the frail man would fall, crashing into him. But he didn't fall. His hug felt surprisingly hearty—there was much more power in this man than his appearance revealed.

Marko watched through a crack in the hug while his mother and grandmother dragged his huge suitcase into the house. He regarded the yard, overgrown with grass and weeds but also wildflowers—sprays of unexpected brightness through the drab. A fruit tree, its branches heavy with orbs, bent toward the tall grass.

"What kind of fruit tree is that?" Marko asked. The question prompted his grandfather to finally pull away from his tight embrace. As he did, Marko noticed that his grandfather was crying. He wiped his face with a pale blue handkerchief, honked his nose quickly into it, then folded it and shoved it back into his pocket.

"Pears," he said. "And we have grapes in the backyard and beautiful blackberries all around the edges." He beamed with pride. "Would you like to taste them? All but the pears; those aren't ready yet."

"Sure," Marko said. His grandfather stood there as if waiting for Marko to get up and walk around with him.

"Can you bring my wheelchair around?" Marko pointed toward the back of the car where his chair was unloaded and waiting on the ground.

"Oh, yes yes," the old man said and retrieved the chair. Just then Marko's mom came back out.

"I got it, Dad," she said quickly. Marko's grandpa stood and faced her. He wasn't smiling anymore. His eyes were swimming. Marko couldn't tell whether the old man had bad allergies or was overcome with emotion. He reached his arms out and said something in Bulgarian. Marko watched his mom walk into her father's embrace. She looked stiff and uncomfortable there and she pulled back quickly. It was hard for her to get away because he was trying to hold on. After an awkward moment where he pulled her shirt, the old man finally let go of her and she stepped away.

The old man turned and walked out into the yard. Marko's mom got the wheelchair and helped Marko into it. She had the same frown that Marko's grandmother had when helping him do things, and it made him feel bad. It probably meant that she was ashamed of him and hated having to do everything for him. But then he saw his grandfather wandering in the yard and thought maybe she was frowning because of him, the old man.

His mom pushed his chair up onto the paved walkway around the house, pivoting him up two small steps along the way. Once up, she let him take over. Marko turned his chair and faced her but she was already walking away.

"Mom," he called. She turned and walked back. She leaned down to him and smoothed his hair.

"Are you okay?" she asked and kissed his forehead. He felt its warmth radiate through his whole head and down his neck.

"You okay?" he asked her. She gave him a fake, tight smile and nodded.

"Go check everything out," she said. "This is where I lived from the time I was about your age, a little older, until I left." She walked down the steps and disappeared into the house. Marko looked through the window and saw stairs. These must be the stairs his mother had told him about—and beneath them, so close, the dream bed portal his mom had discovered as a girl. He felt his pulse quicken. With so many eyes on him, though, he would have to wait until the middle of the night when everyone was sleeping to check it out.

"Try some grapes?"

Marko startled. His grandfather was close, right beside him with a handful of grapes. Marko hadn't seen or heard or even sensed him coming. It was as if he was a ghost. This made Marko feel closer to him. Marko looked at the purple orbs in the old man's large, weathered hand and then peered up into his face. The sun behind his head blacked out most of his features but Marko could see that his jaw was working. The old man lifted his empty hand to his mouth and carefully spit seeds into it and then showed them to Marko.

"Don't eat these part," he said.

Marko ate a grape from the offering palm of his grandfather. He chewed into the seeds, which released a bitter taste to mingle with the sour juice and tart skin. He enjoyed the textures and flavors his mouth contained while he chewed. He squinted up at his grandfather. "Good," he said.

58. May 13, 2015: Sofia, Bulgaria

The old man, Marko's grandfather, pushed him around the perimeter of the yard picking blackberries, and Marko arrived at the end of the tour with blue-stained lips and fingers and a sweet tingling on his tongue asking for more. The old man handed him a soft peach. He bit into it, juice gushing and spilling down his chin, onto the front of his shirt. The old man freaked out about that, shuffling as fast as he could—which wasn't very fast—into the kitchen to grab a wad of napkins, which he thrust, scowling, toward Marko's face. Marko was too busy loving the flavor in his mouth to stop the drool. The rough invasion of the napkin caused Marko's arm to fly up and knock the old man's arm away.

"Stop that," Marko said, spitting out a little more peach in the process. The old man stumbled backward and looked at Marko. His expression was a collage of shock, anger, and hurt. It settled and solidified—wounded, like a chastised puppy—and the old man slunk away into the house. Marko's mom came out.

"What happened?" She looked after her father, concerned, and then back at Marko.

"Why is this so good?" Marko asked and took another bite of the peach. She smiled.

"It tastes like sunshine, right?"

"Exactly."

"Light, it tastes of light," the old man said, wandering back again. "You musn't spill the light." He came back at Marko with the napkin, and this time, Marko let him wipe the juice and pulp from the front of his shirt. Kali walked out and Marko was left alone in the room with the old man. His face, so close to Marko's as he cleaned his shirt, was there for the studying. His eyebrows were bushy white caterpillars with a few coarse black hairs throughout. His face was deeply lined. His breath smelled sweet and slightly rotten. His nose was wide and red. Up close, taken separately, his features were completely alien. Marko had never seen anything like them. But when the old man stood and looked down at Marko from a bit of distance, there was deep familiarity that seemed much older than the generation separating them.

"What happened with you and Grandma?" Marko asked. The old man sat down at the table and faced the window so that Marko was looking at his profile. He sighed and slumped a bit. Marko waited but the old man was silent. "You haven't lived together for a long time," Marko said. "Are you divorced? My parents are divorced."

"No, not divorced," he said and paused. "To keep a relationship on course, there is a need for secrets and lies, for hiding and hoarding. We didn't follow those rules. There has never been a secret between us. No relationship can survive that."

Marko felt feelings number six and fourteen. He watched the shape of them rising in his body and felt the dark body press close.

"Can I have another peach?"

The old man smiled. "You've consumed too much light; you're very bright. I need sunglasses to look at you."

"That's just it. I need its lightness so I'm not so heavy. I read this novel of my mom's? Called *The Unbearable Lightness of Being*? And it's about the heavy, physical body versus the light body, the metaphysical body. Like the soul? Anyway, my friend Malik told me that. He read it too."

The old man looked at Marko. His eyes looked like glass, they were so still and unblinking. "Did your mother give you that book?"

"Sort of," Marko said.

"That is no book for a boy to read."

"I'm not a boy. I'm almost fifteen. I'm practically a man."

The old man smiled. Even his smile looked like a frown.

That night, Marko's mom tucked him in. He was to sleep on a mattress on the floor in the den—the room that had been his grandfather's office. Just outside of it and around the corner were the stairs, and under the stairs, the long-awaited second dream bed portal. Marko lay and listened for the sounds of footsteps in the house to stop. Then he listened for a long while more until he was sure everyone was asleep. When he was certain, he dragged himself to his chair. Marko wasn't used to getting into his chair from the floor. He could transition easily from his bed, but found that he could not from the floor. He had no choice but to drag himself to the portal.

Marko moved slowly, trying hard not to make too much sound. But the sounds of his legs dragging and the floor creaking under the weight of his hands were as loud as explosions. He arrived at the small door beneath the stairs and opened it. Inside, the space was filled with books. Stacks and stacks of books. Looking at them, Marko had a sense of déjà vu. There was no way he would fit in there. He'd have to remove the books first.

"Shouldn't you be asleep?"

Marko startled and whirled. It was the old man. He stood near the bottom of the stairs, staring down at Marko.

"Sorry, I . . . I couldn't sleep," Marko said.

"Looking for something new to read? All of those books are in English."

"Yes, actually," Marko said. He reached in and took out a book. *Timaeus*. It was by Plato. Marko was not at all interested in reading it, but he saw the way the old man's face brightened when he recognized it.

"Ah, yes, that book is a must-read. You'll be an expert on the world soul and the nature of the universe."

"Thanks," Marko said and tucked it in his waistband before dragging himself back to his room. His grandfather followed slowly behind.

"An old friend very dear to me gave me those books many years ago. He passed away before you were born. Those books are all that's left of him," his grandfather said. Marko looked at him blankly, not knowing what to say. Did the old man want him not to take the book? He pulled it out of his waistband and held it up to him.

"No no, you go ahead and read that. You seem to be reading well beyond your years, so this should suit you fine. Goodnight," the old man said.

"Goodnight," Marko said.

Marko lay awake a while longer, listening, but all he heard were the howling dogs outside. The city was overrun with stray dogs, his mom had said, and they gathered in the foothills every night to howl at the moon. He didn't hear a sound in the house. It was as if the old man were a ghost.

59. May 14, 2015: Sofia, Bulgaria

It was the dying man's wish that they visit the Black Sea together as a family. Marko's mom, when she was young, had travelled there annually with her brother and parents. Marko drove in the small car with his mom and his wheelchair. Marko's grandparents drove in a separate car. His grandmother drove and his grandfather rode as a passenger. There was a lot of concern before departing that the old man would not be up for the long drive—about five hours from their house in Sofia to Sozopol, a small town by the Black Sea.

"Why is he dying?" Marko asked. He was in the back seat with a tower of bags and food beside him, making him feel small. His mom didn't answer. Perhaps his voice was drowned out by the roar of the tires, the wind around the car. He asked again, louder. She turned her head slightly in his direction.

"Everybody dies," she said.

"But what's killing him?" Marko remembered his grandmother telling him that it was cancer. Or, had she said it was something *like* cancer?

"Living his life is killing him. Dishonesty is killing him."

Marko considered this answer. He sat back in his seat and looked out the window. It was true that everybody died and that living life for a long time, too long of a time, would kill a person. What Marko was looking for was a medical condition that would be the final cause, but his mother knew that and chose to give him this general and ambiguous response instead.

"He had a small heart attack, I guess. He's convinced he'll have another, final one before long," she said.

Marko didn't say anything. He found that, more and more, when he could manage to stay silent, more information would leak out of his mother. She would tell him things that she didn't mean to tell him if he just stayed quiet. Then at some point, she would say, I shouldn't be telling you this. That was the tactic he'd used on the airplane when she told him so many stories about her childhood and about her brother before he died. Marko. The man he was named after.

The tactic didn't work this time. His mom stayed silent. Marko thought about the heart having an attack. It was one of the dangers doctors had warned him about for his own heart. Its bovine part could eventually tire or deteriorate to a point that would make him more vulnerable to a heart attack. They'd given him a list of symptoms— warning signs to watch out for.

To pass the time, Marko watched out the window for expressions of the numbers seven and nine. He would count things and divide totals or add digits, whatever he needed to do to get back to either seven or nine. Then they came upon a sunflower field: a rolling sea of yellow that extended toward infinity.

"The literal English translation of the Bulgarian word for sunflower is sun looker," his mom said as they passed. Marko noticed only then that the sea of yellow was punctuated by small, dark faces: the centers of the flowers all pointing in the same direction.

"Their faces follow the sun through the sky all day, from sunrise to sunset," she said. "They follow the sun through the sky?"

"Yes."

"I never knew that." Marko stared at the sunflowers. How could that be? Was it magnetic and automatic or was there a shared consciousness? Something like intelligence?

"Where do they point their faces at night? Toward the horizon? Waiting for the sun to rise again?"

"Down."

"Down at the ground?" Marko was shocked.

"Yes," his mom said and smiled. Marko wondered why the bowed heads of sunflowers in the night would make his mom smile. To him, it seemed depressing.

60. May 14, 2015: Sozopol, Bulgaria

They arrived at the rental and Marko's grandparents were already there, settled in. It was a gated group of attached condominiums with a shared pool. Their condominium was right in front of the pool. Marko was unable to get up on the front porch because there were stairs. His mom had to go inside and get help. She came back out with his grandmother and they lifted him with his chair up onto the porch. Marko rolled through the beaded curtain hanging across the threshold. Beads got stuck in his wheels and it took a few minutes for his mom to untangle them. When she did, she took the beaded curtain down from the door and set it on the porch.

When they finally made it inside, the old man was nowhere in sight. Marko's grandmother was busily making lunch. But she had also packed them sandwiches for the car and Marko had eaten one of those.

"I'm not hungry," he said. She turned and flashed a frown at him.

"I'm not either," his mom said in little more than a whisper. She pushed Marko's chair back out on the porch.

"Swim?"

Marko looked at the pool. There was a small circular pool that was shallower than the large rectangle pool. He pointed to the shallow one.

"I'll go in that part."

His mom helped him change into his bathing suit and then carried him from his chair to the pool. She grunted when she lifted him and Marko could hear the strain in her breathing as she carried him. The math swirled and showed him that her arm supporting his weight underneath was slipping. Marko got nervous that she would drop him and he clung to her neck, pulling her hair accidentally. She yelped in pain and dropped him, but he wouldn't let go.

"Marko let go, you're at the pool," she said. He looked down at the water and saw his legs were already submerged. He let go of his mom and plopped the rest of the way in. Kali looked red and was sweating a little. Wearily, she turned and walked away. She disappeared inside the house and came back out with Marko's water wings. It was harder and harder to get them on his arms because they were meant for small children. Marko had been growing fast since the growth hormone, and the wings now stretched tightly across his upper arms, digging into his skin.

Kali walked away again. Marko sat in the pool, blue water gently lapping at his chest, his big body buoyed up by the ridiculous, child-sized water wings. There was nothing to look at but the chairs around the pool and the gate that surrounded the property. He looked back toward the house and saw nobody on the porch. Soon he saw his mom again, coming back up the walk with bags from the car. She smiled at him as she passed and then went into the house. Marko thought of the door to the house as a mouth that had just swallowed her. There was a scarf tied to the door handle that blew outward in the breeze, like a snake tongue. He laughed and felt uncomfortable. The thought was 40 percent disturbing and 60 percent funny. Disturbing because a swallowing void made him think of the dark body. A chill rose up in him and gave him goosebumps. He shivered.

Out of the snake mouth came the old man. He was clad in long sleeves and long pants, a sun hat, and large, dark sunglasses. He stood at the edge of the porch and looked out. With the glasses obscuring his eyes, Marko couldn't tell whether the old man was looking at him or not. Maybe from up there, the old man could see a bit of the sea. Marko turned around and gazed at the gate and its perimeter, confirming that there was nothing to look at from his vantage point.

The old man sat down on a chair beside the pool. Marko waited for him to say something, but he remained silent. Marko tried to think of something to say but came up empty. The old man stared at the blue water, then turned his gaze to Marko and smiled. Marko smiled and looked away. When he looked back, the old man was again staring at the water. Marko stared at the water in the larger, deeper pool, too. The tiles lining the pool were a deep blue. They glinted and danced under the rippling surface.

61. May 15, 2015: Sozopol, Bulgaria

At the beach on the second day, they found a battered ramp of
wooden planks leading from the road to the sand. Marko's
mom bumped his chair along the narrow ramp, which was
only just wide enough to accommodate his wheelchair. Several times
one of the wheels fell off the edge and lodged in the sand. Each time it
happened, Kali struggled to lift and right the chair and Marko's grandmother scurried to help. The old man walked ahead, unconcerned.
When they arrived at the end of the ramp, there was a rectangular
wood platform opening into nothing but sand.

Marko applied the brakes on his chair and took off the lap belt. He
reached for his mom, expecting that she would help him down out
of the chair and he would drag himself across the sand. It was what
they did at the lake back home. But this time, she lifted him and held
him tight, then carried him all the way to the spot beneath one of the
umbrellas.

"The sand's too hot," she said. She plopped Marko down in the
shade and walked back to get the chair, but Marko's grandmother was
carrying it along with their beach bag filled with towels. The old man
moved slowly behind her, carrying nothing. Marko squinted toward
them, the bright sand assaulting his eyes, and watched as his mom
took the chair from his grandmother. They seemed to wrestle over it

briefly before Kali prevailed. Marko dropped his gaze to his lap and then turned and saw the sea. It looked impossibly blue, almost the same brilliant blue as the pool at the rental house. Waves tumbled gently here and there. Marko watched them swell, peak, and fall in small bursts everywhere on the surface, not just at the shore. It made him think of the tides below and their swirling, sucking force.

Nearby, a lifeguard shrieked through a whistle poking from his angry lips. He paced the shore, whistling, waving his arm, beckoning swimmers out near the buoy to come back toward shore. One swimmer, who seemed to Marko to be very far out from shore, stood to reveal a depth only reaching her thighs. The buoy was just beyond her. Marko wondered why they would prevent people from going deeper than that. But then he saw it: closer in were deeper pockets of water. The place where the woman stood must have been the sandbar.

The whistling was upsetting. Marko's grandmother was arguing with Kali in Bulgarian. The old man sat in the shade, staring at the sea with his back to Marko, silent. He wore a white linen shirt with half sleeves, and the arms protruding from the sleeves were bones. He wore a large sun hat, sunglasses, and long pants. Marko wanted to ask him why he wasn't going to swim, but the old mad had a sad aura around him that discouraged questions. Marko closed his eyes and felt the dark body near. He worked his hands in front of his face, brushing his nose with each twist of his wrists and swipe of his fanned fingers. It steadied him, helping him to be less afraid of the dark body.

"You ready?" Marko opened his eyes. His mom was holding his swim shirt up, crouched in front of him in the sand, smiling. Marko smiled automatically. His hands were still up. He let them drop and pulled off his shirt. The skin of his chest seemed to glow white, almost translucent. In his periphery, he saw the old man looking at the scars on his back and felt exposed. Kali smeared sunscreen on every inch of Marko's body, rocking him gently as she did. It felt good in the places where he had feeling. And below, it started the math swirling. He closed his eyes and gave himself over to it.

"Arms up," his mom said. Marko lifted his arms and she tugged the swim shirt over his head, then wrenched his arms in.

"You will swim?" It was the old man. Marko looked at him, his own brow wrinkled in concern. Marko was turned around at the trunk, twisted at the spine in a way that looked like it shouldn't be possible.

"He swims all the time," Kali said. "He's a water baby, always has been. He's my little seal." She smiled and brought her face close to Marko's face, nudging his nose with her nose. Marko smiled automatically. He felt his whole body lighten. This day, his mom was a brightness that pushed back the shadows.

"But he will swim in the sea?"

"Dad, we live by the ocean in Boston, the Atlantic. Marko will be fine, just watch."

Kali lifted Marko, struggling to get upright. Marko's grandmother swooped in and lifted his legs, carrying his lower half while his mom had him under the arms. They hauled him this way to the water, dropping him in at about knee's depth. The sea was surprisingly warm. A swell lifted him and dropped him; then a whitewater break crashed around him. For a brief moment, Marko was capsized and he tumbled back, under the wave. A current sucked from below and he panicked, reminded of the dark body taking him over without warning. Marko surfaced and panted. He tasted the brine on his tongue and the sting of salt in his sinuses. He snorted then swiped his hand across his nose. Kali lifted him and he clung to her, afraid.

"Just relax," she said, "let go." She tried prying his hands from her body but he clung harder. She held him close and kissed his head.

"Trust me, sweetie, the sea is your friend." But the sea here was too much like the dark body: the tidal effect of darkness washing over him, filling his eyes and ears, rushing down his throat, tangling everything, saturating and choking him.

"I'm scared," he said, still clutching her. He pressed his face against her neck and closed his eyes. Warm water lapped up between them. The air was warm and the sun felt hot but Marko shivered.

"Do you know what seals do? They body surf." Marko lifted his head and looked at her. Her eyes sparkled, although Marko could still see the sadness within them.

"Are you my seal?"

Marko smiled and nodded.

"Can you be my brave seal?"

Marko looked at the waves coming toward them: large swells carrying rough white water.

"You see this wave coming? When I say, I want you to let go of me and go with it, ride it, let it take your body."

Marko tensed.

"Just relax." Marko watched the oncoming wave and saw its darkness, its appetite. But he saw something else, too, something new: a light. The wave seemed to have a band of light across the middle like a horizontal spine. He pictured his own spine and imagined it glowing like the wave's spine glowed. When it arrived, right at the point when the spine of light in the wave connected with Marko's spine, he reached his arms out and completely relaxed his body. Easily and swiftly, the wave carried him along a gentle ride and then tumbled apart around him, pressing him into the sand. Again, the saltwater came into his mouth and nose and eyes, but this time it felt harmless, easy to wipe away and spit and snort out.

Marko sat up and laughed. His mom was near, the concern on her face melting, and she laughed with him. "You did it!"

"I did it!" Marko pumped his fists into the air. "Mom, can you take me back in deep? I want to do it again."

Kali carried Marko with his back to her, the two of them bobbing across the surface of the sea, squinting and smiling with tangled, wet hair. Marko saw the next wave he wanted to ride taking shape. It bulged up from the depths, pregnant with darkness and light.

62. May 15, 2015: Sozopol, Bulgaria

"Let's not talk about the boy or Kalina or our lost son or the past. Let's practice the art of conversation like we did when we first met hundreds of years ago." Todor shouted the words into the wind, walking beside Lydia on the beach. The sun was setting over the Black Sea and they were barefoot. The sand was wet and firm beneath them, sturdy, giving Todor uncharacteristic courage.

"I'm an old man now," he said. "Time moves so fast."

"Time does not move," Lydia said. Todor smiled. "We move, the Earth moves, the solar system moves, the universe moves. This constant motion through space gives us the dimension we measure in time, but time, the measure, does not move. It is not a dimension in itself. It is a measure, and not always such a useful one."

"Time is absolutely a dimension and it does move. It is the fourth dimension."

"Kant disproved that ridiculous theory. Time is neither an event nor a thing. It cannot itself be measured or travelled through."

"Kant proved nothing. What he had was a theory, no different from Newton's theory that time is a dimension. How else would you explain its elasticity? How it moves quickly when we're together and slowly when we're apart?

"No."

"That's not an explanation."

"No."

"Yes."

"No."

"Why no?"

"You brought up that idiot, Newton, so I cannot continue talking to you about this."

Todor laughed. "The founder of physics is an idiot?"

Lydia stopped walking and glared at Todor with such disgust he thought she might actually spit at him. "He was the founder of nothing. He was a lazy mind who took credit for his students' observations. He became famous for stating the obvious and calling that science. And it wasn't even him that observed such obviousness! The ancient Greeks understood quantum physics long before Newtonian physics took over. Then quantum physics was resurrected again by Planck, and Newtonian physics was disproved."

"Disproved only on the Planck scale."

"Disproved absolutely! How can one set of physical laws abide at a certain scale and a whole other set take over once you look closely enough? Nonsense!"

"An object in motion tends to stay in motion. An object at rest—"

"And what is an object but a collection of particles? Or energy waves, for that matter? And the particles, when you look closely, they're blinking in and out of existence. Where are they when they're not here? If we were travelling at light speed in a space shuttle, time would stand still for us. No, please stop citing Newton to me. Your brute man logic does not hold up against the real ways of the universe."

"What is brute man logic?"

"Logic that is founded in the ignorant, male ego."

"And what about the female ego? Is it not also ignorant?"

"Facts are not ego, male or female."

"Exactly."

Lydia growled. "Why do you have to argue with everything? Question everything?"

"You would prefer that I just always agree with you?

"See?"

Todor saw that her agitation was growing. He enjoyed goading her, but this wasn't the time for that. She didn't enjoy it, and he didn't want to drive the wedge between them even deeper. He decided to switch tactics.

"Your interest and knowledge of physics is much bigger than I knew. You always talked about biology."

"I'm not interested or knowledgeable about physics. I am interested in natural philosophy, which encompasses all of the sciences. I'm sorry for my anger over Newton. It's not proportionate."

Todor misheard her. He thought she said, *I'm not a laureate.* He assumed she was using the term wrong. But what took his attention the most was her apology. It was highly uncharacteristic. Todor tried to remember the last time she had apologized to him for anything. He wondered if maybe she never had before, and this was the first time. The apology was for her anger over Newton, not her anger toward him. Or was it? He wanted to clarify. He saw this extraordinary apology as an invitation. A doorway.

"Do you think I'm a good person?" he asked.

"That is not the right question," she said.

"I need to know if—"

"The right question is how ordinary, *good* people can come both to allow and commit monstrous acts against others. What follows is the question of how we can prevent this from happening: how we can cure ourselves."

Todor held his breath. They were actually talking about this. They were nearing the end of the beach and Todor thought they should turn around, but Lydia kept walking. Her pace quickened. Todor realized that he had, in fact, asked the wrong question, because it implied something false: that people could be either *good* or *bad*. The truth, he knew, was that humanity is inherently both and neither.

"Maybe the answer is in the quilts you have made, and the knit blankets."

Lydia flashed him an annoyed look.

"When I look at a blanket of yours, I admire both the flaws and the fineness inherent in it and, flipping over the fabric, I see how they have been woven from the same threads."

Lydia stopped abruptly and turned to him.

"You are not a blanket. You cannot justify the way that you've hurt people by saying that you have flaws."

"Lydia, I am sorry for the ways I have hurt you."

"I'm not talking about how you've hurt me."

Todor knew then: she was thinking about their son, Marko.

"You blame me for his death?"

"You wanted him to be in the military."

"You *blame* me?"

"You drove him away when he needed you."

"You kept him from me!" Todor realized he'd raised his voice.

Lydia bent and picked up a piece of driftwood from the sand. For a moment, Todor thought she would hit him with it, but instead, she hugged it to her and resumed walking a hundred, maybe two hundred feet to the wall at the end of the beach. Todor stood still, watching. Lydia stopped at the wall and turned toward the sea. Briefly, she paused; then she walked in. Todor watched her bare feet hit the softly lapping waves. The water made a whorl tunnel around her ankles as it turned back in on itself. The moon illuminated her feet and ankles—it was as if they were lit from within. She continued on, up to her knees, up to her thighs, her dress floating on the water's agitated surface, lifting and falling with its ebb and flow. Soon, she was all the way in, floating on her back in the slick, silver-black water, face moonward. Todor stayed on the shore and watched her. He knew she wanted him to follow her in, but his fear of the sea was too great, especially at night.

"Come back ashore, there could be jellyfish!" he hollered out to her, but she made no move toward him, nor any sign that she'd even heard him. Todor began pacing, his face tingling with pricks of fear. But he felt more than fear. He felt curiosity. These were new facets of his wife she'd never before shown him. He thought he knew her as well as anyone could know anyone, but he'd been wrong. He suspected, watching her floating under the moon—her dress and her hair flowing and snaking along the surface, glinting with the swells and retreating into darkness with the ebb—there was much more to her than she would ever show him.

63. May 15, 2015: Sozopol, Bulgaria

Marko sat with his mom in the rental watching television. They were sharing the fold-out couch for a bed while Marko's grandparents used the bedroom. It was late and they were both trying to sleep without success. Kali thought turning on the television might help them fall asleep. On the television, a beautiful woman filled the screen, singing in impenetrable Bulgarian. Marko watched his mom staring at the front door. She was agitated and anxious, he could tell. She kept reaching around to her back, scratching and rubbing that spot that seemed to only bother her when she was upset or stressed. Marko had already asked her what was wrong, but she told him what she always told him: nothing.

Earlier in the evening, after they had finished dinner, Marko's grandparents had shouted at each other in Bulgarian. The old man left and Marko's grandma closed herself in the bedroom. Kali followed her in there and stayed for a long time while Marko sat out on the porch watching the blue pool. Then Marko heard them shouting, and a few moments later Marko's grandmother left the house. She gave him a quick, tight smile and a pat on the head when she passed him on the porch and said, "I'll be back later, taking a walk." Neither his grandmother nor the old man had come home since.

"Mom, what's wrong?" Marko asked now as he lay next to Kali on the couch.

Kali looked at Marko like she was surprised to see him there. She sighed and shook her head, lying back on her elbows.

"I'm worried about your grandpa. He left upset and didn't come back. Grandma got mad at me and left too and it's late and neither of them is back."

"Well, they're adults," Marko said. Kali laughed. She sat up and reached out to touch Marko's face. She held his face in her hand and he felt his head leaning into it, savoring the sensation of being completely known and loved. Her touch, combined with the look in her eyes, communicated: *There has never been a time when you were alive in the world and unknown to me.* Marko understood that this was a touch and a look that could only ever be delivered from a mother to her child.

Abruptly, she stood and went to the window. She pulled the heavy curtain aside and peered outside. She turned, wearing a wide smile.

"Marko, it's the fullest moon I've ever seen."

She retrieved his chair from where it was parked and helped him into it. They went to the porch and took in the moon. Marko stared at the vague shapes on its surface. He imagined the terrain of the moon as mountainous, casting shadows, carving the shapes. The air was warm with a hint of cool that rode a light breeze.

"Let's go for a swim," Kali said.

"What time is it?"

"I don't know, it's late—but who cares? We're on vacation."

"In the pool?"

"No way, the sea!"

Marko was skeptical. He didn't want to go into the sea at night. The thought of it made him nervous. His hands came and twisted in front of his face as he thought about the possibility. Kali disappeared into the house then came back out with a bag filled with towels.

"Let's go," she said and pushed Marko's wheelchair to the edge of the porch. She pulled it back into a wheelie and guided it down the three steps to the ground. They threaded through side streets silently, the moon above them so bright it seemed closer to dusk than what it really was: nearly midnight. The streets were lined with closed down shops, darkened apartment windows, sleeping houses. Marko couldn't remember the last time he'd been up so late, let alone out so late. His sleep schedule was important and it made him both nervous and excited to have this break in the routine. His hand worked quickly, crossing back and forth across his field of vision. Cutting it three times, then seven times, three, seven, three, seven. The pattern calmed him.

The ramp to the beach was well lit and the air smelled sweet.

"Do you smell that? It's ripe fig on these trees lining the ramp." Marko heard the smile in his mother's voice and it made him smile.

At the beach the water seemed much further up on the shore than it had been earlier that day. The wooden platform was only a few feet from the waves that slid along the sand. Kali put the bag down and dug through it.

"I forgot our bathing suits," she said. "Oh well, we don't need them!" She started taking off her clothes. Marko looked around.

"Mom!"

"We have the whole beach to ourselves; look."

Marko looked up and down the beach and saw nobody. A cloud crossed the sky under the moon and darkened everything for a minute. Kali began pulling Marko's shirt off but he pulled it back down.

"No, I don't want to!"

She stepped back and looked at him. She wore only underwear and a bra.

"Are you sure? It will feel amazing."

"Yes, I'm sure. You go ahead, I'll stay here."

"Okay," she said and walked off toward the water. She ran in until she was up to her knees, then stopped and took off her underwear and bra. She threw them up on shore then turned and dove in. She seemed to be under for too long. Marko started the pattern again with his hands. She surfaced and howled, "Woooooo, yeah! The water's warm, it's perfect!"

She stood in the water with her arms out to the side, her palms up, and her head thrown back, and then fell backwards, letting the water catch her. She did this over and over, chanting softly as she did. Marko looked up and down the beach again, worried that someone would hear her and come. But there was no sign of anybody. Marko turned his attention back to his mother in the black water. She splashed and giggled, swam and smiled. He couldn't see her face to know the smile but he could hear it and sense it. This raw joy she was experiencing— this letting loose, naked in the Black Sea under a full moon at midnight—perplexed Marko. He closed his eyes and concentrated on what he was feeling. There was happiness (seven) reflecting her happiness, but that was a small part, 23 percent. The rest was a mixture of fear (one), anxiety (two), and sudden exhaustion (one hundred and nineteen). This last, he knew, was a byproduct of realizing that he had not before been and should not be up so late. He tried to overcome it. He sensed something important was happening for his mom, or maybe for both of them.

Eventually, after a long while, she marched back toward shore, knees thrusting high, hair snaking black and wide across her shoulders. The moon made the water liquid metal and it fell away from her bare body, a bronze sculpture in motion. Marko looked away, then looked back. Her breasts, the fur between her legs—the moon was like a spotlight on them. Marko burned with embarrassment; he quickened his hands, his count. But she was not embarrassed. She was exhilarated. As she approached, she retrieved her undergarments from the beach and Marko looked away again.

"That was great," she said. She plucked a towel from the bag and wrapped herself in it. She dressed quickly, slung the bag heavy with the damp towel over her shoulder, and began pushing Marko's chair back up the ramp.

"I can do it myself," Marko said. He began pushing the large wheels forward, feeling her support behind him.

"Mom, let go, I want to do it myself." He felt her let go and his momentum slowed. He kept pushing forward with all his strength, head down, determined. The bumping over the slats and the uphill climb made it nearly impossible, but he couldn't quit. He heard his mom's voice but couldn't make out what she was saying over the sound of his labored breath and pounding heart. The full moon lit the path before him and he saw a sand pile coming up, obscuring the ramp. His wheels slipped and he idled momentarily in the sand. He thought his arms couldn't keep going for one more second. His neck and shoulder muscles burned; his hands felt chafed, almost raw. He saw himself rolling backward and crashing down off the side of the ramp into the fig tree brush and sand. He looked at the looming moon, white and silver; he saw its light on his arms, his flat thighs. It was giving him strength, he realized it then. He could never have gotten so far up the ramp without it.

Renewed energy flooded him and he pushed through the sand on the ramp. In moments, he crested the peak of the hill and was headed down the other side. Marko whooped and pumped a fist into the air. He heard his mom behind him laughing and cheering. He felt stronger, more independent than he'd ever been in his life. Even the spent feeling in his arms and shoulders made him feel strong. Invincible. He navigated the chair all the way down the ramp to the street and kept pushing himself. Kali fell in beside him, walking at a clip. He slowed down when they rounded the corner to their street, feeling the exhaustion again, but different this time. It wasn't a helpless fatigue. It was a rewarding, deeply satisfying fatigue he had earned.

When they were close to their gated complex, Marko noticed something on the side of the road by the curb, squirming there in the shadows. Was it a large bug? Marko rolled up beside it and peered down.

"What is that?" he asked. Kali crouched down to look and then stood up straight. She dropped the towel bag and pulled out her towel.

"It's a baby bird!" There was panic in her voice. She scooped up the tiny animal in her towel and Marko heard its frantic chirps. Kali looked up into the trees, the moon lighting her worried face.

"It must have fallen from its nest," Marko said. Kali lowered her cupped hands to Marko's line of sight and opened the towel. The bird, tiny and black tinged with red, its little wings pasted to its side helplessly (reminding Marko of his legs), immediately hopped out, landing on a wall separating the street from another gated property. The bird hopped off the wall to the other side, into the bushes lining the property. It chirped loudly and wildly, filled with fear and flight.

"Oh no!" Kali dropped the towel and covered her mouth with her hands. Her eyes were wide and wet.

"He'll be okay," Marko said, "the mother bird will come back and find him and teach him to fly."

"No, he'll die! The cats will find him!" His mom was crying now, tears spilling from her eyes, her breath erratic, hyperventilating into her hands. The bird's loud chirps continued on the other side of the gate. Kali gripped the black iron bars and pressed her face to them, searching wildly for the bird.

"He's so brave!" she wailed. Marko rolled close to her and pulled her arm. She turned into him and collapsed against him, sobbing. She knelt on the street in front of his chair and he wrapped his long arms around her. He felt her tears soak his shirt. He was stunned silent. Never had he seen or heard his mother cry, much less sob this way in his arms. And all this for a little bird? But it wasn't just about the bird, he knew. Marko closed his eyes and held his mom tighter. The bird chirped. He concentrated on the baby bird, willing it to stay quiet and hide in the bushes. The chirping stopped. His mom cried harder.

He held her, still feeling tired and strong, while she cried. But now there was a new strength Marko felt, one he never knew he had. It was a strength that allowed him to stay still and quiet and calm while his mother fell apart in his arms. His mother, the one who was always so strong, the one who held him whenever he fell apart, which had been often. Eventually, her crying softened, then stopped. The tension in her body dissolved and she lay relaxed against him, her torso across his lap, her head on his chest.

When she pulled away from him and sat back on her knees, she dried her face on the towel then looked at him. He met her gaze and smiled. She stared at her son, slack-mouthed, dumbfounded. She looked at him like he was new, someone she recognized but only barely. Marko worried that she was upset with him. But then he saw it: she was proud. In Marko, she saw a strong and competent young man— not, as he had often felt, a living, perpetual source of grief.

Marko looked back at her and saw, for the first time in his life, a vulnerable and fallible woman. One who was scared, filled with profound sorrow, and liable to make mistakes, both in judgment and in deed. Marko wasn't troubled or threatened by this recognition—he was relieved. The relief was mutual, he could tell. It was so apparent that it was nearly palpable between them. Marko imagined a neon sign flashing in the night above them, screaming: I LOVE YOU! I'M SORRY I NEVER REALLY SAW YOU BEFORE! I NEED YOU!

64. May 16, 2015: Sozopol, Bulgaria

The following morning, the morning of their last full day at the sea, Marko's grandmother helped with his catheter and enema as usual, but her customary high stress level clashed with the relative calm between Marko and Kali. At breakfast, she asked, "Where were you two last night? What happened?" They were eating breakfast on the patio outside. The air was soft and warm.

Marko used the food in his mouth as an opportunity to stall his response and think about what to say. He looked at her and chewed slowly. Her face was pale with heavy, dark wedges beneath her eyes. Not just her mouth but her whole face seemed to frown. "We went for a walk and had a swim. Where were you?"

Her frown deepened and she said, "Did you get enough sleep? Are you tired?"

"I'm fine, but where were you and grandpa last night?"

She waved away his question and turned to walk in the house. Just then Marko's grandpa walked out. He put his arm around Lydia and said, "We were out on a date." Marko's grandma blushed and pushed him away, but Marko could tell she was pleased. Marko smiled. His grandmother disappeared into the house and the old man sat across the table from him.

"Are you having fun?" the old man asked. He took a piece of toast, spread fig jam across it, and forced it as far into his mouth as it would go before taking a humungous bite. Marko stifled a laugh and nodded.

"Fhat? Fhat's funny?" he asked with his mouth full.

"Nothing. Don't choke," Marko said. The old man continued chewing and stared at Marko.

"What really happened last night?" Marko asked. It made him a little nervous to ask and normally he wouldn't have, but the effect from the night before was still with him. He felt strong. He waited while the old man finished chewing and then swallowed.

"Why do you do that with your hands?" The old man mimicked Marko's hands, twisting them one atop the other from the wrist in front of his face. There was no cruelty in his mimicry, only curiosity. Marko dropped his hands. He hadn't even been aware that he was doing it again. He opened his mouth to answer but thought better of it.

"I asked you first," Marko said. The old man smirked and took another large bite of toast. Marko watched him chew patiently.

When the old man was finished he said, "There are things you don't need to know about this family." The lines on his face deepened and his eyes sealed the finality of his statement. Marko was aware that his hands were back up but he didn't care. The math and the thoughts crowding his skull were too much.

"Moving my hands—I think it's like defragmenting a hard drive," Marko said. The old man scowled.

"Like doing what to a what?"

"Do you have a computer?"

"Yes but I don't know how it works."

"Well, my hands have the effect on my mind that walking has on your mind, I think. Like when people are troubled and they go take a walk? They do that to calm their mind or organize their thoughts? I can't walk so I use my hands." The old man nodded and his face relaxed. His eyes, too, relaxed.

"They look like wings, your hands. Like a bird flying." The old man smiled when he said this. Marko sensed another shift inside him. He looked out at the sky behind his grandfather's head and imagined a bird soaring, black against bright blue.

65. May 16, 2015: Sofia, Bulgaria

Marko's time in Bulgaria ended quickly. There was another swim in the sea complete with fearless body surfing, dinner at a restaurant where barefooted women danced on hot coals, a video call with Malik, and some baseball watching with his grandpa. They drove back to Sofia to spend one last night at the family house.

That night, after the house was quiet, Marko went again to the space under the stairs, pulling himself along the floor of the house to get there. One by one, he moved books out of the space to make room for himself. There were too many to move them all, so he moved a few stacks and then pushed the others back against the wall and smashed in among them. He closed the door and sat there. He closed his eyes. The space was tight the way the dream bed had been. He imagined he was there in the dream bed. The math slowed and stopped and he started to lose sensation in his body. He was close to the formless place when light poured over him and he opened his eyes.

"Marko? What are you doing in here?" It was the old man.

"I'm not Marko. I'm Emil," Marko said, wishing it were true. The old man's eyes widened and his mouth opened. Tears spilled down his wrinkled face.

"Emil! It's you? Oh, I've waited so long," he said and began to sob. He grabbed Marko and hugged him tight, pulling him from the portal and onto his lap. Marko tensed and the math resumed. He was himself; he couldn't feel his legs. He knew then, all at once and with certainty, that his grandfather had been the Ambassador. His name was Todor. The Ambassador was Marko's grandfather! And now he was a sad, confused, old man grieving a long-lost Emil. The old man cried on Marko's shoulder, making his night shirt wet.

Marko patted his back and said, "I'm Marko. It's me, Marko."

The old man continued crying and holding Marko. "My son! Oh my son! I was a terrible father! It's my fault!" Marko held still and em braced his grandfather. He sat there in his grandfather's lap with the math gridding out the shape of his legs against the floor.

"I just wish I could feel my legs again. I wish I could walk again," he said. His grandpa lifted his head and looked at him. His face was red and streaked, his hair disheveled.

"My son, Marko, your legs are the sea. You have the whole Black Sea for legs."

Marko looked at his legs and remembered the way they looked in the sea, how they disappeared beneath its surface and were suspended there in the water. Seeing the water stretching out forever and thinking of it as an extension of himself made him feel powerful and strong.

Marko's grandpa looked at him and his eyes refocused. He gasped, realizing, Marko thought, that he was clinging to his grandson and not his son. He stared at Marko for a few more seconds and then placed his hand gently on the side of Marko's face. "Let's move these books back," he said.

Marko and his grandfather moved the books back into the space and closed the door. Marko hugged his grandfather goodnight one last time and went to his room. He fell asleep that last night to the sound of howling dogs. The howling was so loud that Marko imagined a horde of furry bodies covering the whole lower half of the mountain, muzzles skyward, dog-lips pursed. The sound was melancholy. He worried that he would be kept awake by all the noise, but the exhaustion in his body had accumulated to unprecedented heights and he fell quickly to sleep.

When Marko woke, everything was already packed. The car they had used while they were visiting had been returned and Aleks was there to take them to the airport. For breakfast, Marko ate cut-up peaches in yogurt, which he thought might be the best thing he'd ever tasted in his life. He sat out on the patio beneath the grapevines on the eave and looked out toward the mountain. He wanted to save the image in his mind with as much detail as possible in case he never made it back there again.

"When I was a younger man, I used to walk from here straight out and straight up to the top of that mountain," the old man said. He sat at the table with Marko not eating. Marko's grandmother and his mom were inside the house.

"How long did that take you?"

The old man looked at Marko thoughtfully. "I don't know. I never paid attention to the time. When I climbed the mountain, time went away."

Marko didn't believe him. He would have had to return eventually and when he returned, he would have seen what time it was. Marko always kept track of time, down to the minute and seconds and, whenever possible, fractions of a second. He had a stopwatch at his house that included two decimal points past the whole second. It took his mom one minute, three seconds, and point seven-two seconds to go to the bathroom one time, for example.

"Your mother gave me something on the computer so we can see each other," the old man said. Marko looked at him. He slouched in his seat and frowned. Marko realized that the old man was sad they were leaving.

"You mean video conferencing?" Marko asked. The old man nodded.

"Okay, we can do that, sure." Marko felt better about leaving now that he knew it wouldn't be the last time he would see his grandfather.

But the old man looked very sad. Marko watched him watching the mountain, his grey eyes bright in the daylight, and tried to picture himself as an old man. He looked up the spiral staircase of time, but it didn't reach that far. After a few years, it faded away as though into a fog. Being an old man wasn't something Marko could see for himself.

When they left, Kali hugged her father for a very long time. Lydia watched from the door of the house. Marko watched from the car and worried. Something about the hug wasn't right: it wasn't a happy hug; it was a very sad hug. It was the kind of hug you give to dogs you feel bad for because they look so sad and pent up. The kind that Marko wished he could give to the gorillas at the zoo because they always looked so depressed. If he could give the gorillas hugs, those would be the saddest hugs in the world.

As the car pulled away, Marko waved to his grandparents. Lydia would return to the ashram, though he didn't know when, and he knew, video conferencing aside, that he would never see his grandfather again. Aleks dropped Kali and Marko off at the airport and gave them each a happy hug.

When they were alone again, Marko could still sense the effect of the thing that had happened between them that night of the full moon. Every time Kali looked at him, he noticed it: she really saw him now. All of him, not just the parts that made her sad.

When they landed in Paris for the layover, Kali pushed Marko's chair all the way out through baggage claim to customs.

"Why do we have to come all the way out to change planes?" Marko asked.

Kali smiled and said, "I have a surprise for you."

They put their bags in a storage locker and caught a cab into the city. Marko was thrilled—he had always wanted to see Paris. His mother had lived in Paris for a short time before he was born and was fluent in French. They had a full day to explore; Kali had changed their flight back to Boston to the last one departing that day, an overnight flight so they could sleep. They went straight to the Eiffel Tower.

"They call this Old Dame," Kali said. "Also, *La Dame de fer*, or the Iron Lady. But I call it Old Dame."

"Why?"

"Because she is very old," Kali said and smiled. Marko didn't want to go up inside the Old Dame; it didn't look safe. Instead, he sat underneath and counted its rivets, marveling at all the heavy iron it took to build such a structure. His mom took pictures of him as he counted, which made him lose count. After a while, Marko wasn't interested in counting anymore. They were getting too far away to count, anyway. They walked along the park around the tower and then caught a bus on the other side.

"You have to see Notre Dame," Kali said.

When they stood at the bus stop, Marko noticed a sign with the time to expect the bus. They were strange times; not whole, round times like 12:30 and 1:00 but staggered, random times like 12:37 and 1:16. To Marko's amazement, the bus came at the exact scheduled time, to the minute. Fascinated by this level of punctuality, he insisted that they stay and watch, when they got off the bus, to see if every bus came on time. He waited for five more buses and they all arrived exactly as scheduled. Kali was uncharacteristically patient with Marko, letting him sit there and watch for the buses and check the time as they approached. Marko was grateful for her patience because the buses coming on time made him very happy. It was a tremendous relief to find such order and predictability in the world.

They went to the Louvre where they spent six hours. Marko could have spent six days in the Louvre. Its large halls and high, ornate ceilings alone were hard for Marko to look away from. But the art! Marko found so much life trapped inside so many paintings: Lifelike moments with stilled activity. An instant frozen in time but, somehow, kinetic—still humming with life. The layers of paint and the level of detail and the sheer size of each canvas created dynamic, expressive landscapes. They contained entire worlds

Their last stop in Paris before going back to the airport was the Luxembourg Gardens. When they arrived, they walked the perimeter and Kali told Marko a story.

"In Bulgaria, when people have babies, they save the umbilical cord that gets cut away." Kali pulled up Marko's shirt and poked his belly button. Marko's belly button was numb, being right on the line of where sensation turned into abstract math, and her touching him there produced an interesting marriage of the two: a physical sensation on the skin accompanied by a mathematical mapping of that single point in space inside his mind. This was the first time Marko had experienced them simultaneously and it made him want her to touch his belly button again. He kept his shirt pulled up, hoping that she would.

"The part that gets saved by the mother is to be buried in the place where she wants her child to end up one day. This garden is my favorite part of the city. It's a place where I've always felt peaceful and happy. So I buried your umbilical cord here. I would love it if you ended up here, feeling happy like I did." Then she did it again, touched Marko's exposed belly button. This time, he felt it, saw the math, and got chills: ripples of that feeling cascading through him.

He smiled and placed his own large hand over his belly button, covering it. He looked into the garden—every inch of it bursting with life—and the chill happened again: a blossoming. The air was filled with the scents of flowers and pure sunlight. The concrete under his wheels glittered. Marko closed his eyes and inhaled it all. The light and the air and the smell of life, it filled him like water, from the feet up. It made him almost think he felt even his faraway feet. He opened his eyes. Across the distance of the city, across the rooftops and the warmth, there was a gonging of church bells. Announcing what? He wondered. Looking into the garden, he let his focus go soft and all the colors and shapes turned blobby and indistinct. Summer had tossed its green into the air.

"Isn't this where we belong?" he asked. He looked at his mom and realized he hadn't asked it out loud. Kali crouched beside him and placed her hand on top of his. They sat, hands stacked over Marko's belly button, and watched birds flit into and out of the garden. This, Marko thought, was a fine place to end up.

BIOGRAPHICAL NOTE

Elizabeth Earley is the publisher of Jaded Ibis, a feminist press publishing socially engaged literature. Her first novel, *A Map of Everything* (a Lambda Literary Award finalist), was inspired by her own experience growing up with a sister who had sustained a traumatic brain injury. Her writing continues to be informed by her interest in family dynamics, healing, disability rights, and the nature of consciousness. Earley has an MFA in fiction from Antioch University Los Angeles and lives in San Diego.